"WEAPONS ARE FOR AMATEURS, REMO, HAVE I TAUGHT YOU NOTHING?" GRUMBLED CHIUN.

He had finished off his fair share of leather-clad Smoke Hogs.

It was the machete wielder he was referring to. The man had somehow extracted the weapon from his face and neck and was bearing down on Remo, the howls of outrage bubbling out of his neck. Remo stepped around him and whacked him hard on the back of the head. The machete wielder became airborne, dead already.

Chiun *tsked* over the body when it fell. "Very messy."

"I was just playing around," Remo protested.

"Are you prepared to enter the bus? Or should we take our rooftop perch again and see what other surprises they have in store for us?"

Remo sighed. "I guess we go in. But let's not try to kill *everybody*, Little Father."

Chiun sniffed. "Don't insult me."

Other titles in this series:

Created by Murphy & Sapir

THE Destroyer™

BLOODY TOURISTS

®

A GOLD EAGLE BOOK FROM
W🌐RLDWIDE®

TORONTO • NEW YORK • LONDON
AMSTERDAM • PARIS • SYDNEY • HAMBURG
STOCKHOLM • ATHENS • TOKYO • MILAN
MADRID • WARSAW • BUDAPEST • AUCKLAND

First edition January 2004

ISBN 0-373-63249-5

Special thanks and acknowledgment to Tim Somheil for his contribution to this work.

BLOODY TOURISTS

For the Glorious House of Sinanju,
sinanjucentral@hotmail.com

1

Arby Maple began the day a nobody, but by day's end he would be famous.

First the evening news would introduce the world to this unlikely celebrity with the basset-hound face. Within a day all the news networks would hastily assemble their panels of experts to discuss the Arby Maple phenomenon. Their in-depth analysis of Maple's psyche, distilled into twenty-second sound bites, would be the official confirmation of what the people of the world already knew: Arby Maple was completely insane.

Within a week the garish tabloids would be on the racks in the grocery checkout lines, full of gory crime-scene photos.

A paperback book entitled *Maple the Man, Maple the Mass Murderer,* written by a team of crack journalists, would be in the stores in under four weeks—a tremendous literary achievement. Three made-for-TV docudramas would be produced in time to air during sweeps. By then Maple was more than just another mass murderer; he was a trendsetter. Once he started doing it, it seemed as if everybody started doing it.

All the excitement wasn't going to kick off for a good twenty minutes. Arby Maple didn't know it was coming. Fact was, he was bored stupid and there was no relief in sight.

"I can't decide where to go next!" Natalie Maple said as they left the Hank Jones Auditorium, home of *The Hank Jones Show.*

"How about the airport?" Arby suggested.

Mrs. Maple's enthusiasm dimmed. "You can't say you didn't adore *The Hank Jones Show.*"

"Sure, I can. I didn't adore *The Hank Jones Show.* I didn't even like it. Have you ever noticed the empty space on the couch at home when you watch *The Hank Jones Show* on TV?"

Mrs. Maple shoved the slick city map into his hands. "Okay, Arby, then you decide what we should do next."

Arby handed the map right back to her. "There's not a single thing I want to do next."

"You didn't even look at it!" his wife protested.

"Natalie, you've had maps and brochures lying around the house for months, and I've looked at every single one of them. I figured out weeks ago that there wasn't anything of interest for me in the entire town of Bunsen, Mississippi."

When Natalie got angry she stuck out her lower lip and blew air up her face. It made her look like a bulldog. "Maybe you should have informed me of this little tidbit of information when we started planning this vacation."

"Natalie," Arby said wearily, "the very day you came home with all those brochures I told you no way. No way I wanted to waste my vacation looking at a bunch of old washed-up country-music people in Bunsen, Mississippi."

His wife's eyes were as hard as glass. "You said no such thing."

"Twenty, maybe thirty times I said it, but you had your mind made up. I said it anyway, practically every day since then." Arby shrugged. "But you went right on ahead and bought the tickets and booked the hotel and here we are."

"But it's Bunsen. Where country music was born."

"Eighteen years we been married. How come you haven't figured out yet that I hate country music?"

Lips compressed in a bloodless line, Natalie struggled to come up with a zinger that would put Arby in his place. "You are a real wet blanket, Arby Maple," she declared. "It isn't fair of you to ruin my vacation."

So Natalie went her way and Arby went his. Natalie took the map, and within minutes she had immersed herself again in the magic that was the Bunsen Theater District—America's Country Music Main Street.

Arby, Natalie decided, was an idiot. This town was heaven on earth. There were beautiful shops along Main Street. There was every kind of fine country food, and shops filled with delightful gifts. But the boutiques and restaurants were just the sideshow. The main attractions were the many beautiful theaters.

Natalie had fallen in love with Southern culture when

she was in nursing school. She and the other girls would sit around watching a country variety show called *Yee Haw!* and have a great time. Natalie's roommate, Babsie, was a well-mannered young lady from Georgia who loved to talk about the South.

"Everybody has nice manners in the South," Babsie said. "Everybody calls you ma'am." She would giggle and say, "In the South we think this show is a little, you know, wild, but I like it anyway."

Natalie was from Brooklyn. Brooklyn was crude and filthy and she hated it. Anyplace where the mild shenanigans of *Yee Haw!* were "wild" was where Natalie wanted to be.

She carried around her impression of the South for decades. Now she was really here. In a delightful little park between two gift shops she relaxed on a bench and looked over the schedule of daily entertainment. That's what Bunsen was truly famous for—all the wonderful entertainment! You were never more than a few steps away from a first-rate performance by some of the biggest names in show business.

Natalie Maple gasped in delight when she realized there was a show by a Russian comedian starting in just twenty minutes. He was her absolute favorite! Talk about big-name entertainment.

As she strolled down Main Street, hoping to get to the theater early and maybe snag a front-row seat, Natalie realized Bunsen, Mississippi was everything she had hoped it would be. Polite, friendly people. Clean streets. She didn't feel the need to clutch her purse against her side for fear of having it snatched.

But then there was her nitwit husband. Arby was not what she had hoped he would be. He was too stupid to know he was in paradise.

Natalie Maple decided something right then and there. *This* was where she wanted to live. *This* was the life she wanted. What was Arby going to say when she delivered that little piece of news?

Arby would never move to Bunsen, Mississippi. Not in a million years.

Natalie smiled. This little town just kept looking better and better.

ARBY WAS TRYING to explain that arguing with Natalie was like trying to convince a dog not to dig a hole.

"I'm very sorry to hear that, sir." The bartender couldn't care less and left.

"I know just how you feel," said the young man a couple of stools over. "My aunt decided this was the place to go for our family reunion. They're all down the street watching some banjo players."

"Banjos!" Arby Maple said in disgust.

The young man went across to the bartender and came back with two drinks, handing one over to Arby. "It's on me."

"Thanks, friend." Maple accepted it gladly.

"The modern-day victims of *Yee Haw!* must stick together," the young man announced and raised his glass in a toast.

The Scotch whiskey went down all right, but when it was done Arby had some grittiness on his tongue.

"You know," his new pal announced, "the worst

thing about this place is the people. The people here are very rude."

"Naw, just the opposite. They're too damn polite," Maple said. "Wait. You know what? You're right. They are rude. They *act* polite but they're really being rude, right to your face, all the time, and just dressing it up as Southern manners. At least in New York they tell you to your face if they think you're an asshole."

"Drink up, friend," the young man said.

Maple drained the Scotch whiskey and tried to swallow the grainy residue on his tongue. "They can't even wash a glass right."

"You do not like these people," the young man stated.

"You got that right."

"Especially the assholes who work here."

"Yeah, they're the ones who lay it on thick. They're the worst."

"You know who's the worst?" the young man asked.

"It's that bartender," Arby Maple growled, rising from his bar stool and clenching his fists.

The young man said quickly, "No, not him! There is somebody much worse."

Maple looked around the small bar, modeled after a quaint gentlemen's tavern that had operated in Charlotte, North Carolina, in the late 1800s. It was empty now. Just the two customers and the asshole behind the bar. The bartender was a miserable piece of dog crap who deserved to get the living shit kicked out of him. But there was somebody Maple hated even more. He just wasn't sure who....

"Who is it?" he demanded.

The young man leaned close and held his mustache in place, pointing with his other hand. Maple looked. Out the front windows, across the immaculately clean Main Street, was a small public courtyard.

"Him," the young man growled.

"The guy with the cart?"

"The guy with the cart," the young man said earnestly. "There is nobody you hate more than the guy with the cart."

Arby Maple's lower lip curled. Hot breath stuttered from his nostrils as his body inflated with his passion. The young man was right—Arby abhorred the man with the cart. It was a soul-filling, mind-expanding malevolence. There was no reason why, and this kind of complete hatred needed no excuse. And there was only one thing to do about it.

The Cobbler In A Cup guy had to die.

ARBY MAPLE STRODE from the tavern, crossed Main Street and grabbed the vendor by the collar. The vendor's smile disappeared and his clip-on bow tie landed in the grass.

"Hey!"

But that was all he said before Arby Maple flipped open the lid to the hot-box cart and shoved his head inside. The vendor's face disappeared into the steaming tray of gooey cobbler.

Arby Maple loved the sound of his enemy crying out in pain, but he was disappointed to find that he could only get the man's head and one shoulder through the square opening. He pushed on the other shoulder, then heaved against it and felt a crack of bone as the shoulder went in. The vendor was screaming and kicking his feet.

Maple brought the hot-box lid down, hard, on the backbone of the trapped vendor. Then he brought it down again. The lid was polished stainless steel and was heavy enough to do the job. Maple kept slamming it until he saw the spine give. The legs stopped kicking.

Arby Maple experienced profound satisfaction.

His eyes fell on a decorative iron gate, standing permanently open alongside one edge of the park. The crossbar that slid into place to secure the gate was also of solid black iron with a nice hook at one end. Maple wrenched it out of its socket.

He didn't see the people running away from him. He didn't hear the screaming. His hatred would turn on them in a minute or so, but for now he had one thought only: he was going to wipe the floor with that smug son-of-a-bitch bartender.

As soon as Maple left the tavern, the young man strolled quickly up Main Street and took cover in the door of a souvenir shop. He was tentatively pleased when he saw the body of the cobbler seller go limp.

Maple wasn't through yet, though. He grabbed a hunk of metal from the fence and went back for the bar. Well, that wasn't unexpected. The man had already been irked by the bartender.

Maple emerged from the tavern with his iron bar dripping blood and matted with hair.

Stop now, stop now, the young man pleaded silently.

Arby Maple rushed a crowd of onlookers and began bashing their heads in.

THE YOUNG MAN WALKED despondently through the parklike town, against the flow of security carts and interested visitors heading for the action. His subject was supposed to kill just the one guy. Instead the man was on some sort of rampage.

When he reached his car he started the engine, but paused to pull out his notebook. There were pages of unrelated scribbling inside, but in the middle was a carefully printed chart. At the top of the first column was the entry GUTX-ED-UT1. "ED" stood for Evaporative Distillation, the method used to create this particular batch. "UT" was for Utah, home state of the manufacturing lab, and "1" was the first sample from that lab. Carefully, with his treasured fine-tipped Mont Blanc pen, the young man recorded his findings in the results field.

He wrote just one word: "Imperfect."

Police, fire and SWAT vans were careening into the parking lot as the young man left. A TV news truck was close behind. The young man had to smile when he saw that. Well, at the very least, he thought, this place was going to get some mighty bad publicity and folks would be staying away in droves. And everyone knew what that meant.

Less competition.

2

His name was Remo and he was ordering off the dinner menu, à la carte.

"Meatballs."

"A man like you needs more than meatballs." The waitress chomped her gum provocatively.

"Meatballs," Remo insisted.

"The customer is always right. But why not get the dinner? It comes with pasta and garlic bread and a salad."

Remo considered that, then nodded. "You talked me into it. I'll have the full dinner. In fact, make it four meatball dinners."

Her jaw froze midchomp.

"There will be others in my party," he explained.

"Hope your friends like meatballs," the waitress said, trying to sound witty. She cocked a hip at him, just to be sure he was getting the message.

But the customer in the circular booth looked right past her. "Is that a pie case? I haven't seen one of those in ages."

"We have apple and coconut cream, but I recommend the cherry pie." She leaned at him, thrusting out her impressive bosom.

"I'll take it," her customer said.

"Four slices? Or how about a piece of cherry pie for just you?"

"No, no, bring the whole pie. Two if you've got 'em."

She stood up straight, looked at him quizzically and departed, her heels clicking on the linoleum. By the time she came back with four salads, she was prepared to make another go of it.

"Doesn't look like your friends are going to make it," she pronounced. "How about you and I get a room at the Hilton down the street and order room service?"

"Here he is now."

Remo slipped out of the deep vinyl booth and approached the man who was standing inside the entrance, smoothing his lapels and looking displeased. When the waitress saw who it was, she vanished into the kitchen.

"Michelangelo, good to see you!" Remo said with a hand outstretched.

"Good to see me? Good to *see* me?" The new arrival declined to shake hands. "Buddy, you got some serious balls, I'll give you that much. But you got serious troubles, too, you know what I mean?"

"I have a table." Remo gestured to the huge booth.

"I know you got a table. You think I don't know you got a table? You think I haven't been watching you, trying to figure you out?"

"Please." Remo was conciliatory. "Join me for dinner. We'll talk."

"I don't feel like dinner. I feel like bustin' your ass."

Remo kept a firm grip on the smile. He never claimed to be an actor and this good-to-see-you shtick was getting on his nerves. To his amazement, Michelangelo "The Fig" Figaroa slid into the booth.

Remo joined him. They could have fit another five or six human beings into the booth without crowding, and the vinyl backs were so high it was like being in a room by themselves. Here they could have privacy.

"I got two guys with guns watching the place, just so's you know. I also had the place closed up. For added privacy."

"Very efficient of you, Michelangelo."

"You think I'd be here if I thought this was a setup? I had every square inch of this place checked out the minute I got your phone call and my guys been watching it ever since. I know you came here by yourself. I know that. Got it?"

"Clear as crystal. Have some salad."

"I don't eat salad. So whoever it is you're expecting to come through the door, they ain't coming. Got it?"

"Read you loud and clear. Here comes the garlic bread." Remo turned to the waitress. "Thanks very much."

The waitress knew Figaroa. She set down the breadbasket and fled.

"Bread, Michelangelo?" Remo offered the basket. "Nice and warm."

Figaroa shook his head tightly. "I ain't getting through to you, am I? This ain't no business dinner, because you and me ain't doing no business. I'm here to find out what the fuck you got and why the fuck you're waving it in my face."

"Oh. Okay, then." Remo put down the basket, looking crestfallen.

"So start talking."

"Okay, then. So, I just happened to know that you're a big man around here. I know you've been having some trouble, too, with people moving in on you, like Boss Jorge and the other Mexicans, and I heard you got muscled out of some parts of town and stuff. Then I heard about somebody putting some bad stuff on the street, and some of the stuff is so bad it's killing people and making them go crazy. And I heard people saying it came from the Mexicans and was really hurting their business, and nobody would buy stuff anymore from the Mexicans and so your business was doing nice. I wouldn't have thought nothing of it except that I found out something else."

"Yeah?" Figaroa demanded.

Remo lowered his voice. "The Mexicans are not too happy."

"No shit, Sherlock."

"Boss Jorge's going after you, I heard."

"When? How?"

"Not with men, you know. He's not gonna start a war. He's got a plan that he says will make you a nonproblem for good."

"Huh. That slimeball Mexican ain't got a prayer. How's he gonna do it?"

Remo sat up straighter. "*That's* what I'm selling, Michelangelo."

Figaroa nodded, then shook his head. He looked at

the man across the booth as if he didn't quite believe what he was seeing.

The man who called himself Remo Vu was slim, neither tall nor short. He had dark hair and deep-set eyes that were cold, but the goofy look on his face told you more about who he really was. Michelangelo had noticed the expensive Italian loafers, which were a point in his favor, but Remo Vu was also wearing black Chinos and a black T-shirt. A T-shirt! There's class for you.

"You telling me you want me to pay you, some sleazebag off the street, somebody I don't even know, you want me to pay you for information that may or may not be true."

"Oh, it is true, Michelangelo, I promise."

"You *promise?* Let me tell you something, Remo Vu, whatever the fuck kind of name that is. I know who you are."

"Really?"

"I seen your kind before, all over the place. A month don't go by that I don't run into another Remo Fucking Vu. And you're all little guys with nothing going for ya except your little schemes and little ideas, and now you're trying one of your little schemes on me. Well, I'm saying no. I'm doing worse than saying no, 'cause I'm going to make sure all the other little maggots know that fucking with Michelangelo Figaroa is a major mistake."

The waitress arrived with a tray of plates and began setting them on the table, frightened and silent.

"What *is* this?" Figaroa asked. "You invite me to a business dinner and you order me hamburger balls, the cheapest entrée on the menu? You slap me in the face when you're trying to do business with me? You're just proving my point, Remo Vu. You know what comes next, don't you?"

"No. Do you?"

"Better believe it," Figaroa's voice was low and threatening. "Time for you to start serving as an example for the other maggots."

"Okay. Fine. I give up, Figgy."

That was the last straw. Figaroa was fed up with the smart-ass in the T-shirt, and nobody ever called him Figgy. He pulled out his brand-new toy, glad to have a chance to show it off. The piece cost him a bundle, but it was baddest piece of hardware on the streets of this town.

"Okay, dirtbag, time to talk straight."

"Has Figgy got a new popgun? I'm not impressed, Figgy."

Figaroa's brain boiled. "Look, shit-for-brains, this is a Heckler & Koch MP-7. It's got twenty rounds in the magazine, 4.6 mm shockers that go twenty-five hundred feet per second. That's like four times faster than a .45-caliber round. Just one of these bullets would rip your heart out through your spine if you were wearing five suits of body armor, which you ain't."

Figaroa couldn't help notice that he wasn't making much of an impression on his audience.

"It's got about as much rise as a .22 pistol," he continued doggedly. "So when I start shooting, it ain't too likely I'm going to get my aim screwed up by the recoil. It fires at a rate of 950 rounds a minute." Figaroa dramatically lowered the front grip and aimed it two-handed at the front of that damn T-shirt. "Now what do you have to say for yourself, smart-ass?"

"I say whoop-de-do, Figgy. Hey, is that thing made out of plastic?"

Figaroa could have explained that the MP-7 was, in fact, constructed using a polyamide material reinforced with carbon fiber. This exotic composite possessed greater tensile strength than aluminum but made the weapon extremely lightweight—not even three pounds with a full magazine. But Figaroa was too furious to explain all that, and a second later he was too surprised to say anything.

The machine pistol was no longer in his possession. Remo Vu had it. He actually had a finger in the barrel and was peering at the very expensive weapon with a slight twitch of amusement on his mouth.

Then he pinched the stock of the weapon with two fingers. The entire rear end crumbled.

"I think they should have stuck with steel, don't you?" Remo observed.

Figaroa was now on his third major emotional shift in the past seven heartbeats: his confusion turned to outrage, even as part of his brain was trying to reconcile the impossible thing he just witnessed.

"You can't do that!" Figaroa blurted, not sure himself what point he was trying to make.

"Can. Did." Remo spidered his fingers around the machine pistol, and Figaroa watched it disintegrate as if it were a bread stick.

"You asshole! You know how much that cost me?"

"Chill, Figgy, you'll ruin your appetite. First thing

on the menu tonight is a hertz doughnut. Ever have a hertz doughnut?"

Rage and disbelief battling for dominance in his head, Michelangelo Figaroa never saw the hand come at him, fingers pinching his earlobe. And then Figaroa felt pain. Whopping pain. He opened his mouth but nothing came out, and tears rolled down his face—*that* kind of pain.

"Hurts, don't it?" Remo quipped, then looked expectant.

Figaroa tried to nod, but the pain paralyzed him. He managed to shudder a little.

"I guess you've heard that one. You know, nobody laughs at my jokes," Remo complained. "Now, let's get this first little bit of business over and done with. Listen closely."

Figaroa swiveled his bulging eyes to Remo, which was about all he could do to prove he was listening.

"Okay, here's something you'll want to keep in mind," Remo said. "It's about the pain."

Figaroa knew about the pain. His whole existence was pain.

"I made the pain," Remo began.

Figaroa wanted to say "Oh, yes, I understand and I hope you realize I'm being extremely cooperative," but his vocal cords were locked up

"The important part..." Remo added slowly.

Figaroa quivered in anticipation.

"Is that I can make it stop."

Figaroa blinked in agreement.

"Now, Mr. Fig, would you like me to make it, ahem, stop?"

More blinking.

"Yes? No? Maybe?"

Frantic, teary-eyed blinking.

"Okay," Remo said reasonably. "One blink yes, two blinks no."

With more determination than he had ever mustered for anything in his forty-seven years of life, Michelangelo Figaroa blinked just one time.

"Oh. Okay."

Remo let go, and the pain was just—gone. Completely. As if it had never been there.

"You wouldn't try anything sneaky?" Remo wondered aloud.

Figaroa worked his jaw and shrugged, amazed and relieved. He was perfectly okay. His ear wasn't even bleeding. He didn't know what Remo Vu had done to him, but it left him without a scratch.

It also left him as mad as hell.

"Figgy, I asked you a question."

Figaroa reached for his backup piece but found his second holster empty. A new collection of metal lumps rolled out of Remo's hand. They were all that was left of Figaroa's precious old 9 mm Glock.

"You son of a—!"

"Very nice couple from Arizona." Remo took Figaroa by the ear again.

The first pain had been excruciating, but that was nothing. A new explosion of fire filled Figaroa's skull and cascaded down his spine like a lava river. He started to scream.

Something like a steel vise clamped around his jaw.

"Use your inside voice, Fig," Remo said. He released the ear and the pain vanished. "Eat your dinner."

"What?" Michelangelo Figaroa sobbed.

"You heard me. Eat up."

Figaroa tried to bolt from the booth, not once but twice. He scooted no more than an inch before the pain pinchers were on his ear again. Tears of frustration on his face, he began to eat.

A minute later Figaroa's companions in crime entered the restaurant.

"Hey, Mikey, you okay?" asked a mountain of flesh under an ugly mess of wavy black hair. His partner was a bald cherub, just as wide but a foot shorter. Neither of them looked like they wanted to become friends with the man named Remo.

"I'm fine," Figaroa said, voice cracking with strain. "Leave us alone."

"Hey, Mikey, you eating a salad?"

"Hey, Mikey, you been cryin'?"

Figaroa quivered like a poodle standing at the back door with a bursting bladder. He could have ordered his men to gun down Remo Vu, but the memory of the pain was too vivid. He couldn't risk it. He was a reborn coward.

"Go away," he ordered.

"Sure you okay, Mikey?"

"Get lost, would ya!"

The pair left the restaurant hesitantly. Not until Figaroa had polished off his fourth salad did Remo begin asking questions.

"Tell me about your inventory problems, Figgy,"

Remo said, sliding the first plate of meatballs and pasta in front of the Mob boss.

"I got to eat this, too?"

"Yes. Answer the question."

"I got no inventory problems." Figaroa distastefully pushed the first forkful of spaghetti into his mouth.

"What about all the freaked-out junkies uptown?"

"Hey, they didn't freak out on my stuff!"

"Yuck. Say it—don't spray it." Remo wiped tomato sauce spatters off the tablecloth in front of him. "I heard you sold poisoned crack. Bad crack. Turned a bunch of peace-loving crack heads into violent lunatics. Four people died, Figgy."

"Maybe it was some of my regular customers that got all wired and went all crazy, but my stuff didn't do it."

Remo watched the mobster closely. "You're telling the truth," he said resignedly.

"Damn straight!"

"Eat your dinner."

"What for I have to eat more of this crap? I told you the truth, didn't I?"

Remo didn't seem to hear him, but one hand was suddenly on Figaroa's ear. The fingers held Figaroa's earlobe with so little pressure that the crime boss almost couldn't feel it. Still, the threat alone would have convinced him to kiss his own sister on the lips. He shoveled in more spaghetti and meatballs.

"Okay, so who did supply the bad stuff?" Remo asked.

Figaroa just shrugged.

"You know."

Figaroa swallowed hard. "I don't know, I swear on my mother's grave."

"Got any suspicions?"

"No. Uh-uh."

"A hint? A clue? Back-fence gossip? Give me something, Figgy."

"I heard they was freebies."

"Yeah? That means somebody is trying to muscle his way in."

"You'd think, but it wasn't that way. It was just five or six giveaways, and it was just the one time. If somebody wanted to take my business he would have unloaded a whole shitload of cheap junk."

Remo looked dejected.

"It has got to be the Latinos," Figaroa said.

"It's not the Latinos. I questioned Jorge Moroza this afternoon, and he said it was you. Eat your dinner."

Figaroa was dismayed when Remo Vu pushed a second plate of tepid pasta in front of him. "I'm full up," he complained, but he dug in.

"You think you got problems?" Remo said. "Upstairs has got me out here playing freaking Columbo. They've got more computer hardware than the IRS, and Smith puts *me* on the street to try to figure out what's going down."

Figaroa listened desperately, looking for any tidbit of information that would tell him who this man was and what he wanted—and how he did what he did. So what did this mean about Upstairs and computers? The guy had to be a Fed, right? But not like any Fed that Figaroa had ever heard of.

"And all I get for my trouble is a bunch of ethnic attitude from you and Moroza," Remo continued. "You two are a real pair of curly-lip slimeballs. The only way to tell you apart is by the accents."

Figaroa gagged. He had been likened to Moroza once before, and the fool who made the comparison was compost. This time he decided to let the insult pass.

Remo was on a roll. "Cripes, between Moroza's favorite restaurant and this place I've got a coating of grease in my lungs that'll take me a week to hack up. And you know what the worst thing is? All this effort is for nothing. 'Cause when it comes to providing me information, you're just as useless as he was."

Figaroa caught the past-tense reference and knew with certainty that his archenemy Moroza was dead. That should have made him happy. It didn't. He knew who was next on Remo Vu's list. He slurred something through a mouthful of meatball.

"Don't talk with your mouth full."

Figaroa forced himself to swallow the partially chewed mush. "I know something."

"No, you don't."

"I do! I swear I got something that'll help you break this thing open!"

Remo rolled his eyes, seeing right through Figaroa's bluff. So Figaroa was going to die.

Then came salvation. It appeared in the form of Angelo Vichensi and Franco Ansoti, his right-hand men. They had sensed trouble when they came in the first time, and now they were back to put things right. They emerged silently from either side of the booth with their weapons aimed at Remo Vu. Can't-miss shots. Remo Vu wasn't even looking in their direction

"Shoot him!" Figaroa bleated.

The shots never happened. Remo Vu reached up as if to scratch his right shoulder. Angelo Vichensi and Franco Ansoti fell over.

"Oh, my God!" cried the waitress, who stopped dead as she emerged from the kitchen.

"We'll need clean forks for Mr. Fig," said the man whose name was Remo.

Figaroa half rose from his seat so he could see the bodies of his bodyguards. One inch of a fork handle protruded from a tiny wound in Angelo's forehead. Franco had a nasty opening in his throat where his Adam's apple had been.

"My men."

"Killed by cutlery," Remo said. "I could hear those two tromping around in the kitchen like a pair of walruses. But don't worry about it. You don't need them anymore, Fig."

"I don't?"

"Eat up."

Figaroa didn't even consider disobeying. He used his hands.

"Hello? Forks?" Remo said to the paralyzed waitress. "And whatever happened to that cherry pie?"

3

Greg Grom pulled the rental Buick to the curb and extracted the photocopied newspaper article. The editorial from a concerned citizen was titled Nashville's House Of Shame.

"The Nashville Police Department has raided the house ten times in eight months. When will they put some of these resources behind a long-term solution?"

The concerned citizen had included the address of the building in hopes of embarrassing the owner into taking action, such as locking the place up. It didn't help. Nothing helped. The dilapidated three-flat continued to serve as a flophouse for crack users and sellers.

Just what Grom was looking for.

The building was a trash magnet, the sidewalk piled with soggy paper and other unidentifiable filth. Guess the residents don't have much civic pride, Grom joked silently to relieve his own tension.

He was startled when one of the trash heaps moved, looking at him with baleful eyes.

The human ruin that he had mistaken for a pile of garbage began to lose interest when Grom just sat there. The head swayed and the eyes narrowed to slits as catatonia reclaimed him or, possibly, her.

Grom lowered the window four inches and called out, "Hello, you there. I have free samples."

The eye slits became as round as quarters and the heap of trash staggered to its feet. At the same time a head emerged from the half-open front door and shouted, "D'you say free samples?"

"Free samples," Grom said.

The human trash pile reached out one shaking hand, and Grom fed a small package through the window opening. The hand snatched at it, and Grom withdrew his hand in panic. The human trash pile missed the little package and fell to the ground, scrambling for it.

The woman from the building was eyeing him suspiciously and approaching Grom's car with her arms crossed resolutely. She was black, twenty-something, and her limp clothing and sallow skin showed the effects of dramatic weight loss.

"Why you giving free samples?"

"It's a method of damaging the local narcotics traffickers' hold on market share."

"You doin' what now?"

Grom winced. "I want a piece of the action," he said, the words sounding stilted.

She sniffed disdainfully. "You think Fumar is gone like you taking some of his what-choo-call 'market'?"

"That's between me and Fumar."

"Maybe I get Fumar right now and see what he says about that."

Other faces now peered from the dingy darkness of the half-opened door and the shattered windows. They all had the starving look of addicts, ruled by a nasty craving that they would do anything to satiate.

Grom saw the same need in the black woman's eyes. Her bluster couldn't mask it. He was already on firm ground.

"Look," he said reasonably, "you don't have to take any if you don't want any."

The woman scowled at the human trash pile as he or she crept into the nearest smelly alley with Grom's little plastic bag.

"I guess Fumar ain't goin' be after us 'cause we took some freebies. But he sure goin' be after you, white bread."

"You let me worry about Fumar." He forced a reassuring grimace and thrust a plastic sample bag through the window.

She took it and hurried into the condemned building. That had to have been the signal the others were waiting for, because the crack house residents came pouring out. Suddenly it was Halloween, and Grom couldn't hand out his treats fast enough to satisfy the eager queue of red-eyed ghouls outside his car window.

When the last of them had scurried back inside, Grom still had three samples in his grocery sack. The black woman reappeared, chin bobbing to unheard music. The free sample had improved her mood.

"I was wondering if you had more samples, white

bread," asked the emaciated woman, who inserted her face in the window opening.

"Here you go," Grom said pleasantly, passing them to her.

"You okay, white bread."

"I'm more than okay," Grom said. "I'm a great guy."

She nodded slowly, then vigorously. "You sure are the greatest."

"I'm the nicest guy you ever met. That guy Fumar? He's an asshole. He's always ripping you off."

"Yeah. Yeah! Fucker!"

Grom spoke carefully now. "You are going to tell everybody what a bad person Fumar is."

"Tell 'em?" she cried. "I can do more'n that!"

The crack heads jittered out of the condemned building, agitated and looking for focus. Grom spoke loudly and hurriedly. "Fumar is a very bad man. He is always ripping you off. You want to tell him how mad you are."

The crack heads showed rapt attention now.

"All of you, you *hate* Fumar and you want to spread the word," Grom exhorted. "Tell everyone what a bad man Fumar is."

"I wanna cut him, don't I?" demanded a buzz-cut Anglo man with a steel stud in each nostril.

"You do not want to cut him—none of you wants to hurt Fumar. All you want to do is spread the word."

"Spread the word." The black woman nodded, her eyes now bright with fervor.

"Spread the word. Spread the word about Fumar," the crowd agreed.

"You right," the black woman cried suddenly. "You

right about Fumar, and you right about you! You the greatest!"

She came at him, and Grom groped for the window switch but was too slow.

"I love you to pieces, white bread!" Her upper body wriggled into Greg Grom's car, forcing the window down, and she wrapped her bony arms around his neck, mashing her mouth against his. Her breath was putrid. Grom struggled, but his paramour was powered by passion. When she opened her mouth and probed his clamped lips with her tongue he felt the bile rising.

He was saved by a shout from the crack-house crowd.

"It's Fumar! He's coming!"

Grom's admirer joined the mob. Every one of them faced the same way, watching Fumar come. And they chanted.

"Spread the word."

"No violence," Grom announced loudly, then added, "Unless he starts it."

"We hate Fumar," the crowd growled. "Spread the word."

"Spread the word."

"Spread the word."

The chant quickly became a battle cry as a tight knot of toughs rounded the corner. Grom pulled the rental car into Reverse.

"You! Yeah, you! Where you think you're goin'!"

The towering Latino stalking down the middle of the street had to be the man himself. Fumar was outfitted in embroidered jeans tight enough to profile his manhood and a green polyester sports jacket loose enough to hide his piece. A small army of powerful-looking bodyguards was at his heels, and every last one of them carried a persuader—a crowbar or a section of steel pipe.

Grom knew they had guns, too. The question was if they could get them out and get a bullet into him before he got the hell away. He stomped on the gas, gripping the wheel as the rental screeched backward down the decrepit street.

Fumar grabbed inside his coat just as Grom over-steered and sent the back end of the Buick into a brick building facade. A giant crunch came from the rear end and left Grom momentarily dazed.

He rubbed his temple and blinked to clear his blurry vision, and by then he found the whole scene changed.

Fumar and his boys had forgotten about Grom. They were too busy with the chanting crack house crowd.

"Spread the word. Spread the word. We hate Fumar!"

The neighborhood drug dealer wasn't used to this lack of appreciation from his loyal customers. They moved in on him, a congregation united by a common hatred.

Grom was so enthralled he forgot his predicament. Had he done it? Was it working? He could see the intensity in their clenched faces, but the crack heads didn't lash out.

There was no violence.

At first.

All it took was a shove. Fumar pushed one of the crack addicts out of his way. She was a skin-and-bones teenager who didn't look as if she had enough muscle mass to lift a cigarette, but she struck back at the drug dealer in a blinding fury. Her jagged fingernails sank into the flesh under his eyes and dragged down, tearing skin off his cheeks.

Fumar staggered away, mouth dangling open, but the girl wasn't done. Flinging away the scraps of human tissue, she leaped at him again, clamping her scrawny arms around his rib cage and sinking her teeth into the open wound on his cheek.

Fumar's boys moved in to help, grabbing the girl by her amazingly quick stick arms. The other crack heads crowded around, shouting belligerently, but they didn't touch Fumar's boys.

Now Greg Grom understood. His suggestion had been that they should not resort to violence unless the other guys started it. The suggestion was holding, but the impulse to violence was too strong. They were exploiting the loophole he had provided them.

The inevitable happened. The enforcers began thrusting the addicts out of the way, which was good enough to qualify as "starting it." The crack heads turned on Fumar's boys with sudden savagery.

The crack heads grabbed and bit and slashed with their fingernails. Fumar's boys gave up on their big sticks in a hurry, and there was a flurry of gunshots. Bodies started falling, but the addicts got their hands on a few metal clubs and started cracking skulls. Their obsession gave them a huge battlefield advantage—a disregard for their own safety.

In just seconds the tide turned against Fumar's boys, who quickly came to a conclusion—these weren't just crack heads and waste cases. They were mad animals. They were maniacs. Fumar's boys tried to flee and didn't get far.

Grom was intrigued by a few desperate crack heads dancing around the fringes of the bloodbath and trying to maneuver themselves into the thick of the fighting. His suggestion was still holding. They were in hysterics, but they couldn't break the no-violence suggestion until and unless they were physically assaulted by one of Fumar's men. Grom observed this behavior with the fascination of a true scientist.

But inevitably they managed to insert themselves into the fray and get shot or pushed or hit by one of Fumar's men, and then they were released into a frenzy of violence. Grom thought of a mad dog at the moment the leash snapped—and the cat that had been taunting him was just sitting there, ready to be snapped up. Grom's eyes grew bright. There was none of the scientist in his appreciation for the ensuing slaughter.

Then the mayhem became stillness. Fumar and his boys were obliterated.

One pathetic crack head, the human trash pile who had accepted Grom's first sample, danced around the massacre shouting at the bloody remains. "Spread the word! We hate Fumar!" Somehow, he or she had never managed to get into the fray.

The other crack heads were disoriented and muddled, several of them wounded and some of their number sprawled in the street with Fumar's men.

Of Fumar himself there was nothing recognizable left. The teenage girl who drew first blood had torn the flesh from his body until her fingers broke, then hacked at his corpse with a pry bar until her adrenaline was used up.

Sirens. Greg Grom was startled back to the reality of his situation. He pleaded with the rental car to start, and it did. He begged it to actually roll on its wheels and it did that, too, although some part of the crushed rear end was rubbing against a tire.

The rental car got him across town, which was good enough. He pulled to the curb in a Nashville industrial park. When no one was looking, he yanked off the stolen license plates that covered the rental car tags. He tucked the plates into a sewer, along with his hairpiece.

Then he pulled out his notebook and flipped to his chart, scanning the left-hand column of alphanumeric identifiers. The column next to the list was headed Results.

He found the entry GUTX-SPF-OR1. The Oregon lab had held out high hopes for its patented system called slow-process fermentation. Slow-process fermentation, however, looked like a big fat failure. Greg Grom meticulously penned in his one-word summation of today's trials.

"Imperfect."

4

Dr. Harold W. Smith didn't pick up the phone. Mark Howard, his assistant, did.

"Hi, sonny," Remo said, "could you put your old man on the line?"

"Dr. Smith is tied up at the moment, Remo. Give me your report."

Remo stood at a small end table using a house phone in a parlorlike sitting area, which was dwarfed by the vast hotel atrium. It was a classy place, but Remo had stopped noticing hotel lobbies after the first few thousand. "This is grown-up talk, youngster," he said. "I think I better speak to your dad."

"Dr. Smith is tracking an event, Remo," Mark Howard explained.

"Right now?" Remo asked. "Where is it?"

Suddenly Remo found himself on a speakerphone, and he heard Dr. Harold Smith's lemony voice over the bad acoustics. "Nashville, unfortunately, Remo."

"Crap. I'm still in Boston."

"The event has concluded anyway," Smith said without emotion. "What did you discover?"

"I discovered exactly how much spaghetti and meatballs are lethal to an adult male scumbucket."

"That's all?"

"Eight plates, and then the stomach bursts. It's quite a sight."

"That's all you learned?" Smith pressed.

"That's it."

"The bad narcotics didn't originate with Figaroa or Moroza?"

"They didn't deal them and they don't know who did. Figaroa said somebody claimed the drugs were give-aways, but there wasn't enough of it to look like new competition."

"What do you mean, not enough?" Smith asked.

"Huh?" Remo asked. "Not enough means you need more before it's enough."

Without thinking about it, Remo's stance was an instinctive balance of muscle and bone, but it was more that just your average good posture. His stance took into account a hundred factors that any other human being would have failed to sense.

Maybe someone standing beside him would have felt the slight movement of the circulating air, if they concentrated. But they never would have been able to sense, let alone make sense of, all the other shifting pressure waves flickering through the atmosphere.

Remo did feel them, and balanced his body to them just as he adjusted himself to the force of gravity. He didn't feel these dynamics in a conscious way, but absorbed them as part of the ebb and flow of his environment.

The part of his environment he was trying to ignore at the moment was the concierge, an outgoing woman in her forties with mannequin-perfect grooming. She caught his eye and gave him a sultry smile.

Well, Remo thought, you ask somebody to point you to the phone and you're just looking for trouble.

"I am asking about the quantity of the drugs that were distributed," Smith clarified.

"I told you, Smitty, a handful of samples."

"You don't know that," Mark Howard observed. "There could have been thousands of samples distributed on the streets and only a small percentage were contaminated."

The concierge was coming out from behind her desk, moving languidly, cycs locked on Remo Williams as she sauntered in his direction. Remo gave her his back.

"That's true," Smith said. "Figaroa's customers wouldn't be forthcoming with that kind of information so he might not have known. Remo, you could survey the populace."

Remo's exasperation crested. "Okay, Smitty, First, no. Second, the Boston Freak Party happened on one street corner, so even if there's a thousand other untainted doses floating around out there, so what? Third, here's the important part—I'm not Peter Falk and the word *investigator* is not on my business card."

"I know this—"

"Fourth, you've got so much computer brainpower in the loony bin basement that even Bill Gates would be hard-pressed to monopolize it. Why haven't *they* figured this out?"

"The data coming in to the mainframes is only as good as the data our gatherers can uncover," Smith explained with forced patience.

"So put the Folcroft Four on the streets," Remo insisted, referring to the mainframes that collected and served data for Upstairs. "Have your Boy Howdy slide 'em in the ass end of that rustbucket battleship you call a car. When you get here you can put them on toy robot treads to move around town."

"I don't think that is a reasonable plan."

"You know what these people drink?" Remo continued. "Ripple. I didn't even know they still made Ripple. I don't even know what Ripple *is*. But that whole end of town smells like Ripple."

"Remo—"

"I bet the Folcroft Four know what Ripple is. They're way smarter than I am—we both know that. You get them out here, they'll put two and two together in a big way."

"This is foolish. The mainframes cannot serve as gatherers."

"Then get other gatherers," Remo retorted.

"We have the best gatherer on the planet. You."

"Just when I think I've heard it all you go and lay some flattery on me," Remo grumbled. "Well, there was the one time you thought I was just the right one to be framed for murder and electrocuted, but since then, no compliments. So today you don't have any credibility."

There was a sigh. "Remo, it was not a compliment,

it was a statement of fact. When no one else can get people to tell what they know, and tell the truth, you can do it."

"There's lots of things I can do better than other people—" Remo said.

"I'll bet there is." It was the concierge. She lounged on the sofa by the phone, one long leg crossed on the other. A dressy high-heeled sandal dangled from her toes. Remo had been pretending she wasn't there, but she didn't get the hint.

"Who's that?" Smith demanded.

"Hold on," Remo said. "Who are you?"

"I'm Madelaine," she purred. If her blouse had not somehow become unbuttoned almost to her belly, her white lace bra wouldn't have been so exposed.

"She's Madelaine," Remo said to Smith.

"I didn't want you to ask her name," Smith responded, his voice becoming more tart.

"I'm the concierge," she said.

"She's the concierge," Remo relayed.

"Remo, I don't care," Smith said.

"I do things for people," Madclaine breathed.

"She does things for people," Remo told Smith.

"I don't care," Smith insisted. "I meant—"

"What kinds of things?" Remo asked the woman.

"For you? Anything."

"Smitty, great news," Remo said into the phone. "She'll do anything. So you can have *her* walk the Boston beat."

Smith came close to raising his voice. "Remo, please stop this foolishness."

"You first." Remo hung up, then severed the cord

from the phone with a tug. Madelaine was delighted. "Now it's just the two of us."

"Yeah, well, not counting the fifty people I can see in the restaurant and the bar and at the front desk."

"Forget them. Let's go to your room."

Remo shrugged. "Sorry, Madelaine. I can't tell you how great you've been. I mean, who'd have thought I'd get so much personal attention just because I asked where the phone was? But I'm off to Nashville."

"Can I come?"

"Without a doubt. But not with me."

Madelaine sat up suddenly. She was alone, just like that. The hunk in the T-shirt had vanished.

She stood and looked all around before glimpsing a figure in a black T-shirt slipping through the stairwell doors. Was that her hunk? He could never have traveled that far through the obstacle course of the lobby in just a couple of seconds.

Could he?

5

"Cue the music," the director ordered.

From the speakers came a swell of steel-drum rhythms with an underlay of romantic strings.

"Action," the director called.

The camera on its lofty crane perch drank in the scenery of lush gardens embracing the base of palm trees, which stretched over the sugar-white sandy beach and the turquoise Caribbean Sea.

The camera crane descended to the level of the woman in the bikini, strolling on the shore with the waters tasting her toes. Her lithe body was deeply tanned but detailed with freckles. Her hair was luxurious and dark, with just enough of an auburn hint to match the terra-cotta trim of the white bikini and the translucent wrap on her waist. She looked off camera, admiring the glorious tropical view, and produced a smile. *The* smile, warm and provocative and friendly all at once.

Todd Rohrman smiled along with her. He always

did. She was something special. You couldn't put your finger on it, but you knew she had a gift of, well, attractiveness. Everybody liked her. Men lusted after her, and women gravitated to her as if she were their best friend. People just *wanted* her.

She turned from her beautiful view of the beautiful ocean, looking directly into the camera with her beautiful blue-green eyes.

Rohrman thought, She's looking right into the minds of every man and woman who'll see this commercial. She's unbelievable.

His trousers buzzed.

Rohrman retreated on tiptoe through the snaking cables and equipment tables. He didn't answer the phone until he reached the pool deck, but the caller hadn't given up.

"Hello, Todd, this is Amelia. I have the president on the line. He would like to speak to the minister."

"It'll have to wait. They're right in the middle of the new commercial shoot," Rohrman said.

"He's calling from the United States, Todd," Amelia Powlik pressed.

"This island is the United States, Amelia."

"The mainland, I mean."

"He'll have to wait," Rohrman said patiently.

"He's meeting with federal officials in two minutes," Amelia insisted.

Rohrman didn't get excited. Sometimes people just didn't understand the pecking order around here. Even people who were a part of the pecking order. "I will not interrupt the minister of tourism in the middle of a shoot."

Amelia pursed her lips with displeasure—Rohrman didn't have to see her to know she was doing it.

Below him they were doing another take of the same shot, this time with a reflector positioned to backlight that beautiful mass of dense hair. Nice, Rohrman thought approvingly. The auburn highlights glimmered in the added burst of backlighting, and the vision of loveliness in the bikini was even more radiant.

"This is the president," said a new voice on the phone.

"This is Todd Rohrman, Mr. President."

"Why am I not speaking to the minister of tourism?"

"As I explained to your secretary, Mr. President, there's a shoot today."

"Mr. Rohrman, I am the president of Union Island, and I want to speak to my minister of tourism. Now."

"Sorry, Mr. President. Not until the shoot is done."

There was a long, tired sigh. "Oh, all right."

"It will just be a few minutes—maybe ten," Rohrman added cheerfully. Then Todd got to do one of his favorite things in the whole world.

He put the president on hold.

THE DIRECTOR WATCHED in the monitors, which received video feeds from all the cameras. It was their eighth take of the afternoon, but the star of the commercial didn't show it. She gazed into the lead camera, and even the director felt as if she were looking directly at him. When she spoke it was both intimate and friendly.

"I am Union Island," she said with her delicious half smile. "Come to me."

She was perfect. She stirred you up when she talked like that.

"You nailed it," he told her as they viewed the shot a minute later. "You got it just right."

"Thank you." She smiled like that even when she wasn't being filmed. "It's good working with you again, Hal. I can't wait to see the finished spots."

Hal, the director, was about to offer to show her the finished spots personally, but the proposal, which he had been practicing for weeks, was laid waste by an announcement from the rear of the set.

"I have the president on the phone for the minister of tourism."

Excitement seemed to ripple through the crew.

"Bye-bye, Hal. Thanks so much." The woman in the bikini threaded her way through the set, shaking hands and offering her thanks to every one of the crew, all the way down to the Florida State University sophomore who was interning with the sound engineer.

"How did I look?" she asked Todd Rohrman.

"You turned *me* on."

"Come on!"

"Almost. Seriously."

She gave him a doubting look and took the portable phone.

She said, "Minister Summens speaking."

Todd Rohrman strolled away to watch the set teardown.

After all, government leaders needed their privacy when discussing matters of state.

"MINISTER SUMMENS, what's our communications status?"

"Wide open, Mr. President," replied Dawn Summens, professional bikini model and Union Island minister of tourism.

"I see," the President said.

The president always had a hard time improvising on an unsecure phone line.

"How are your visits going with the U.S. officials?" she asked leadingly.

"Good. Yes, productive. Constructive. I would like to discuss them when you have time."

"I'll be available in my office between seven and eight this evening, Mr. President."

"Fine. Talk to you tonight, Minister Summens."

"Goodbye, Mr. President." Summens killed the connection.

"Moron," she muttered under her breath.

6

The white man wore only a T-shirt. If he was cold in this unseasonably chilly evening, he didn't show it. If he was concerned about being alone in the worst part of town, he wasn't showing that, either. Maybe, Antoine Jackson thought, he was a crazy man. He'd heard some white men did some mighty stupid things.

But in sixteen years he'd never seen a white man acting this stupid.

He dragged on the front window of his mother's second-story apartment and yelled, "Man, what are you doing here?"

The white man looked right at him as if evaluating him for a moment, but he never slowed his pace.

"You ought to stay out of that place! They'll kill you in there!"

The white man ignored him.

"I'm just trying to help you out."

The white man waved and went to the door of the crack house without hesitation.

Antoine slammed his window. He tried to be a good kid—Lord knew that was tough enough living in the Nashville slums. He tried to be decent to his fellow human beings. But sometimes people just didn't want your sincere help. Let the white man go get himself killed if that's what he wanted. Nothing more Antoine could do about it.

THE WHITE MAN PUT his hands on the door and waited until he saw the shadow of the young man disappear from the window. The kid was partly right. *Somebody* was going to get killed.

He felt the movements of people inside the condemned building, and his nostrils were assaulted by the acrid fumes of burning trash.

The quick slap with the flat of his hand looked feeble, but the blow cracked the door at the bolt and sent it swinging open.

"Special delivery!" He stepped inside and nudged the door closed. "Candy-gram! Pizza boy! Anybody home?"

The foyer of the condemned apartment building was empty. At the foot of the stairs anyone else would have heard only silence, but he detected activity in the ground-floor rooms and movement upstairs.

The ground-floor inhabitants were his first consideration. But those upstairs might try to make a break while he was otherwise engaged. And he hated to do a half-assed job. He grabbed at a broken steel folding chair and dismantled it into components with a few snaps of his fist, then straightened the longest section of black metal tube and jammed it between the wall and the stair rail six inches off the ground.

That would slow whoever descended from the upper floors.

He strolled through the door of the first ground-floor apartment. The tiny living room was bare, but the burning stench was potent.

"Fire inspector! You need a license for a cookout in this city, you know."

The simmering coals of a fire glowed on a makeshift fireplace of scavenged bricks in what had once been a bedroom. The charred remains of rotted timber, old wooden signs and melted plastic soda bottles littered the floor.

He heard his assailant coming and waited until the noisy footsteps were close, then he intercepted the attacker with movement that looked like quick-seeping mercury.

The attacker was street scum, a crack dealer who used a little too much of his own product. His clothing and hair were filthy; his face had dirt crusted in the creases.

His dirty creases grew when his mouth gaped open. His mouth gaped open because he suddenly found his handgun flying out of his grasp as if it had sprouted wings. The man he thought he was sneaking up on was now holding him by the collar, and there were several inches of empty air between his dangling feet and the floor.

"Cleaning service!"

"I didn't order no cleaning service, man!" the drug dealer wailed.

"Somebody did, and man, this place needs it."

"I ain't payin' for no fucking cleaning service!"

"Somebody else is footing the bill."

Before he protested further the dealer's skull was knocked against the wall hard enough to crack it open—and then he was beyond complaining about anything. The corpse got nudged into the closet as it collapsed.

A buzz-cut man scrambled out of his closet hiding place to escape the cadaver that tackled him.

"Who are you, man?" he demanded.

"I'm the florist," Remo Williams lied.

"You killed Drago, man. Killed him with your bare hands. How'd you do that, man?"

"Even we florists need to know self-defense—they taught judo at the Flower Arranging Academy of Chicago." Remo was lying again. He had never attended the Flower Arranging Academy of Chicago. Or any floral trade school, for that matter.

"You killed Drago. You killed Drago!" The young man snatched a switchblade from his jeans pocket, "You killed Drago!"

"Are you trying to tell me I killed Drago?"

The young man leaped at Remo with a screech like a rabid beast. Remo extended his arm, letting the flying man connect with his fist, cutting off the noise. The knife wielder's nose exploded across his face and his body cartwheeled before he slammed to the floor. Remo made a quick punt and the knifer's head arced through the air.

In the door a straw-haired woman, as clean-cut as Janis Joplin, issued a grunt of horror and bolted.

Remo followed her out of the apartment and into another down the hall. Her pig snorts of panic were joined by the howling and grunting of two other people who stormed out of the bedrooms to stand by her side.

More addicts-dealers. But there was something else going on here. The three of them stood in the empty apartment living room and screeched and howled wordlessly, crouching like apes, clawing at the air in front of them. Remo came at them slowly, but their howls became throat-tearing screeches.

"Is that all you have to say for yourselves?"

Apparently it was.

"You the nice folks that offed a local distributor named Fumar?"

One of them, a tall white man in torn jeans, managed to get words around his howls. "Kill you!"

He bent and charged Remo. Maybe he played football before crack claimed his brain. Remo applied a palm to the top of his head, creating a tremendous amount of force that compressed the attacker's vertebrae into one fused bone-mass.

The other man whirled a crowbar overhead, issuing a catlike yowl. Misjudging his clearance, the crowbar lodged in the ceiling and he looked up to see what the problem was. Remo drummed his knuckles on the man's chest as if he were knocking on the neighbor's front door.

The druggie forgot the crowbar and concentrated on the fact that his heart had begun pounding as wildly as a rubber ball in a tiny box. He ran blindly into a wall and fell to the floor, dying in spasms.

The woman made singsong wails that came with each exhalation, her mouth pulled back over her teeth like a chimp in a snit. Despite her apparent mania, she calmly leveled the mini-Uzi she had grabbed from somewhere and squeezed the trigger.

Her chemically altered state left no room for skill, and she emptied the entire magazine in a single continuous stream of rounds that crashed into the wall of the room and somehow managed to get nowhere near her intended victim, who slithered away from wherever she directed the fire.

Remo lifted the Uzi out of the crack queen's grasp when she still had a single round left in the magazine and, with a blow to the head, snapped her off like a light.

He heard footsteps and the tumbling of bodies tripping over his booby trap on the stairs. He found two men scrambling to their feet. They were junkyard warriors. One had a piece of old chain, while the other possessed a ragged steel bar. They spotted Remo and instantly began howling, bansheelike.

Whatever was going on here wasn't pleasant, and Remo considered the possibilities as the two howlers came at him. Remo had run into his share of drug users in his day, and none of them made such a racket. It wasn't just ghoulish; it was annoying.

"Oh, be quiet!" He grabbed the iron bar from the first attacker and used it to absorb the blow of the second attacker's chain. The chain looped around the bar and lifted it out of the attacker's hands. Suddenly the bar was descending on them both, the point crashing through the first skull with such momentum it was carried well into the second skull. The first attacker collapsed with a good portion of his brains splattered on the walls and floor around him. The second fell on his back with the bar sticking straight up like a flagpole.

The deaths were witnessed by a group at the top of the stairs and started them all yowling, which got on Remo's nerves. He loped up the stairs in long strides and grabbed the first crack head he came to, hurling him over the railing to the landing below, where his vocalizations stopped with a bony crunch.

A crack head bashed his vodka bottle on the floor. Half the contents spilled out, and the air filled with the smell. Remo lifted the glass weapon out of the crack head's hands and inserted it in his chest, twisting and slicing a perfect circle of empty space where much of his rib cage and heart should have been.

The final crack head ran into an empty apartment and tried to slam the door behind him, only to find his attacker standing right there at his side. His howl died to a curious "Urk?" and he died with it, as his trachea shattered and his breathing apparatus stopped functioning.

There was a rustle from above and Remo drifted up to the third story, following the sounds to the doorless entry to another apartment. A zinc trash barrel stood in the middle of the room, smoking slightly from a fire that had been allowed to die out. A hairy, greasy man was struggling to claw his way through the narrow window, snuffling and grunting like a dog digging its way under the fence.

"Let's talk," Remo suggested.

The hairy man's mouth fell open.

"Please?" Remo added.

All he got was a high-pitched hyena wail.

"Oh, can it!" Remo swept the metal garbage container across the room, where it slammed into the screamer and crushed him into the window frame, shattering most of his skeletal system and silencing him instantly.

Remo listened. There were no more animal-like howls. More importantly, he could hear no other heartbeats or furtive movement inside the building.

Grabbing the boneless dead man, he tromped to the second floor and collected an armful of corpses. On the first floor he sat all the dead druggies together, rifling their clothing for paraphernalia and coming up with a few large plastic bags of white powder, a few plastic-wrapped rocks of crack cocaine and a couple of syringes. He broke the needles and pocketed everything else.

Down the street was a tiny neighborhood grocery that looked like a miniature prison. The windows were barred. A heavy steel gate covered the door.

Miraculously, the pay phone on the sidewalk functioned. Remo depressed the one button and held it. Somewhere, magic computerized connections were made. A wind blew and his body adjusted automatically to the chill.

"Luigi's Pizza," said a computer-simulated voice on the other end of the line.

"I want an extralarge pepperoni, delivered," Remo said.

A scrawny man stalked to the phone booth, wearing so many gang colors and insignias he looked like an Eagle Scout who had gone over to the dark side.

Remo nodded. "Evening. The weather outside is frightful. Dum, dum, delightful."

"Man, what're you doing on my telephone?"

"Remo? What did you say?" said a new voice on the line.

"I'm talkin' to you, boy. What're you doin' on my phone? You know this is my place of business."

"Hold on, Luigi," Remo said, then turned to the gang-banger. "I thought you guys used cell phones these days."

"Usually I do, but there's times I need a public phone, and it's that phone right there. Now you get off my phone."

"You work with those clowns in the big green build-ing down the street?" Remo asked.

"What's it to you, boy?"

"I just took this off them," he said, pulling one of the largest of the plastic bags of white substance out of his coat pocket. The dealer became very still, steam hiss-ing out of his nostrils.

"Remo, what's going on?" Harold Smith demanded.

"Just hold on, Luigi."

"You a cop?" the dealer demanded.

"Just an interested bystander."

"If you ain't a cop, then you're moving in on my ter-ritory!" Reaching into the back of his pants, he yanked out a snubby handgun. "Hand it over."

Remo extended the dope and let go of it. In the mo-ment the drug dealer's attention was distracted by the plummeting bag of controlled substance the handgun somehow became turned around in his hands, with his thumb depressing the trigger. He started to shout, and Remo nudged the muzzle of the weapon into his mouth. A great red mess suddenly covered the sidewalk. Remo snatched his bag of drugs before it hit the ground.

"I'm here, Smitty."

"Are you calling me from the middle of a job?"

"No, job's done. I just got tangled in some superfluous details and now they're untangled."

A man in a sleeveless undershirt and a dirty apron stepped out of the front of the grocery, looked down at the corpse and the mess on the sidewalk, then peered quizzically at Remo. Remo shrugged. The grocer retreated inside.

"You get any samples?" Smith asked.

"Got 'em. You were right about the perpetrators. They howled like dogs."

"Get those samples shipped here ASAP and maybe we'll figure out what's making it happen."

The wail of a siren filled the dingy block, and a Nashville Police Department squad car rolled around the corner. As the crowds gathered, Remo slipped through the cops trying to take control of the scene. A scene that appeared, as unlikely as it seemed, to be a suicide. The victim was on the ground with the front end of his handgun wedged squarely in his mouth, hand on the trigger.

If only a few more drug dealers took care of themselves like that, one of the cops observed, the world would be a better place.

The police never even saw Remo slip past them.

7

The colors of the late-afternoon sun played over the peaceful community of cookie-cutter duplexes in Stamford, Connecticut, painting bright colors on the windows and lengthening the shadows of hopscotching children. Inside one of the duplexes a phone started to ring.

The ringing lasted twenty minutes. It stopped, then rang again, for twenty more minutes.

The childlike figure in the kimono sat cross-legged on the mat in the empty-looking living room, performing a nearly impossible feat: ignoring the ringing. Truly ignoring it. The endless electronic jangling did not annoy or even distract him. This was not a child at all, but an old Asian man. So old, in fact, he could have used his age to make himself a celebrity, had he chosen to.

There was a sheaf of empty parchment pages on the mat. There was another such stack on a mat across from him. A quill pen was placed next to each stack of paper. He ignored these as well. He was staring into space, not smiling, but somehow with contentment on a face that was as dry and pale as the parchment but far more wrinkled.

When the phone paused and started to ring yet again, the Asian rose and lifted the receiver from its wall mount. He put it to his ear, saying nothing.

"Master Chiun, is that you?"

"Yes, Emperor Smith."

"Were you out?"

"Out of what?"

"Is something wrong, Master Chiun? Were you sleeping?"

"I have been reciting Ung."

"I see. I've been letting the phone ring for the better part of an hour."

"I was reciting Ung. It is an absorbing and beautiful literature."

"I see. Well—"

"The people of the Western world cannot allow their attention to rest on any one thought for long. They are children who become bored with playthings and look for another plaything and then another."

"I suppose that's true—"

"I blame Homer."

HAROLD SMITH HAD been struggling to change the direction of the conversation. He knew little of Ungian poetry, other than it was extremely lengthy and endlessly repetitive, and he knew the old Korean named Chiun could lecture about it for hours, interweaving his diatribe with discourses on the inadequacies of those who didn't enjoy it—a population that likely included everyone on Earth save Chiun himself.

But now the old Master of Sinanju had piqued his interest. Smith studied the classics during his university years, which was decades earlier, and was proud that he retained much of his classical education.

"Surely you don't mean the Greek poet Homer?" Smith asked.

"Of course I mean the Greek poet," Chiun sniffed. "Has there ever been another famous Homer?"

"Not that I know of," Smith agreed. "But Homer penned the great epics." He knew he shouldn't be having this conversation, but somehow he couldn't steer off the subject.

"Pah. He made outlandish adventure tales," Chiun retorted. "He put sex and violence and low-brow ribaldry on every page to keep the dim-witted entertained, and he broke his stories into convenient segments that could be read quickly before the reader lost his concentration. From there it was just a few short centuries before that abominable playwright popularized the formula for the masses. Now the West produces hackneyed films and miserable, fatuous 'literature' that is all derivative of the abhorrent formula Homer scribbled on vellum three thousand years ago."

"I don't think you understand the true impact his writing had on the world," Smith insisted.

"Ungian poetry, on the other hand, is written without the artificial structure of a series of events that lead a character careening without purpose into one hair-levitating quandary after another. Ung explores a single, simple aspect of nature. It gives full value to its subject, be it a flower or a cliff face or a lichen mass in a tidal pool. It is truly in harmony with the nature it celebrates."

"But Homer can be appreciated by the common man," Smith countered. "In fact, the *Iliad* was likely a transcription of stories that had been in the oral tradition for centuries—the *Odyssey* may have been, as well."

"Circuses for the rabble," Chiun declared. "Thank goodness his rivals in certain neighboring empires saw wisdom in hiring competent assassins to carry out a literary coup de grâce before he could distribute his other stacks of quill scratchings. I can't imagine what seventeen more 'epics' would have done to further degrade the Western intellect."

Smith was flabbergasted at the implication. "Are you saying Homer was assassinated by Sinanju?"

"Trust me, Emperor, the other epics are as lacking in merit as the two that are known to the modern world."

Smith's dismay deepened. "Master Chiun, are you saying Sinanju possesses them? That you've read them?"

"What is the purpose of your call, Emperor Smith? Remo has not yet returned, and when he arrives he will be indisposed for many hours."

Harold W. Smith, with an effort, forced himself to focus on the cold data windows filling the display under the surface of his great, black onyx desk. These dispassionate reports were his world. Why had he become so distracted? "I am afraid Remo's not returning to Connecticut tonight. He's in Nashville."

"I see," Chiun said after a frosty silence.

"There's been another event. I'm hoping he'll be

able to catch up to whatever person or group is making it happen."

"I understood that was the purpose for which he was dispatched to the city of beans and arsonists," Chiun retorted acidly. The old Master and his son had lived in Boston for years, the sole inhabitants of an old, renovated church. It was the closest thing to a real home the pair had known in all the years they were contracted to the organization Dr. Smith headed, but the building burned to the ground in a fire set by irate mobsters. The irate mobsters were extinguished not long after the blaze they set, but Chiun was still bitter over the loss of his Castle Sinanju.

"Remo was unable to identify the perpetrators in Boston," Smith explained.

"That is to be expected. He is a good son but, between you and I, Emperor, he is not the brightest bulb in the toolshed."

"Uh." Smith had to think about that one for a moment before he sorted out the mixed metaphor. This conversation was definitely not going as efficiently as he would have hoped. "Yes, Master Chiun, which is why I was hoping you would join Remo in Nashville. He could benefit from your incisiveness."

"Ah," Chiun said in a singsong sigh. "I understand. But I have no wish to leave my home at this time."

Smith continued. "He is a skilled Master and he has been trained flawlessly—"

"Yes, that is certainly the case."

"But he lacks your wisdom."

"I understand completely, Emperor." Smith could

almost see the appreciative half smile on the face of the Korean centenarian. "In the ways of the mind, he is a child, really."

"An amateur thinker," Smith added.

"Yes! Those are the perfect words," Chiun agreed with a squeal of enthusiasm.

"He may be biting off more than he can chew in Nashville if there is much deductive reasoning called for."

"We can only imagine what sort of mischief he might cause. I believe I should join him immediately."

"An excellent notion, Master Chiun."

Dr. Smith hung up feeling satisfaction with how he had handled Chiun. Getting Chiun to change his mind on anything was a major victory. Smith still shuddered at the memories of the contract-negotiation sessions he endured with the old Master.

In recent months Chiun had been somewhat of a recluse. Smith knew that, after the Rite of Succession, when the Reigning Master of Sinanju passed the torch to his protégé, the elder Master often retired to a life of seclusion. Smith was aware that there was a cave outside the Korean village of Sinanju that was the traditional hermitage of retired Masters.

Smith had mixed feelings about this possibility. Remo Williams was extremely capable in his role, but Chiun could be a godsend at times.

It wasn't even that Chiun had time and again been the catalyst to success in the organization's various undertakings. It was that he was a part of a team. Remo and Chiun. There had never been a time when it had not been the two of them working together.

The pairing had come about many years ago, when Smith needed muscle—when his organization remade itself from being simply a clearinghouse of information to an agency of enforcement.

The agency was named CURE. Smith steadfastly thought of the name in all capitals, like an acronym, but it wasn't. The name had come from the mind of a U.S. President who decided that the escalation of crime and mayhem needed a solution—a CURE for a sick nation.

This President, as young and idealistic as he was, understood that the government agencies designed to rein in crime, within the limitations set by the U.S. Constitution, weren't doing the job. The laws of the land tied the hands of law enforcement, but the criminals ignored those laws.

So CURE was set up to maintain the integrity of the Constitution by ignoring the Constitution. To protect the freedom of Americans by violating their rights to privacy and due process.

Creating CURE would have decimated the reputation of even a wildly popular President if it became public knowledge, but the bigger worry came from the potential for abuse. CURE, operating virtually without accountability, represented incredible power. And power corrupts.

So the young President looked for an incorruptible man to run it. One whose ethics were incontrovertible, whose self-discipline was steel, whose patriotism was unquestionable.

Somewhat to his own surprise, the President, not long before he was assassinated before the eyes of the world, found a man to fit the bill. An ex-CIA computer expert, not the most charismatic man you'd ever meet, but Harold W. Smith had all the qualifications to take on the awesome responsibility of CURE.

That burden of responsibility expanded when it became clear that simply finding and exposing illegal activity had minimal impact. Smith and his network of oblivious operatives uncovered more illegal acts than the FBI and the CIA combined, but all Smith could do was surreptitiously pass the intelligence along to other agencies to take action. Sometimes they could not act, did not act, were prevented by manpower and corruption—and the credibility of the intelligence Smith funneled their way—from acting.

So CURE changed its strategy. It became an agency that took action, and the action it took was just as illegal as its blatantly unlawful intelligence-gathering.

CURE hired an assassin. They found him in the form of Remo Williams, a New Jersey beat cop and war veteran. Smith's right-hand man, Conrad MacCleary, made the choice. What CURE needed, after all, was a natural-born killer. Conn had witnessed Remo Williams in action in wartime and never forgot it.

Officer Williams, with a fiancée and a solid reputation and a bright future, was framed for murder. He was found guilty. He was sent to the chair and executed.

But the execution didn't take, thanks to Smith and MacCleary, who arranged the entire charade, and Remo Williams woke up with a surgically altered face and a decision to make. Join the team. Or die. For real this time. No hard feelings.

Remo Williams joined the team. He was trained in weapons and stealth. He was trained in Sinanju.

Chiun was another one of MacCleary's choices. Smith had such faith in his old friend from the CIA that he acceded to what sounded like a bizarre training regimen. Sinanju, MacCleary said, produced the finest assassins the world had known. Ever.

Smith didn't quite buy into it. MacCleary wasn't known to exaggerate, but the feats that he claimed for these Sinanju masters were beyond believability. But Chiun proved Conn right.

Before long, Remo proved Conn right, as well. Even Chiun was surprised by Remo's ability to absorb Sinanju. No child of the village of Sinanju ever mastered the art as Remo mastered it. No adult had ever been able to learn more than a few rudimentary basics.

But Remo became Sinanju, and Chiun deemed that this American orphan would become his protégé, a last-minute godsend for an elderly master who had lost two heirs already—one to tragedy and one to betrayal.

Chiun would not leave Remo, so CURE found itself with the most potent pair of assassins on the planet under its employ.

They worked side by side, a perfect team. The disasters that had been averted by Remo and Chiun were unfathomable in their scope.

Harold Smith didn't know what the future held for the world, but he knew the world wasn't ready to exist without CURE and its enforcement arm. Its enforcement team.

But he might have no say in the matter. If and when Chiun made up his mind to seek the comfort of retirement in a dark cave in North Korea, Smith certainly wouldn't be able to talk him out of it.

There was something else on Smith's mind. He had enjoyed his parlay with the old master about the merits of Ung and Homer. It had hearkened back to the discussions he enjoyed years ago, when he was considered a scholar of sorts. It was the kind of pastime he had looked forward to during that brief interlude in his life when he was retired from the CIA and had accepted a position as a university professor. All too quickly that future was erased with a summons from a U.S. President in need of a man just like him.

Smith hadn't refused the CURE assignment. His patriotism would not have allowed him to refuse. But there had been no personal considerations, really. From the moment of that meeting with the President until this day, decades later, CURE came first. Everything else in Smith's life came second. Wife. Family. Home. Enjoyable diversions.

That give and take with Chiun had been quite satisfying and novel. It had been a long time since he had that kind of, well, fun.

8

Greg Grom evaded his security detail without trouble. He always did. Still, he followed orders and did the circle-the-block thing and tailback thing. There was no sign of the others.

He looked for a likely dark alley to do the park-and-wait thing. Sitting in the shadows for fifteen minutes watching for the tail he knew would not come. What a waste of time. Just this once he'd skip it and nobody would ever have to know.

But that was a fantasy. When it came time to report in, he wouldn't be able to hide his rule breaking. And then he'd be in big trouble.

"Dammit!" He shouted at the steering wheel, then turned the car quickly into a convenience store lot, parking in the shadows alongside the building where a security floodlight was inoperative. He waited and watched for fifteen minutes, as ordered. There was no sign of pursuit.

"Told you so," he said to nobody.

It was a two-hour drive to Lexington. It was a two-hour drive back.

He stopped for a short while at the Big Stomp Saloon, which *was* big. It had been a roller rink once. The "Stomp" referred to the type of dance favored by the clientele. It seemed to include a lot of cowboy-boot stomping.

The Big Stomp was now famous throughout Kentucky and Tennessee as the birth of country rave, the newest evolution in country music. The original raves had sprung up in the U.S in the 1990s, when the designer drug Ecstasy became all the rage. Kids took it and danced all night. That was a rave.

An Ecstasy high gave the user a high-adrenaline rush that lasted for hours, and rave music had a rapid, thumping beat. Country music took years to come up with a hybrid that fit the bill. It was mostly just Garth Brooks remixed over a disco rhythm track. Whatever. It was awful.

Greg Grom smiled broadly, at no one in particular.

"Look like you got a stick up your butt and you really are enjoyin' it," commented an acne-scarred teenager in grease-blackened jeans and shiny, new imitation-rattlesnake cowboy boots.

"Do I?" Grom asked.

"What the hell you all smiley about?"

"I just made a big score," Grom explained.

The teenager looked around. "Oh, yeah? So where's she now?"

"Not a woman. Business. A deal. I just closed a big deal, and I made a hell of a lot of money off it. Buy you a beer?"

"Oh. Sure. Yeah." It was hard to stay antagonistic to a guy who paid for your brew.

"Give this man a beer!" Grom shouted at the bartender. He slapped a twenty on the counter. The twenty made the bartender his friend, too. "What the hell! I want everybody to celebrate—give everybody a beer!"

He thrust a few hundreds at the happy bartender and the party started. Word spread throughout the place and the dance floor emptied as the patrons crowded in for the free drinks. "Let me give you a hand," Grom shouted, and the bartender had no objections when Grom stepped behind the bar to help him man the tap and shove beer mugs across to the eager customers. The bartender never noticed that Grom's beer mugs received a quick sprinkling of white powder before they were rotated under the open taps.

"This is party night!" Grom shouted. "This is the most fun we have ever had! We need to keep dancing all night long!"

The bartender gave him a bemused smirk, but Grom thrust several more hundreds at him. "That should cover things for a while."

The bartender quickly estimated it would cover every customer's bar tab for the whole night and maybe the next.

"The rest is yours, friend! Keep 'em coming!" Grom shouted, "This is the best night ever! We want to celebrate all night long!"

He sounded like an ecstatic idiot drunk, and that was perfectly okay to the Big Stomp patrons. The bartender figured he had to be some sort of foreigner. The guy didn't talk right, sort of. But the bartender wasn't about to upset this apple cart.

After the first free round was distributed, Grom slapped the bartender on the shoulder. "Thanks, friend! I need to step out for some fresh air."

The bartender just grinned and kept pouring.

"Hey, you're the greatest, businessman!" shouted the acned teenager, waving his free beer at Grom. Other patrons came at him, shaking his hand, offering compliments. Grom was careful not to say anything more. One careless suggestion could ruin everything.

Every batch so far had technically *worked*. The formula he was searching for—the perfect formula— would be the one without side effects.

The original formula of GUTX, derived from nature, had no side effects. But there was no more natural source. Grom had one alternative only: a synthesis. It had cost him serious cash to have certain laboratories synthesize versions of GUTX, none of which perfectly replicated the natural substance. They were close, but, so far, not close enough.

Tonight he was taking a different approach to his suggestion-making, too. All positive statements. Have fun! Be happy!

Greg Grom had not even reached the door when he heard the sounds of violence. A stomp dancer had been jettisoned off a raised section of the dance floor into a table below.

A livid couple stomped off the lower-level dance floor. "You spilled my beer!" screeched the plump young woman. "His, too!" she added before her plump young boyfriend could add his two cents' worth. They started stomping all over the offending beer-spiller.

Their victim twisted free of the bruising boots just long enough to stab one finger viciously skyward. "'Twarn't me!" the poor man yelped. "Johnny Ogden throwed me!"

Suddenly the plump couple and their heavily stomped victim were at peace with one another and forged an instant alliance against a common enemy.

"Johnny Ogden, you sheep-fucking son of a swine!"

The woman had a piercing quality that cut through the disco-country soundtrack. Everybody looked at her. Nobody stopped stomping. The fallen man, one arm hanging limp, struggled to his feet and even he resumed stomping.

Oops, Grom thought. He'd suggested something about dancing all night long, hadn't he? And this was what these people called dancing.

The music stopped. The stomp dancing continued, but it was now the march of soldiers into battle, filling the vast saloon with the clomp-clomp rhythm.

The woman and her pair of male followers stomped up the ramp to the upper-level dance floor.

Other patrons stomped out of their way.

The plump young woman stomped at a big stomping man that could only be Johnny Ogden.

Greg Grom noticed the bartender. The only non stomper in the place. He was punching numbers into a cell phone and looking frantic. Calling the cops. Time to go, Grom decided.

The bartender looked right at him.

Grom's heart sank.

The guy would remember him. Recognize him. He would be lucid enough to give the cops a description. That would ruin everything.

Grom felt foolish. But he couldn't stop to berate himself now.

He had to solve the problem.

"Stop!" he shouted.

They stopped fighting, Johnny Ogden and his three attackers. Everybody in the bar turned to Greg Grom, still stomping. The grinned and waved at their good friend, the guy who bought them the beer.

"Johnny Ogden is not a bad man," Grom declared. "Johnny Ogden is your friend! But there is someone else here who is the enemy! Someone you all hate!"

The stomping grew furious as fifty-three enraged beer-swillers craned their necks, trying to find the enemy.

"Who?" squealed the plump lady. "Who is it?"

"It is—" he paused, just for the drama "—the bartender!"

The bartender looked stricken. He didn't understand why this was happening, but suddenly, with perfect clarity, he knew how it was going to end.

Grom left as the stomping became deadly.

He pulled out his little black book. With regret, he found the entry for that night's batch and penned in next to it, "Imperfect."

9

The quartet of sky marshals scowled at Remo Williams. They scowled at the nervous young lady at the check-in desk. They scowled meaningfully to one another to make it appear they knew what was going down.

But they didn't have a clue.

"You sure there's no problem here?" the head sky marshal asked the airline ticket puncher for the third time.

"They say everything is fine," she protested.

"What about the complaints?"

"The passengers issued an apology through a spokesman," she explained reluctantly.

"Since when do a bunch of passengers have a spokesman?" the sky marshal demanded.

"I guess they're traveling together," she said. "A tour group from Paris."

Uh-oh, thought Remo, who now had an inkling as to what was going on aboard the 737 that had just landed. Its pilot had relayed a passenger-disturbance complaint minutes before landing. That brought the sky marshals in a hurry, but after the aircraft landed the pilot called back to say the complaint had been retracted. The sky marshals weren't buying any "retraction."

"Let me get this straight," the head sky marshal said to the ticket puncher. "This tour group issues a complaint against another passenger and asks for law enforcement. Then the passenger apologizes, so the Paris tour group says no hard feelings and expects us to just drop it?"

The ticket puncher seemed to shrink into herself. "Not exactly, Officer."

"Marshal."

"Not exactly, Marshal. From what I understand, the Paris tour group apologized to the passenger. You know, the one they issued the complaint about."

"Well, why'd the bejeezus they do that?"

Remo knew the answer. The answer strode out of the debarking door, scowling. The scowl became worse by degrees when Remo approached.

"Bad flight, Little Father?"

"Do you know what was on that flight, Remo? Can you possibly guess?"

"Hmm. When you screw your face up that tight, it's got to be, oh, French?"

"Yes!" Chiun exclaimed, pleased to share his outrage. "They spent the entire flight behaving like French. They spoke French. They *smelled* French. I was harassed for hours."

"It's a fifty-minute flight."

"They gave me no peace. They insulted me in their hideous tongue, thinking I could not understand their meaning. It was a mob of uncivilized nonbathers against a frail but hygienic elderly man. I was on the verge of being physically assaulted."

"You were lucky, I guess."

"Excuse me," asked the sky marshal, "where are the rest of the passengers?"

"There was some trouble with the lavatories after landing, Marshal," Chiun said, croaking out the words like the weak, failing senior citizen he wasn't. "Apparently a great many of them became wedged in the lavatory cubicles."

"Oh, my God!" the sky marshal said. "How did that happen?"

Chiun looked at the floor, a sad and pathetic old man. "They are French. Who can say with the French?"

CHIUN THE ELDERLY, Chiun the Frail, Chiun the Dying became Chiun the Obstinate when he was informed that he was to board another aircraft at once. His wrist bones, as brittle as sun-dried pine needles, nearly broke when the old Korean master illustrated his displeasure by backhanding the motorized cart that had just transported them to a two-engine prop plane.

The airport staffer on the cart knew his little putt-putt vehicle couldn't possibly go as fast as it was suddenly going, and it sure the hell couldn't do it in reverse. He was still trying to figure all this out a half second later when the cart stopped against the protective concrete pillar at the base of the airport gate. It was hours before he thought about anything again.

"Do you have my trunks?" Chiun demanded.

"Yes. The Reigning Master of Sinanju is faithfully jockeying all six of your trunks."

"The Master of Sinanju Emeritus expects no less," Chiun replied with an offhand wave. "See that they are not scratched."

"They're not scratched," Remo said.

"You handle them irreverently," Chiun complained.

"Hey, you were lucky I grabbed those things just when you were sending the poor driver halfway across the tarmac. They'd have been scratched and dinged and who-knows-what all."

"Dinged?" Chiun stopped on the third step up into the charter plane. "You shall *not* allow my trunks to be dinged, or scritched or danged or any other thing."

"I didn't, no thanks to you."

"Of course there are no thanks to me," Chiun said with a sniff. "There have never been thanks to me, especially not from the adopted son to whom I have given everything." Chiun was speaking now for the benefit of the flight attendant who awaited them inside the doors at the top of the steps.

"I gave him my title. I gave him an education and a vocation," Chiun explained to her. "I gave him what orphans the world over dream of. What do I get in return?"

"Bellhop service for life," Remo answered.

"Disdain." Chiun's quivering head shook sadly.

"Oh, dear," the flight attendant murmured, her mechanical smile melting into genuine sympathy.

"Don't believe a word of it," Remo warned.

"You poor man."

"Ask him how poor," Remo called from behind. "He could buy this airport."

"Poor in the currencies that matter. Loyalty. Understanding. Respect."

"Yo, Emeritus! We got places to go."

Chiun leaned close to the young woman in the starched navy blue uniform. "You see how it is for me," he whispered, his lungs, weary from a century of breathing, were barely able to get the words out.

The flight attendant wiped away a single drop of moisture from the corner of her eye and tenderly embraced the little man's crippled body in her arms, then gently assisted him to the window seat. When she was sure he was comfortable—as comfortable as his weak, failing body could possibly be—she turned and shot a lethal look of disgust at Remo Williams, Reigning Master of Sinanju.

THE FLIGHT WAS chartered for just the two of them, and in no time they were taxiing to a stop at a tiny regional airport. A rental car was waiting, and Remo followed the directions that had been faxed to him, with a hand-drawn map, from Folcroft. Remo still felt disoriented by the three words that were printed in neat block letters at the big X that indicated their destination. He knew what "Saloon" meant. What was "Big Stomp?" Was Smitty experimenting with some more code words? If so, Remo missed the meeting. Or he'd missed paying attention at the meeting. Did Big Stomp indicate he was supposed to go in and assassinate everybody in the place? He was thinking he'd better call Upstairs and clarify the message before he actually carried out such instructions.

His destination came into view in the form of a massive lighted sign, fifty feet off the ground, bright red with white letters. Then he understood the words on the map.

"Big Stomp Saloon is the name of a bar?"

"The Big Stomp?" Chiun said, perking up from his introspective sulk. "Is it *the* Big Stomp Saloon?"

"Don't tell me you've heard of the place?" Remo asked as they parked amid squad cars and unmarked vehicles.

"Hey, you!" said a state trooper just inches from the driver's-side window.

"Who has not heard of it?" Chiun asked as they stepped from the car.

"Mister, I been waving you off since you started up the drive," the trooper said. "Now you tell me, you blind or just stupid?"

"I'm with the federal government, so you make the call," Remo said, pulling out an ID and giving it a quick glance before presenting it to the trooper. "Remo Baggins, National Tobacco, Firearms and Alcohol Association."

"From who now? You mean ATF? Partner, this ain't a federal case. No nationwides are invited."

"There was something in the booze that caused it, so that makes it the business of the booze bureau."

The trooper's lips went tight. "You wait right here." He scurried off, never noticing the pair was silently tailing him, but the Masters halted when a white limousine turned into the lot and rolled to a stop on crunching gravel.

"Do you see, Remo? People of wealth come here. It is a place of importance in musical history."

"Yeah." The limo received personal service from one of Tennessee's finest. A trooper chatted with the driver, but Remo was more interested in the figures behind the dark glass in the back seat. "You mean they aren't reopening tonight?" asked a voice from the rear. Whoever he was, he was hidden behind the bulk of a bodyguard.

The trooper chuckled politely and explained that it would take hours to process the crime scene and, no, the place would not be reopening tonight. The figure in the back stared past his hired muscle, taking it all in. Then he stared fixedly at Remo—it was the voyeur gaze of a man who knew he could see but, behind the dark glass, not be seen.

But this time he was wrong. Remo adjusted his vision to compensate for the refraction of the flashing light that turned the windows into mirrors, at the same time adjusting the angle of his face so that the headlights of the nearest squad car put his own face in shadow.

But the man in back never moved out from behind the bodyguard. Remo saw only the eyes.

Then the limo rolled away.

REMO AND CHIUN FOUND the cavernous interior of the Big Stomp crowded with uncollected corpses, shattered furniture, and the stench of spilled beer turning sour under hot crime-scene lights.

"Yeesh. The Big Stomp is a big dump," Remo said. "So how come you've heard of it?"

"It is renowned throughout the world," Chiun said.

"Which world we talking about?" The stark white police lights hid none of the shabbiness of the peeling wall paint, the scratched floor or the water-stained ceiling tiles.

"This is where the career of Wylander Jugg blasted off," the old Korean explained.

"Launched?"

"Before she became a star, the comely Wylander was performing here without appreciation of her marvelous talents, until a musical agent came to see her show. Even in this foul place her brilliance shone, and the musical agent took her under his wing."

"Ah. Many things now makes sense to me about Wylander Jugg." Remo looked down at a body inside a chalk outline. The broken end of a beer bottle protruded from the stomach of a man with a week's growth of shaggy beard.

"Nasty, ain't it?" asked the man taking pictures.

"Looks like a prop from a Patrick Swayze movie," Remo commented.

The photographer screwed up his face. *"Dirty Dancing?"*

"I wish. Who did all this running amok?"

"Who didn't?" the photographer said. "The whole place went nuts. Started out with one little fight on the dance floor, and next thing you know everybody was brawlin' everybody. We had five bodies when we got here and we musta sent fifty wounded to the Methodist hospital."

"Were they lucid?" Remo asked.

"Were they who?"

"You know, were they thinking clearly? Or kind of confused?"

"Oh. Definitely more like kinda confused. None of 'em seems to know what happened. None of 'em even knows who did the killin'."

"Can I help you?" demanded a county official with a sheriff's badge pinned on his rumpled white shirt. "You federals are not supposed to be here."

"Just asking a few questions," Remo said. "Won't take long."

"Let me see your identification."

Remo thrust his badge at the sheriff. "Where's your witnesses?" he asked the photographer.

"Don't answer that, Aberle!" the sheriff snapped. "What about him? You gonna try and tell me he's ATF, too?" The sheriff nodded at Chiun, who watched stoically with his hands tucked neatly in the sleeves of a scarlet kimono.

Remo tried to remember what Chiun's ID said. "Who're you with again, Little Father?"

"CLECIC," Chiun chirped without hesitation.

Remo and the sheriff were equally befuddled. "Hùh?" the lawman demanded.

"Congressional Law Enforcement Corruption Investigation Committee," Chiun explained in his pleasant singsong.

"There ain't no such thing!" the sheriff insisted. "Let me see your damn—"

The sheriff stopped talking and stopped moving. His mouth hung open, ready to complete the expletive.

The photographer found it very curious. He also

found it curious that the little Korean man was now holding the sheriff by the earlobe. "What just happened?" he asked the skinny Caucasian ATF agent.

"We were being rudely interrupted. You're done blathering, right, Sheriff?"

The sheriff had tears rolling down his face, but he managed a terse nod.

"Okay. Now tell me about the witnesses."

The photographer looked questioningly at the sheriff, who gave his permission with very emphatic head jerks. "Okay," the photographer said. "Well, there was just one witness. The bartender."

"Yeah. He among the living?"

"Oh, yeah, not a mark on him. He got out. Went into the manager's office and locked the door behind him, then watched the whole thing through the peephole."

"What about the manager?"

"He's at a restaurant trade show in Chicago."

"Wait staff?" Remo asked.

"Two beer gals usually, but tonight one of them called in sick, and she's lucky she did. The only serving girl who was working the place is over there."

He nodded at a nearby mess of flesh that had erased its own chalk outline with spreading blood.

The photographer expected a gag or a gasp, but Remo just sighed.

The little old Korean man rolled his eyes. Then he strolled to the long, L-shaped bar and gingerly lifted a plastic beer mug, sniffing the contents.

Remo, too, had noticed the odd aroma that permeated the place. Even masked by the stench of spilled beer, the smell was obvious and alien. Chiun looked puzzled.

They left the sheriff with the photographer and found the bartender still in the manager's office giving his statement, and the tale came so automatically it was clear he'd gone through it all several times.

"Relax," Remo told the good-cop trooper and his hulking, silent partner, the bad-cop trooper. "We're Feds. We'll just listen in."

"Like hell," growled the bad-cop trooper, a colossus who knew he didn't even have to stand up to be intimidating—so he didn't bother. His shoulders were powerful, his arms massive under the specially tailored uniform. "This ain't your jurisdiction until I hear otherwise. Amscray."

"No, thanks." Remo nodded pleasantly, hoping the good-cop trooper would continue the questioning.

The colossus got to his feet. He did it slowly, as if moving his monstrous frame into a standing position required a mighty challenge to the forces of gravity.

"Don't make me go local on you, U.S. boy," he growled.

"Okay, Unincredible Hulk, you made your point. You're big and tall. Ooh. Ahh. So what. Sit down."

The trooper with the notebook went white. Wrong thing to say! he communicated to Remo Williams silently.

Remo Williams didn't care. He wasn't here to make friends. In fact, he didn't know what he was here for. Upstairs had him running around doing all this look-into-this stuff and investigate-that stuff. He wasn't experiencing job satisfaction and he wasn't running into a lot of friendly, cooperative people. Even the cops were giving him crap.

So when the hand the size of a manhole cover made a grab at his collar, he broke it.

Even the giant didn't get it at first. He thought the skinny little guy had simply batted his hand away. Then he felt the sensation of shattering bones and the pain that traveled up his arm like a flood tide. With a bull-sized bellow he went for a full body tackle, and stopped midair. The skinny guy from the federal government caught him in the chest with his palm, and it should have sent the little guy flying halfway across the state. Somehow it was the giant state trooper who crashed to the floor.

"The bigger they are, the smarter they are not," Chiun observed.

"But they are louder," Remo added, groping around the back of the giant's neck and making a small adjustment. The bellow ended.

"Ah, peace and quiet."

"What'd you do?" the good-cop trooper demanded.

"Don't worry, I just hit the mute button. Please carry on."

"But he's wounded! He's paralyzed!"

"Criminy!" Remo opened the door and gave the giant a nudge with the bottom of one expensive Italian shoe. The paralyzed trooper rocketed out the door and down the short hall, still moving fast when he hit the messiest of the corpses. Sliding on blood, he actually seemed to pick up speed. Remo didn't bother to watch the dramatic end of the wild ride, grabbing the pen and notebook from the hands of the other trooper and tossing them out the door, as well. The trooper stared at Remo dumbfounded.

"Well? Go fetch."

The trooper nodded sadly and left.

The bartender was, if anything, mildly amused.

"I hate to do this to you again, but could you tell us what happened here?" Remo asked.

"Hell, sure. You two are the first law enforcement I seen all night that act like they could actually do something about it." The bartender quickly related the events that led up to the violence. "That door saved me," he said. "It's like a safe door. Solid steel. Anything less they would have got me and killed me for sure. When they couldn't get in, well, it was like they had to take it all out on somebody. They started fighting each other. Somebody would go, 'Hey, ain't you the bartender?' and they'd go after one of the other customers and kill him and then do it again."

"That's sort of unusual, isn't it?" Remo asked. He knew the guy was telling the truth, but it sure made no sense.

"Weirdest damn thing," the bartender agreed.

"The one who purchased the intoxicants for your patrons was gone by this time?" Chiun asked thoughtfully.

"Yeah, he left right after he sicced everybody on me."

"But you don't know who he was or what his home address is or anything like that?" Remo prodded, knowing he was grasping at straws.

"Naw. You know, you don't ask questions like the other cops."

"Yeah, this ain't my gig," Remo explained dejectedly.

"He is not skilled at speech or thought," Chiun added helpfully.

"But I can tell you he was disguised," the bartender offered. "I saw him in the parking lot. I lock myself in here and grab the phone for the cops and I look out back." He nodded at the grimy window over his shoulder. "There he was, writing in his notebook."

"Huh?" Remo asked.

"That's what I thought," the bartender agreed. "Just a quick note. Then he rips off his eyebrows and his hairpiece and he drives off."

"In what?"

"The car? Couldn't tell."

"See what he looked like without the fake fur?"

"Naw. Back's dark."

"You been a lot of help."

"I think the state of Tennessee is really mad at you guys," the bartender offered as a megaphone down the hall demanded the surrender of all occupants of the office.

"That's just perfect," Remo grumbled.

"Really?" Chiun asked with raised eyebrows. "You mean to say this is going as you had intended?"

10

"The State of Tennessee multidepartmental task force has established an irrefutable link between the incident at the Big Stomp Saloon, the Mafia and the Yakuza." Harold Smith's voice was more sour than usual.

"Is that so?" Remo replied in his best not-in-the-mood-for-it voice. Trouble was, he'd been using that voice a lot lately, and nobody seemed to get the message.

"They report their crime scene was aggressively compromised by two men posing as federal agents."

"Us?" Remo asked.

"It was not us, Emperor," Chiun called out, never turning away from the television set. He was sitting on the hotel-room floor staring at the screen.

"One elderly Asian and one Caucasian male, age indeterminate," Smith reported.

"That's what they're going on?"

"There's more," Smith said. "I'm getting into the Tennessee crime database now."

Remo sat on the hotel bed and listened to Smith tap the keys. The tapping stopped but Smith said nothing.

"Let me guess," Remo volunteered. "It's the shoes and kimono."

Smith spent a long time saying the word "Yes."

"So we go in there and get what you asked for despite a bunch of Southern-boy attitude, and all they see is a pair of Italian loafers and an Asian guy in a bright robe. I don't know what's more amazing—that they came up with the Yakuza and Mafia theory or the fact that you think we blew it."

Smith considered that. "You may have a point," he admitted. "Still, you overreacted. You put an investigator in the hospital."

"We could have put him in the morgue," Remo countered. "On the other hand, we could have left when they said, 'Sorry guys, no Feds allowed at our crime scene.' For future reference, which choice should we make next time, Smitty?"

While Smith hemmed and hawed, Remo watched two Mexican actresses with flawless makeup have a conversation in Spanish, one on either side of the small silhouetted skull of the Korean Master of Sinanju. As the poorly acted discussion became more dramatic, the woman with the artificial mole began extruding tears. The camera moved in for a close-up of the perfect glycerin drop just as the drama faded to commercials. Then came a news break with a video clip from some political dinner, where the guest of honor looked about twelve.

"So what now?" Remo prodded. "You want us to go run some prints through the crime lab, maybe? How about we round up some usual suspects? Maybe we could do something *really* useful like look through the mug books."

"I hope we'll have some direction for you by morning," Smith said.

"Which means right now you've got nothing."

Smith made a weary sound. "That's right. Nothing."

"You feeling okay, Smitty?" Remo asked.

"I feel fine," Smith snapped back.

"You oughta take a nap."

"I don't need a nap, and it's a luxury I can't afford regardless."

Remo hung up slowly, but his thoughts were interrupted by a seething hiss.

"What's the matter?"

"You did not notice this? *This?*" Chiun spun on him and jabbed a bony hand at the television screen.

"The television? The news anchor? Give me a hint."

"Fah!" Chiun uttered in disgust. "This news break is now in its *second* minute, coming after two one-minute commercials. This dramatic series is edited for breaks of three minutes each."

"Since when do you know all this kind of programming junk?"

"Since I watch the program and happen to pay attention to the world around me. You do not. How you notice the door is closed before you walk into it is a mystery of the ages. The point is, they are butchering the drama with irrelevant anecdotes that pass for substantive journalism."

Another video clip now showed the same youthful-looking honoree in an expensive suit. "What is he, the world's oldest Boy Scout or something?"

"Less important still—the idiot president of an island that is vying for independence," Chiun said with disgust. "He is some sort of hero to the Puerto Ricans who watch this television channel."

Remo sneered. "That kid's too young to be president of the chess club." Then a thought occurred to him. "You mean vying for independence from us? America?"

"Cretins!" Chiun spit as the news break ended and returned to some Mexican soap opera sobbing, already in progress. "They defile art to show us their foolish news footage of feasting imbeciles!"

"*Art?*"

"Hush! I know your taste in drama and it is as valid as your negligent appreciation of literature."

"What's that supposed to mean?"

"Silence. I have missed too much of the story already. If I had not already watched the episode this afternoon, I would be forced to have the programmers of this station coerced into replaying it at once."

Remo didn't argue the point. The last thing he needed was to be browbeaten into paying an unsocial call on the poor engineer running the boards at the local Latino TV station.

It was just the kind of busywork he'd have a hard time squirming out of if Chiun got the idea in his head.

11

The phone buzzed softly. The couple on the veranda tried to ignore it.

She was gazing over the tops of the palm trees, watching the golden blazing ball of the sun descend on the glimmering mirror image of itself on the surface of the Caribbean Sea. The moment they touched was like a melding of fate-linked lovers.

"Exquisite," murmured her companion, his hand creeping atop hers on the stone rail. The phone, thankfully, went silent.

"You're not even watching it," she chided gently.

"It's not the sunset I'm not talking about, Minister."

Union Island Minister of Tourism Dawn Summens felt something special in the unique golden rays of the sun during those precious moments as it was swallowed by the sea. It felt different from the first light of the morning, and somehow she felt it infused her with a special radiance. This notion had come to her when she was just a teenager but stuck with her ever since.

When she joined the government of Union Island she appropriated this office for its unparalleled sunset views. When the former occupant protested, Summens saw the demand as a challenge to her new authority. The former occupant now had a cubicle on the ground floor.

"I don't think you appreciate my view, Senator."

"But I appreciate mine," Sam Switzer, Republican senator from Utah, said glibly.

Summens all but rolled her eyes, but her words were complimentary. "Very witty, Senator. But I was talking about my view on the Free Union Island movement."

"What?" The senator looked confused.

"You have not looked at this issue from my point of view."

His mouth hung open and the sagging flesh of his cheeks hung just below his jawline. "You're right. I've never even stopped to consider your perspective. How stupid of me."

"Now, there, not stupid," she assured him. "You're just a little too narrow in your thinking."

The senator was suddenly stricken. "Oh, mother of mercy, you're right. I've got to open my eyes to the world! I've been wearing blinders all my life!"

"No, it's not as bad as all that," she said reassuringly, and at that moment the phone began to buzz again, annoying as a mosquito. "I'll be right back."

Summens strode through the custom French doors she had ordered from a Michigan woodworker and snatched at the phone on the desk. "Yes?"

"Good evening, Minister Summens. This is President—"

"I can't talk now."

"Come on, Dawn, I gotta talk to you about something. I'm getting worried."

"Call later. One hour. Make it two."

"Aw, come on!"

Dawn hung up and practically sprinted onto the veranda, but the damage was done. The senator had run with her suggestion and was by now way, way out in left field.

"How can I vote against abortion rights when I've never had an abortion?" he demanded, tears of shame in his eyes. "Why did I fight for tax cuts when I never even listened to my opponents' reasons for wanting tax increases? And will you please tell me what gives me the right to introduce antigay bills when I've never even gone to the trouble of experiencing sex with another man?"

Summens thought furiously. What was it she'd said exactly? Had she suggested he needed to see all sides of the story? It had been *something* like that. Christ, this was the only dose she had been entrusted with in a month and she was on the verge of blowing it, big time. "Senator, listen to me," she said in a clear, loud voice.

He stopped talking, his attention riveted on her.

"The freedom of Union Island is the most important issue before the Senate right now. You must make it well known that you now support the Union Island Freedom Bill, and you need to put resources into corralling support for the bill. It must pass."

"Of course. It *must*."

"With enough votes to override a veto," Summens added. "And there can be no amendments to the aid package."

"I won't let them trim so much as a single dollar," the senior senator agreed emphatically. "Union Island needs U.S. dollars just as fervently as it needs independence from the U.S." His old, wrinkled eyes drew together. "Now, why is that again?"

Summens patted his arm. "You'll come up with very clever arguments to support your position. You can't wait to get started."

The senator nodded, his posture erect with new purpose. "My dear, you must forgive me if I cancel dinner and our little tryst. I have suddenly realized how vital it is for me to get involved in this campaign immediately."

"Of course I am disappointed," Summens said, although the truth was she never intended to sleep with the man. "But I understand. It's for the cause."

Before she could suggest he not do it, the old slimeball had mushed his slobbering lips against hers. It was over in an instant, though, and he left in a hurry.

He'd better come through for her, she thought, or next time she'd suggest he go for a long walk off the short roof of the Congressional Office Building.

Summens was angry with herself. She had handled the senator badly. She could count on one hand the number of times she had been entrusted to perform a dosing alone, and this time she almost lost control. She'd probably ruined the senator's career as it was—his constituency might not go along with his new views on contentious issues. No matter, so long as he kept his job long enough to help ram through the Union Island Independence Bill.

She needed a good dinner to get the taste out of her

mouth. She had reservations for two at Café Amore, but maybe she could just order in.

Then she remembered that the president would be trying to reach her in the office in a short while.

That was a very good reason to be anywhere else.

12

"Sheriff Pilchard here," said the monotone voice on the other side of the door.

Greg Grom unlocked the dead bolt and tried to open the door, but the little brass security thingy brought it to halt. Grom closed the door again, silently swearing at the little brass thingy for making him look like an idiot. The worst thing ever was to look stupid.

"Sorry, Sheriff," he said to the unsmiling statue of a country sheriff.

"Quite all right." The sheriff followed Grom inside and sat without invitation in an easy chair in the parlor.

"I don't suppose you'd accept a drink when you're on duty."

"I suppose I would. Scotch."

"Oh. Okay." Grom found a bottle of Scotch whiskey behind the bar and poured while his guest looked casually around the expensive suite.

"Some room, huh?" Grom observed sheepishly.

"Cleaned up a triple in this room 'bout nine months back," the sheriff announced.

"What's a triple?" Grom asked, sucking on a bottle of Corona beer.

"Homicide."

The beer went into his lungs, and he hacked it up for two minutes. Then he said, "I see."

"Looks like they recarpeted. Guess they would've had to." The sheriff chuckled without losing his dour expression.

"Yeah. Heh."

The sheriff looked Grom dead in the eye. "Guy used a fan blade off an International Harvester OTR rig." The sheriff shrugged and reclined with his drink. "It was convenient. Trucker had it parked at the motel next door. So the guy just tore it off and came in here swinging the thing."

"Imagine that," Grom said.

"Not a sharp edge to it. Took some work on the murderer's part. Made a hell of a mess."

"I bet...."

"Poor trucker started his rig the next morning and heard this awful noise and popped the hood. Found his fan all out of whack and some of it missing and he reported the vandalism. That's how we know what we know."

Grom had been trying desperately to think of a way to steer the conversation in a new direction, but now he said, "You mean you didn't find the weapon."

"Oh, yeah. Few weeks later. Twenty miles outside town alongside the road in a culvert. Couldn't get prints or anything useful off it by that time. So, well, you know."

"I know what?" Grom demanded.

"You know, we couldn't positively ID the killer. Know who he is, of course, but the son of a bitch is walking around free as a bird until we get physical evidence...and what was it you wanted to talk to *me* about exactly?"

Grom drank more beer as he tried to catch up to the conversation. "What about the Big Stomp?" he finally managed to ask.

The sheriff nodded, revealing nothing, but his cooperation was a foregone conclusion. The man wasn't stupid enough to not cooperate with a man like Greg Grom.

"The investigation continues," the sheriff said. "There was an interesting development at the crime scene."

"Like what?"

"The crime scene was infiltrated. Based on the evidence at hand, we're fairly certain the Nashville Azzopardi Family has formed a joint venture with a Yakuza branch. Their purpose is undoubtedly to launch a protection business specializing in high-profit, private, unregulated businesses, such as the Big Stomp. Their interest in our crime scene is obvious—whoever poisoned the well needs to be taught not to tamper with organized-crime businesses in the Kentucky-Tennessee district. In other words, they want to find the bad guy before we do."

"Oh." Grom's head was swimming. "Do you think they will?"

The sheriff finally showed an emotion in the form of a smug twitch of the colorless lips. "Mr. Grom, we're professionals. Highly trained. Superbly equipped. We're not going to be outsmarted by a bunch of import thugs."

Grom let out a silent sigh, nodding with what he hoped looked like dispassionate satisfaction.

"Good to know you people are on the job," he said condescendingly as he walked the sheriff to the door. "What did these men look like, anyway? The men who came to the crime scene?"

"Well, that's not an easy one to hammer down. Nobody seems to have gotten a good look at their faces. But I'll tell you this much. One of them was a Far Easterner, old as Moses and no bigger than my dog Bert when he gets on two legs to give me a face lickin'. Other guy was just some white feller. I guess he must look like all us white fellers."

As the sheriff was on his way out the door, Grom asked, "That's the best description you have?"

"We have other clues to their identity," the sheriff said, and told Greg Grom about the federal IDs.

The sheriff was the one looking sheepish now. "Who knows?" he said, donning his hat. "Maybe they really was just a couple of nosy Feds."

Greg Grom closed the door, bolted it and moved the annoying little brass thingy into place for extra security. Then he raced to the other doors and windows of the suite, checking and double-checking the locks. All the while he was talking to himself about the possibility of a pair of nosy Feds.

What he actually said was, "Oh God oh God oh God..."

13

At first Remo thought it was the snoring that woke him from an easy slumber, but he was accustomed to Chiun's honking and wheezing. His senses told him there nothing out of place in his environment—just the typical squeaks, groans, smells and grumbles of a hotel in the middle of the night.

So why was he not asleep?

Remo Williams, Reigning Master of Sinanju, was not the type to wake in the middle of the night with a niggling problem. But there was *something.* Wasn't there?

He rose silently from the floor mat that was his bed, strolling to the window and contemplating his view of the gravel parking lot.

"You dreamed it," Chiun squeaked.

"Dreamed what?" Remo asked.

"Whatever scary thing roused you."

"I didn't have a bad dream. I was thinking."

"Of course. And I suppose I was snoring."

"Matter of fact, you *were* snoring," Remo said.

"No, you were dreaming," Chiun said in kindly condescension. "Where else but dreams do you experience one highly improbable thing after another?"

"Like maybe a talking goat?"

Chiun sat up. "Remo, was there a talking goat?"

"Yes, there is."

Chiun's lips came together as tightly as Remo had ever seen them, his face going crimson. Chiun stood, the door slammed and Remo was alone in the hotel room.

Served the old biddy right. Taste of his own medicine. Slice of his own sour-grapes pie. Chiun had been a thorn in the keister for months. It seemed he had been getting increasingly grumpy and withdrawn ever since the Time of Succession, when Remo had finally donned the mantle of Reigning Master of Sinanju.

Remo hadn't really expected much change. He didn't believe that Chiun was going to start following Remo's lead or stop trying to drill his head full of five thousand years of Sinanju history, and in truth that hadn't happened.

But there had been changes. Chiun was less prone to being the harping teacher to Remo's inattentive student. Sometimes. Well, almost never. For a while the old Master had become extra-antisocial, spending hours watching TV, or pretending to. Remo knew he was engrossed in deciphering whatever it was that had happened to him in Sinanju at the Time of Succession.

Remo didn't know what actually had happened to Chiun, and Chiun wasn't talking.

Chiun appeared in the gravel parking lot, slowly strolling away from the hotel in a sort of walking meditation.

Lately Chiun had become impatient with Remo's gaps in learning. The trouble was that Remo had learned the art of Sinanju years ago, and all that was left for Chiun to teach was the boring stuff—occasional bits of obscure philosophy that the old Korean always seemed to be making up as he went along. Legends of Sinanju Masters who were so unimportant or dull that they hadn't been mentioned in all these years. Then there was the stilted prose of the endless written histories.

Remo had experienced a new sense of pride and responsibility when he achieved the title Reigning Master. He had even agreed to undergo training in Chiun's archaic form of Korean calligraphy—

Oh. That was supposed to happen yesterday.

"Ah, crap," he announced to the empty room. "I forgot about the writing lesson."

Far across the parking lot the figure of the Master of Sinanju Emeritus turned and offered Remo a scowl that told him he had at least had the brains to figure out what he'd done wrong.

So that was what was bugging Chiun. But for some reason Remo thought it wasn't what was bugging *him*.

So what was it?

He sensed the tiny surge of electricity inside the phone and snatched the receiver as it started to ring. "Yeah?"

"It's happening." It was Mark Howard. "Not far from you."

"Where's your dad, Doogie?"

"At home, getting some rest. Remo, listen—there's a disturbance going on at one of the bars in town. The police scanner feed says there's some bikers tearing up the place."

"Let me get this straight. You think a brawl in a biker bar is out of the ordinary?"

"Of course not," Howard said. "It's the Nashville Rock Hard Café. It's strictly an upscale place—you know, all kinds of expensive rock-star memorabilia and stuff. Caters mostly to tourists. The bikers are outsiders. I don't know what they're up to, but it sounds like they're laying siege to the place."

REMO DROVE across the lot and pulled to a stop behind Chiun, who was facing resolutely in the other direction, his scarlet kimono shimmering in the distant lights.

"The Fresh Prince of Folcroft says it's time for work," Remo called.

For a moment the old Master was motionless, then he turned, the picture of dignity, and entered the car. They drove into the heart of Nashville.

After some silence, Remo spoke. "Little Father, I am sorry I blew off the writing lesson."

"You deliberately avoided it," Chiun said evenly.

"Hey, no, it wasn't like that. Smitty needed me here to look into all the crazy types."

"You could have delayed the trip."

"Aw, come on! What good would that have done?"

"What good have you done since you arrived?" Chiun asked innocently.

"All right, so I'm batting zero. I told Smitty to get his investigators on this instead of me."

"But you did not insist. All this is a sham. Do you

even wish to learn the most basic of skills necessary for a true Master of Sinanju?"

Remo was getting ticked. "What the hell have I been wasting my time on for all these years?"

Chiun stared at him coldly. Then he faced forward again. "You have learned just enough to make you the most uncouth and unmannered Master in five thousand years. You're a Mongol. A barbarian."

"Remo the Barbarian?" Remo asked.

"Yes. Exactly. That is how I shall address you in the scrolls. Remo the Barbarian is what I shall call you as I record your history during my waning years—because clearly you will not be able to record your own history."

"You make me sound illiterate," Remo protested.

"Your scrawl is hideous. It is an abomination made worse by the unbeautiful Roman characters you choose to use and the despicable hodgepodge of a language you employ. You must learn to make graceful hangul characters in order to keep the chronicles of Sinanju history."

"I'm not gonna be keeping the books in Korean, Little Father. I'll keep them in English."

Chiun turned his head sharply at Remo. "What are you saying? You absolutely will not allow mankind's most important historical record to be sullied with the use of English! It is unthinkable!"

"But that's how it is," Remo said firmly.

"I will not allow it! The writing of the Sinanju Masters has always been in Korean dialects."

"Yeah, well, up until a few years ago the Masters were always Korean. That's changed, too. Now I'm the Reigning Master, and I'm not Korean, mostly."

"The blood of the Sinanju Masters flows in your veins."

"True. But every Master before me was born in Sinanju and grew up speaking Korean and I wasn't. I was born in America and I grew up reading and writing American."

The large and garish Rock Hard bar and hotel came into view. It was past two in the morning, but the lights were blazing and the music was thumping from inside loud enough to rattle the dashboard of the rental car. Crowds seethed in the streets and on the sidewalk.

"Lively place," Remo commented.

A human being crashed through one of the glass doors, moving fast, moving backward, and his feet never touched the ground until he crumpled in a broken heap.

"Getting less lively every second, though," Remo added, pulling to the curb.

VIRGIL "VIRGIN KILLER" Miller liked the way the body sounded when he hoisted it into the doors. The doors cracked and the body made breaking noises, too, and then made more breaking noises when it landed. At some point during his brief flight the victim had stopped being alive.

Served him right!

Virgin Killer didn't dwell on the fact that he really didn't have a reason for hating these people. Him and Bork and all the guys, the Road Sharks, they was finally doing what needed doing.

He spotted a weasel in a light blue sport jacket.

"You!" Miller's meaty hand shot out and intercepted the man as he bolted for the exit. Virgin Killer spun Mr. Blue Sport Coat, and the man's spine met the steel support beam between the front doors. Miller grabbed him again just before he fell.

"You make me wanna puke!"

"I don't even know who you are," his prisoner stammered.

"But I know you! Coming in here in your prissy clothes like some fairy boy! I hate you all!"

Virgin Killer Miller turned on the interior of the bar, carrying Mr. Blue Sport Coat over his head. "You hear me, you people! I hate you like I hate my own mother!" He hurled his victim into a lounge area, breaking tables, chairs and bones.

A large crowd of patrons was trapped in the middle of the Rock Hard Café. Miller and the other bikers were blocking the doors and the rear emergency exits. Virgin Killer had lots of choices.

"Well, look at all these fancy clothes," he snarled. "You people must spend a lot of money to make yourselves look so fine. You sure are a bunch of prissy-assed bitches and pretty boys."

Miller grabbed one young man by the shirt collar. He went limp with terror. "You know I can't stand pretty boys. I want to do things that'll make them look really ugly. And hey! You're about the prettiest of them all."

"Well, it sure isn't you I'm going to see on next month's *GQ*," said somebody just behind Virgin Killer Miller. Miller could have sworn there was nobody there a second ago.

Then a hand with unnaturally thick wrists came from behind him and clamped onto Miller's forearm. Miller released his hold on the pretty boy because he couldn't help it. Over his shoulder he saw that the thick wrists belonged to a skinny guy with dark eyes.

Miller put all his considerable body mass into an explosive roundhouse punch with his free fist, but somehow he missed. Miller's weight carried him in a circle, and he found himself facing the same direction he had started in. His head gyrated wildly, but now he was alone. Could he have possibly hallucinated abut a skinny guy with thick wrists?

Something blurred at him from very nearby. Miller's last thought was, Oh, there's the skinny guy now.

DON "FORK" BORK, leader of the Nashville Road Sharks, couldn't believe what he was seeing when the shrimpy little guy did some sort of a judo jab that sent Virgil into a sudden spin. Virgin Killer Miller was a massive slab of meat that should have taken hydraulics and diesel power to manipulate.

Then the shrimpy guy who did the judo trick vanished, reappeared out of nowhere and poked Virgin Killer in the face. Not a two-finger Moe-poke to the eyeballs, but a one-finger stab at the forehead. A red blossom appeared on Virgil's forehead. Virgil rolled his eyes up at the gaping hole, then collapsed without a sound.

Fork wouldn't have thought it possible to get more angry than he already was. The Road Sharks had been so filled with their righteous indignation that Fork postponed their plans for the night. That liquor store and its gook owner would be there for the taking tomorrow. The Rock Hard was an insult that needed to be avenged *now.* Every man and woman in the place was an enemy of every Road Shark.

And now one of those men had just killed Fork's blood brother.

"You'll pay for that, sonny," he growled.

Remo Williams found himself on the receiving end of a real-estate broker who had been reduced to a mess of wild limbs in a thousand-dollar suit. The real-estate broker made a noise like a siren, which ended in a question mark when he was intercepted with amazing gentleness.

Remo put the guy in the expensive suit on his feet.

"Well, don't just stand there," Remo said, waving at the door.

The man sped off. Fork Bork bellowed and came at Remo, and Remo moved to intercept. Fork never saw him coming.

What Fork saw was his own arms leaving, one in either direction. The blood was leaving his body, too, in gushes. That couldn't be good.

As sneering bikers closed in on Remo from all directions, he grabbed Fork about the beer belly and twisted the armless one into a spin. His impromptu sprinkler sent blood splattering in a perfect circle in all directions. Bikers slipped and slid until they collided in a messy jumble around the legs of their friend without the upper extremities, who collapsed atop the pile, his eyes fixed and open.

Amid the confusion and shouts, one of the bikers rose out of the tangle of bodies. And he just kept rising and rising until he stood at seven feet six inches.

"Cripes," Remo observed, now standing outside the mess. "The beer-and-cigarettes lifestyle agrees with you."

"You. You will die."

"Not before he trains his replacement," Chiun announced, emerging from the darkness with a pair of bodies skidding across the floor before him. His nimble feet seemed to reach out here and there to nudge the bodies and guide them in the direction he wished them to go.

"Souvenirs?" Remo asked.

"Did you not say we need to get information from the rabble before they are rendered into rubble?" Chiun bent over the battered bodies and asked in his most polite singsong, "Which is the leader?"

The bodies stirred. One of them raised a quivering finger at the armless corpse. "Him. Fork."

"And Virgin Killer." The dying man pointed at the one with the head puncture.

"Fork and Virgin Killer?" Remo asked incredulously.

"Good work, Remo." Chiun sighed. "I see you've managed to kill just two hoodlums thus far and one of them happens to be the one we needed to keep alive."

"Give me a break," Remo answered. "Hey, you." He snapped his fingers over Chiun's bodies. "Who's next in the line of command?"

One of the bikers who still clung to life raised his eyes to the giant. Then he raised his eyes to heaven and said a strange word, which ended in a final hiss of breath.

"What did he say, Belltower?" Remo asked.

"He said Belfagore," intoned the seven-plus-footer. "I am Belfagore."

"What kind of name is that?"

"It is one of the names of Satan," the giant thundered.

"Oh, brother."

"And I will dispatch you straight to hell, little man!"

By this time the surviving ranks of the Road Sharks biker gang were on their feet, and Remo saw deranged vitality in their eyes. He'd seen it the day before in a certain crack house.

Belfagore raised one long arm and stabbed the air, shouting, "Kill them!"

The Road Sharks struck fast, overpowering the throbbing music with banshee battle cries. Their movements were adrenalized out of human proportions as they tore into the two Masters.

The two Masters were gone, though. The small mob stumbled to a halt, shouts dying in their throats until the shouters started dying themselves. Remo pushed a pair of skulls against each other and removed his hands fast before the gore splashed them. He leaped around their collapsing remains and reached wide with both hands, inserting a finger deep into the ear of one Shark and the chest of another.

Chiun stood watching Remo as the heart-puncture victim flopped to the ground. The old Master was the picture of peaceful composure, hands tucked in his kimono sleeves, as if he were unaware of the three Road Sharks sprawled dead at his feet, let alone claimed responsibility for them.

"What was that 'Kill them' all about?" Remo demanded of the Road Sharks' new leader. "You trying to do a whole *Batman* TV show thing on us? Were you expecting some CRAACKK!s and KERPLOW!s? Notice that the real world doesn't work that way?"

Belfagore was astonished at the nearly instant annihilation of his gang.

"So?" Remo demanded. "What's the deal? Why are you doing this? What's your problem?"

The Shark closed his mouth and began to quiver.

"He is mad," Chiun declared resignedly.

"No kidding. Belfagore's got serious bats in his belfry."

"No. I mean he is angry."

Belfagore made a sound like a komodo dragon whose goat haunch has been taken by another komodo dragon.

"Ya think?" Remo asked Chiun, then stepped aside and nudged the charging giant, who tumbled with tremendous momentum across the bloody floor and crashed through the last few upright lounge tables. Then he leaped to his feet, shouting incoherently and charging again.

Charging fast.

Belfagore launched himself at Remo but Remo stepped out of the way, so Belfagore was sliding again, headfirst this time. A wall stopped him hard.

"Ah, crap," Remo said.

But Belfagore wasn't dead or even unconscious. He used the wall for support as he rose to his feet, and his eyes seemed incapable of focusing.

"I'm surprised you don't make accordion sounds

when you breathe, Belf. I think you're three inches shorter. Don't you think, Little Father?"

"Four inches," Chiun said.

Belfagore staggered at the Reigning Master of Sinanju, grunting and croaking.

"Oh, just give it up, would you?" Remo stepped aside and tripped the giant. Belfagore fell down, and it was a long way down.

"That was for your own good." Remo crouched beside the biker. "You'd have killed yourself running around like a maniac, which would rob me of the pleasure."

Belfagore made agonized sounds when he was flipped onto his back. He coughed blood and didn't have the strength to grab Remo by the throat.

"Okay, so you're dying anyway," Remo said. "You've got maybe ten minutes. So why not just tell me what I wanna know?"

Belfagore made animal sounds, gnashing his teeth.

"Why'd you guys get all freaked out? Who put you up to this?"

Belfagore's collection of sounds settled into a long, menacing growl.

"He's mad," Chiun pointed out.

"You said that."

"I mean, he's insane."

Remo nodded reluctantly. "Who isn't? I wanna know." He grabbed the dying biker by the base of the neck and turned him off. Belfagore went limp.

"I am not insane," Chiun said indignantly. "You, however, are behaving oddly. For example, I see you have now taken up the noble pastime of looting the dead."

"Ha!" Remo had extracted the biker's wallet, a huge black leather affair on a stainless-steel belt chain, and flourished the driver's license. "Belfagore's real name? Maurice."

Chiun said nothing, but his brows grew heavy as he observed Remo moving among the corpses, pulling out wallets one after another. "This guy's named Bork. This guy is Virgil. No wonder the weird nicknames!"

"This has some meaning to you?"

Remo grinned and shrugged. "Just looking for the common thread tying these losers together."

"What is common is they are all dead," Chiun noted.

CHIUN WAS STARING at the wing of the 737 as if it might, just might, fall off right then, before they even pushed back from the gate.

"Slowpoke," he said.

"Who? Me?" Remo asked from the next seat. "When was I slow?"

"I've already explained that."

"Did I miss something?"

"You missed me on the way in," said a woman in a blue blazer and a blond hair helmet. "I'm Johlene, and I'll be your stewardess on this flight."

"Fine. Thanks." Remo avoided eye contact and said to Chiun, "Explain it again."

"Who buckled this seat belt?" Johlene demanded playfully. "It's all wrong."

"You know, I've done ten thousand airplane seat belts and I think I've got the hang of it." Remo shoved her groping hands away from his lap. "Now, when was I slow?"

Chiun sighed. "During the poke. As I explained."

"What poke?"

"Against the smelly bicycle riders in the loud nightclub," Chiun said.

"My poke was *not* slow."

"I could use a slow—" Johlene interjected.

"Can it!" Remo barked at the stewardess. Her eyes opened a little wider. They glinted. Remo wasn't looking.

"Your form was imperfect, as well," Chiun complained.

"You're making up stuff."

"Your form is perfect. Don't listen to him," Johlene said comfortingly to Remo.

"What does it take to offend somebody these days?" Remo demanded.

"Who knows?" the stewardess asked, leaning her bosom into his chest. "Why not call me a few dirty names and see if I leave in a huff."

"Addressing the fraudulent nature of her udders should drive her off," Chiun said with irritation.

Johlene stiffened. "What did he say?"

"Oh, yeah." Remo glared pointedly at the sculpted bustline. "Boob implants. I absolutely can't stand fakes. It turns me off big time."

"But look at them," she pleaded. "They're so firm and symmetrical."

"What have you got in there—aluminum softballs? Yech."

Johlene finally left, and Remo ignored the alternately pleading and disdainful looks she gave him during the rest of the flight.

"Your mean form lacks grace, which is a result of your lack of precision dexterity," Chiun explained when she was gone.

"Say that again, Little Father?"

"Your training was unbalanced. I failed to instill the proper respect for the written word. From the creation of beautiful words on parchment comes the appreciation of beautiful movement of the rest of the body."

"You're joking, right?"

"I joke not."

"Listen, Chiun, the training is done. I'm trained. You did the best you could, and it turns out you are a wonderful teacher. I'm good at my job."

"Your job?" Chiun turned to face him finally. "Is that what Sinanju is to you? An occupation?"

"Of course not."

"Is that why you have decided to stagnate? You have deemed yourself adequate and see no profit in improvement? Oh, Remo, you send all my hopes crashing down like fine crystal goblets pushed off high shelves."

"Oh, brother."

"This is a white attitude. It is the blood of your European ancestors that makes you lazy. I prayed that your Korean blood would give you perseverance. Even the Native Americans who have sullied your ancestry will inherently strive for improvement against the greatest adversity."

"I never said I was going to rest on my laurels!" Remo argued.

"Laurels? How European. How Roman. How like you to use those words."

"It's a figure of friggin' speech. I don't even know what laurels are!"

"I feel grave concern for your future, Remo."

"I thought you felt hopeless."

"I am gravely concerned for your standing among the Masters. I do not want to be known as Chiun, Trainer of Remo the Slothful."

Remo said, "That's what this is about, huh? How I reflect on you in the Sinanju scrolls?"

"Of course! The status of a Master depends in great part on the status of the Master he trains."

"And I'm not good enough?"

"You are not trying hard enough."

"So I haven't been pulling my weight?"

"You are complacent," Chiun replied without hesitation.

Remo didn't answer. He looked at the seat back in front of him and thought about Chiun's words.

This was more than an idle insult—and Chiun was the king of idle insults. The old Master had been considering this. He was sincere.

But was he right?

It sure didn't feel to Remo that he was slacking. He'd had a rough ride of it in recent years, starting with his Rite of Attainment and getting worse as he closed in on the Rite of Succession. Even Chiun had admitted that Remo had faced harder obstacles than most Masters reaching their prime.

Was it possible that his attitude had changed for the worse since he became Reigning Master? Was he slacking?

"Okay, Little Father," he said finally. "First chance we get, I promise, we'll get into the whole penmanship thing."

Chiun narrowed his eyes.

"I mean it," Remo added.

"What are you hiding?"

"I'm not hiding anything. I meant what I said, that's all. I'll take the calligraphy lessons."

"I sense a ploy."

"No ploy. No tricks up my sleeve. I promise you I'll give the lessons a shot."

THE WING SEEMED well anchored to the fuselage of the aircraft, but wings and limbs could become separated from their bodies easily enough. What Chiun had never understood was why such great masses of metal could not be made inflexible. But he had been assured that they were designed to wobble in the wind. And they all did. Wobble.

There had been a time when Chiun was worried about his unlikely protégé for much the same reason he was worried now. It was just after Remo had, miraculously enough, passed through the Rite of Attainment.

Common sense decreed that Sinanju skills should never have flourished inside the inherently clumsy body of a white, but Remo had such skills in abundance. His proved Sinanju lineage only partially explained it.

But after his Attainment, after he solved the mystery of his parentage and offspring, there was a time when Remo had become, of all things, content.

Contentment was no good. Contentment led to

complacency, and complacency could get a Master annihilated.

Then came a time of increasing hardship as the leaders of the world seemed to descend en masse into idiocy. The U.S. put in place a puppet president whose only possible qualification could be for entertainment purposes. The challenges to Remo became greater, as well, as he became afflicted with the Master's Disease and was haunted by the manifestation of the Master Who Never Was, foretelling worsening hardship.

It all seemed to culminate at the time of the Rite of Succession, when Remo's ritual assumption of the title of Reigning Master of Sinanju was interrupted by the resurrection of old and powerful enemies. Chiun himself was wounded emotionally and almost broken. He still carried in his mind the image of a decimated village of Sinanju. The image was false, a mirage, but for a short time he had believed it, and the distress he felt had left a scar.

When the danger was over, and Remo was Reigning Master, his strange behavior began. Despite his new burden of responsibility, despite new dangers foretold, Remo seemed at ease. Why?

Even for a man of far-reaching wisdom such as himself, Chiun found answers elusive. Could Remo be bluffing through the burden of being the Reigning Master? Could it be that he was in truth straining under the weight of this awesome responsibility? What if, unknown to Chiun, Remo was in distress and approaching an emotional breakdown?

Chiun had thought Remo was sleeping, but then the

young Reigning Master sat up straight in his aircraft seat and spoke aloud.

"Pork tamales."

Remo sounded quite pleased with himself.

Then Chiun knew the truth. As good as his body was at making the motions of the martial arts Sun source that was Sinanju, his feeble white brain had simply been unable to keep pace and it had finally folded in upon itself.

Ah, well. Folcroft Sanitarium was a pleasant enough place for an imbecile. Chiun would make sure that Smith gave Remo the nicest room in which to spend his remaining years doodling, sloppily, on the walls.

14

It was well past regular hours and the outer office was empty. Folcroft Sanitarium felt abandoned in the depth of the night, and they met no one on their way up to the office of Director Harold W. Smith. As they reached the outer office, domicile of Smith's longtime secretary Eileen Mikulka, Chiun turned to Remo.

"Wait here."

"What for?"

But Chiun was already gliding inside Smith's office and closing the door behind him.

"Hey, Chiun, what's the deal?" Remo asked, following him inside and finding the old Korean leaning close to the gray, patrician features of the CURE director, whispering fiercely.

Chiun wheeled on him. "I told you to remain outside!"

"Yeah, but I didn't. You planning a surprise party for me or something?"

Chiun sniffed disdainfully, but there was a look of worry on his brow. "Yes, something."

Remo tried to read the old man's expression, but it was an inscrutable combination of distrust and—what, concern? Smith revealed nothing. Mark Howard sat in the couch looking like a man who had no clue what was going on around him.

"So let me in on it," Remo demanded.

"Later perhaps," Chiun said, and gave Smith a prompting glare.

"Uh, yes. Tell me about Nashville."

"Southern inhospitality, too much money, too little taste. What else you want to know?"

Smith's gray face puckered sourly. "Anything. A clue. A hint."

"Nope. None of that. Lots of crazy dead dancers, and later lots of crazy bikers. That's about it."

"We're still getting reports on the murders at the Rock Hard Café," Smith said. "All the police are releasing is that the biker gang called themselves the Nashville Road Sharks. The gang stormed the Rock Hard seemingly without provocation."

"That's about the size of it," Remo agreed.

"That's nuts," Mark Howard objected. "There has to be motivation for it."

"You'd think," Remo admitted, relaxing in one of the chairs before Smith's desk. Chiun chose to stand, unusually guarded, Remo noticed. Guarded against what? "We asked the bikers. Politely at first, and then we got persuasive and they wouldn't tell us why. Said they were just really angry."

"Were they hiding their motive?" Howard asked.

"They could not hide their intentions from a Master

of Sinanju," explained Chiun. "They claimed they were simply filled with rage."

"Here's what we found out," Remo said. "They were at their usual hangout, you know, just having a few beers like every night, and they were talking about over-paid monkey suits at the yuppie bar down the street," Remo explained. "Only this time they decided it was time they stop talking about bashing heads and actually go bash some heads."

"Skilled killers they were not," Chiun sniffed.

Remo explained how they stopped in for a visit at the biker bar that had been the Nashville Road Sharks hangout. After delivering the sad news of the demise of Bork, Virgil, Maurice and the rest, they questioned the tearful, mourning patrons about anything unusual that happened in the bar that evening.

"Only one thing out of the ordinary," Remo said. "That night the Road Sharks came in with a friend. A new guy the locals had never seen before. Claimed to be a TV commercial producer looking for a real, hon-est-to-goodness biker gang for a new ad campaign for beer-flavored vodka."

"You think he was just trying to get close to the gang?" Smith asked.

"Looks like it." Remo shrugged. "He bought them a few rounds and said he would be in touch, then left. Half an hour later the Road Sharks had transformed from peace-loving Harley huggers into homicidal maniacs with a taste for yuppie blood. That's when they headed for the Rock Hard."

"And nobody got a good look at the man who claimed to be a TV commercial producer, I suppose."

"The clientele of the tavern were inebriated, Emperor," Chiun explained. "They remembered a man in his twenties with ridiculous face whiskers. Not another pertinent detail could any of them provide."

Smith sighed. Mark Howard put his hands behind his head and stretched back in the couch, staring at the ancient ceiling tiles, so yellowed with age their original color was impossible to discern.

"Well?"

Remo looked at Chiun. Howard and Smith looked at Chiun.

"Well what?" Remo asked.

"Do you not have more you would like to say?" Chiun said.

"Like what?"

"Do you have something more to report, Remo?" Smith asked sternly.

"Uh-uh. What about you?" Remo looked sharply at the old Korean.

"I have said all I know of the matter," Chiun replied leadingly.

Remo asked, "You think I know something about this that you don't?"

"Naturally not. I have been with you over the past twelve hours. All you have learned, so I have learned."

"So what are you fishing around for, Chiun?"

"I am not fishing." The bony hands appeared from within the kimono sleeves and waved airily. "I was merely guessing you had some sort of pronouncement to make to the Emperor."

"I don't think I've ever made a pronouncement in my life."

"Fine," Smith said with weary impatience. "What about the bikers' behavior?"

"It was atrocious," Remo stated.

"Compared to the addicts you encountered in the condemned building," Smith added.

"Well, they did a lot less screaming and they weren't as jittery," Remo recalled. "They were more clear-headed than the crack heads, but that's not saying much. What about the drugs I took from the crack house?"

"The analysis shows nothing out of the ordinary," Mark reported.

"I think it is still reasonable to assume that these killers were drugged," Smith added. "The man in Bunsen, Mississippi, Arby Maple, was reported to have shared a drink with a stranger just prior to embarking on his murder spree. That's the same as with the Nashville bikers and the crowd at the Big Stomp. I think it's safe to say it was probably something similar with the addicts."

"What's the difference between the screamers and the nonscreamers?" Remo asked. "Think it was the drugs?"

Smith nodded. "Makes sense. Whatever was used to bring about these fits of violence could have reacted with the crack cocaine the addicts ingested."

"That does not account for the aftereffects, though," Mark said. "The killers in each case seem to have different long-term reactions to the drug," he explained to Remo and Chiun. "Arby Maple claims to remember nothing—otherwise he seems healthy. The addicts who were taken into custody by the police after the killings have gone from paranoid and uncooperative to uncontrollably demented and violent. Some of them are starting to drop into semiconsciousness. None of them seem to have the power of speech any longer. The customers at the Big Stomp have also started experiencing decreased metabolism and slowing brain function. A few have slipped into comas. The medical teams are trying to come up with a treatment to keep them alive."

"Doesn't add up," Remo said.

"You're right," Smith agreed. "None of it does. Yet."

HE KNEW HIS PLOY would never work, but Remo went through the motions anyway. First he waited for the snores like fingernails on slate to fill the confines of the suite that was their Folcroft home-away-from-home, then Remo slipped into the hall. The cadence of the snoring in Chiun's room never changed, but he hadn't gone far before he knew he was being stalked through the Folcroft corridors.

He ignored it and entered an office on the upper floor. The room was so tiny there was barely room for the desk and the single guest chair, and yet the man sitting at the desk never sensed he was not alone until Remo closed the door and said, "Knock knock."

Mark Howard launched himself out of his seat and started to say something, only to find a very solid hand clamped firmly against his face.

"Shh. Keep it down."

"What's going on, Remo?" Mark demanded when he was released.

"I need a little help."

"What kind of help?"

"I think I've got a line on what's behind the weirdness in the heart of Dixie."

"Why all the sneaking around? Let's go see Dr. Smith."

"No. Uh-uh."

"This is not the time for playing games."

"I'm not playing games, Junior."

"Then why—?"

"Last warning, loudmouth. Keep your voice down." Remo nodded at the big oak desk, which dominated the room like a coffin in a closet. "Start typing."

Howard sat and raised the screen from the desktop, hands poised above the keyboard. "I need to know—"

"Get into the air travel records and flight plans. The airlines, the charters, private aircraft."

"You have to know we've done a search already," Howard said. "Want to tell me what I'm looking for?"

"A delegation from Union Island."

"You must be kidding me."

"Do it."

Mark shrugged, and his fingers started flying over the keyboard. Remo leaned over and stared at the screen for a moment. The electronic windows were hogwash. Howard could be checking the balance in his checking account for all Remo knew.

"Huh," Mark said.

"What huh?" Remo asked.

"The delegation was in Boston at the time of the

drug distribution. Hold on. They were in Nashville. The entire itinerary matches up."

"I thought so."

"But that doesn't exactly prove anything. The time frames were loose enough that we could put thousands of people in the right place at the right time."

"What's this bunch doing all the traveling around for, anyway?" Remo asked.

"Don't you read the news? Their president is on the talk-show circuit. He's trying to drum up support for their independence movement. They want to break away from the United States."

Remo frowned. "Show me what the president looks like."

Howard tapped a few keys and pushed back from the screen. Remo slid around the desk and looked at a Web page for the Union Island Independence Movement. The page was dominated by the smiling face of the elected leader of the island, President Greg Grom.

"What do you know, it's the same kid I saw on TV," Remo said. "He doesn't look old enough to vote, let alone get elected."

"He's not as young as he looks," Howard said, doing something esoteric with the little blinking line on the screen to make the window change to a biography of the kid in question. "Says here he's twenty-nine."

"For the president of the He-Man Woman Haters Club that's old—for president of anything bigger it's young."

"Doesn't mean he can't do his job," Mark protested. "He might actually achieve his goal."

"The independence thing? Just because he's got Puerto Rican go-it-aloners on his side?"

"That's strictly part of the PR campaign to generate sympathy for the cause. What counts is he's getting congressional support."

"How's he doing that? What's the angle?"

Howard shrugged. "I haven't been following it too closely, but it's all kind of confusing. I haven't heard anyone come up with a real reason Union Island should want independence, let alone why anybody on the Hill would support it. But it's happening."

"Is there any possible way they could they benefit from all this killing?" Remo asked.

"That's what I'm looking into," Howard said as he typed furiously. "None of the people involved in the killing have ties to Union Island. There's never been known drug trafficking through Union, so there doesn't seem to be a logical organized-crime link."

"But if they were independent they could run drugs through the place," Remo suggested.

Howard shook his head. "Independence wouldn't help them there. Even if they set up the island as a distribution hub, we'd find out, blockade them and shut them down."

"Yeah, I guess so."

Howard's fingers spidered over the keys for a few more minutes until he sat back in the chair. "I just don't see a connection."

"But it might be there," Remo insisted.

"Might be." Mark clearly doubted it. "Tell me why all the secrecy."

Remo shook his head. "Maybe later. Where's the Union group now?"

"En route to North Carolina for a PR event in the town of Fuquay-Varina."

"You better not be making that up."

"There's a morning talk-show appearance scheduled for the president, then a chartered bus trip through the Smoky Mountains. There's an afternoon photo op for the media at a mountaintop hotel, then on to a late dinner hosted by the mayor of Knoxville, Tennessee."

"Why the long drive? Why not just fly to Knoxville?"

"Maybe they want to see the Great Smokies."

"Yeah," Remo said. "Maybe I do, too."

15

"I would appreciate knowing where we are going."

"Uckfay-Farina, North Carolina," Remo answered as he balanced Chiun's chests on each shoulder and ducked to get them below the top of the airport door. "From there maybe to Tennessee."

"You have not yet told me why we are doing this."

"And I'm not going to. That's the deal if I let you tag along."

"The Master Of Sinanju Emeritus does not 'tag along.'"

The uncomfortable silence continued all the way to Raleigh.

THE REAL PEOPLE HOUR out of Raleigh, North Carolina, was as amateur as any TV talk show got. Some folding chairs and a stage pounded together out of plywood. A couple of digital camcorders from Walmart. One of them had a tripod.

The Real People Hour had been broadcast on the

whim of a retiring station manager and met with unexpected success. Now, as it celebrated its one-year anniversary, *The Real People Hour* was seen in fifteen markets throughout the Carolinas, Georgia, Virginia, even Florida. And more stations were interested.

"It's a barn," Remo said as they emerged from the rental car.

"It sure is," said the boy in the orange vest who was waving cars into parking places on the flattened grass. "This was a working farm up until a year ago. My mom's the one who started the show and my daddy does the production work. Tickets?"

"No, thanks."

"We flew in an airplane to come to this place?" Chiun sniffed. "They raised pigs in this place."

"Yeah. And never bothered to clean out the sty when they made the switch to showbiz," Remo observed.

The kid in the orange vest hustled past and chatted seriously with a pair of older boys at the barn entrance. The pair stiffened and eyed them as they checked ticket stubs, then closed ranks on Remo and Chiun.

"You'll need tickets to see the show," the taller boy declared. He had a face full of patchy whiskers. His younger brother had the girth of a gorilla and was even hairier.

"Shouldn't you be in school?" Remo asked.

"Don't go to school. We got a TV show to run," the taller one explained scornfully. "Now, you got a ticket?"

Remo extracted an ID from the front pocket of his Chinos. "Remo Rottweiler, Secret Service, foreign diplomats detail. Let's see some ID."

The tall one went slack-jawed, then turned and gestured frantically into the barn. A moment later a beerbelly and its owner emerged. The man had the same scruffy whiskers as his sons.

"You the man in charge here?" Remo demanded before the tall kid could get out an explanation. He pushed his ID in the man's face. "I assume you've got federal diplomatic access clearance for all employees?"

"I never heard of federal diplomatic access clearance," the father responded, unable to decide if he should be belligerent or agreeable.

"You've got heads of state on the premises. You'll need FDAC on all personnel."

"Nobody told me that." The beer belly and its owner swung pendulously at them. He apparently decided on belligerence.

"Sorry. You can start the show when you have them. Phone the Department of Justice, and they'll take care of it."

"Oh. Okay. I'll phone right now. How long it'll take, you think?"

Remo shrugged. "Eight weeks is what they'll tell you, but really it'll take twelve."

"What? We got a show to do in ten minutes! You can't make us stop the show!"

"Wouldn't dream of it. But we will be required to escort your guest away from the premises immediately."

"But then we *got* no show!"

"Then maybe you tell Scruff and Scruffier to cough up some ID. You, too."

Remo glared at the IDs, then ordered Scruff the

Youngest and the car-parking kid to go to school. Scruff the Youngest began sobbing. Remo reluctantly allowed the show to go on, under his supervision, and he and Chiun took seats in the audience. *The Real People Hour* got under way just fifteen minutes late.

"Don't worry about it folks. We're on tape anyway, and we want everything perfect before we get the show on the road!" The host was Missy Glossé, whose complicated hair design and makeup contrasted with her rumpled farm-wife dress and the cheap set. In fact, the only change made to the show since the very first program was the host's new hairdo and several new folding chairs.

After a few handshakes and bad jokes, Glossé disappeared into the curtained livestock stalls that now served as dressing rooms. Minutes later the house lights dropped and the show started with a blare of music from a portable stereo. Missy Glossé came on stage and brought out her guest without delay.

"Who is this whelp?" Chiun asked in a voice so quiet only Remo could hear it.

"Don't let his age fool you. The kid is an elected government leader."

Chiun shook his head sadly. "I am not surprised. You elect felons. You elect actors. You elect professional wrestlers. Why not elect a playground brat? Democracy inspires idiocy."

"Well, he wants out of our particular democracy," Remo explained. "He wants Union Island to go independent."

"Ah. Emperor Smith opposes this."

Remo shook his head. "I don't think Smitty give two hoots in a holler about Greg Grom or Union Island."

Chiun's face pinched. "Then why are we here?"

Remo ignored the question. Missy Glossé was effusing to the audience about her recent vacation on Union Island. "President Grom, your island is just the most beautiful tropical paradise! I have never experienced anyplace like it!"

"Thank you very much, Ms. Glossé. You know, we can only try to protect our beautiful country from the ravages we know are coming—no less than total destruction of the entire island."

"What?" demanded a mortified Missy Glossé.

"You know the poor people of Puerto Rico have been terribly inconvenienced by the military exercises on their out-islands," the youthful-looking Greg Grom recited. "The political backlash has been tremendous and the U.S. is looking for another site—one without a minority population. We have it on good authority that Union Island has been designated. It's close, it's a U.S. property and the population is more than fifty-percent white, so the military can't be accused of racial discrimination."

"But what about that beautiful island and those shining, happy people?" Ms. Glossé wailed.

Greg Grom hung his head. He took off his glasses and rubbed the bridge of his nose. He looked up a moment later.

"I am sorry. It just makes me so sad to talk about."

"I can't believe anybody falls for this guy," Remo muttered.

"Most of the charlatans vying for ballots in this failing democracy have some crude acting skills, if nothing else," Chiun observed. "This young faker is entirely insincere."

Grom was looking straight at the camera now. "Our friends in Washington says there is a lockdown on these plans, and we've met with nothing but falsehoods and denials from federal officials. They do not even have the guts to tell us the truth."

"I haven't seen acting this bad since we did Gift of the Magi in fifth grade," Remo complained. "Come on."

"What? Going?" Chiun said. "The show has just begun."

"There's more to see and it's not in here. You coming?"

"Not until I know where."

"Suit yourself."

The entrance had a hand-lettered sign that forbade opening the door during the taping of the show. A padlocked steel bar kept the door firmly closed. Standing guard was another family member—in fact, his age suggested he might be the progenitor of the Glossé species.

"Terlet's in the rear. Can't be opening this door while tape is rolling."

"Terlet's on the stage, if you ask me," Remo replied as he tapped the padlock and it cracked like brittle glass. It clanked noisily on the wooden plank floor. Remo handed the steel crossbar to the dismayed old-timer, but the weight of the bar carried it right out of the old man's fingers. The racket was tremendous. By then taping had come to a stop and Producer-Director Beerbelly Glossé was yelling about "a closed set" and "federal meddlers!"

"I see you are now abusing all the elderly, and not just me." Chiun had slipped through the door of the old pig barn just before it slammed shut.

"I don't know what President Grom is up to, but he's sure telling a tall tale about the U.S. using his island for target practice," Remo commented. "I wonder why."

"There are many other questions one must ask at this time," Chiun said. "Why did we come here? Why did we leave? What insidious plot do you conceal from your Father-in-Spirit?"

Remo led them to the customized tour bus parked in the rear of the barn. The engine was running, and a uniformed driver stretched out on the steps in the open door. He smiled easily but made no move to get up.

"We need to check out the vehicle." Remo flipped out the badge and stalled on the name and agency du jour. The driver waved the badge away.

"Whatever. Coffee's in the pot."

The driver scooted to one side so the Masters of Sinanju could use the steps. Inside they gazed at a vast suite of living spaces created out of compact furniture and built-in appointments.

"Remo!" Chiun exclaimed. "What is this place?"

"The Lost Naugahyde Graveyard?"

"It is beautiful," Chiun enthused, strolling through a small parlor made by a tight grouping of sofas. He descended a few steps into the media center with theater seating and a huge, flat television display mounted in the wall. "Look how carefully it is crafted! See how they have used the finest fabrics and design to create compact living spaces inside a truck!"

"It's a sleazy Vegas hotel room on wheels," Remo said.

"No, it is a *palace* on wheels!"

Remo didn't like the sound of that one bit. "Help me look, will you?"

"How can I help when I do not know what I am looking for? This kitchen is a miracle—small and yet complete down to the smallest detail. There is even a warming drawer!"

"We eat rice, fish and more rice. What would we warm in a warming drawer?"

"The drawers are made with a tiny catch to keep them from sliding open while the vehicle is in motion!"

"Wait," Remo said. He stopped and looked around the room. He sniffed. Chiun creased his eyes at the young Master.

"Smell anything?" Remo asked.

"I smell a thousand aromas. I assume you smell something out of the ordinary."

"Not yet, but I'll find it." He sniffed loudly.

"Pah. You smell like a horse—and I mean that in every sense," Chiun said. "Tell me what we are attempting to locate, if sharing the secret is not too troublesome."

"Well, I don't know exactly. Some sort of a drug or chemical or something that would make people act crazy."

Chiun's white mouth drew up in a hard line. "As in violently maddened? Is that why we are here, Remo, to hunt down the source of the tavern brawl troubles?"

"Yep. That's the reason."

"Why did not Emperor Smith inform me of this purpose?"

"Emperor Smith doesn't know we're here, okay?" Remo said. "It was my idea to come here. I'm the one who started thinking that maybe this bunch of Caribbean nincompoops was making all the bad stuff happen. The only person I told was Prince Junior and only because I needed to get some of my facts straight."

Chiun nodded, uncharacteristically thoughtful. Remo tried to ignore him as he opened cabinets and sniffed under coffee tables.

"What did the Prince Regent think of your deductions?"

"You know what he thought, Chiun! He thought I was grasping at wild geese and I am sure you do, too. So what do you say we skip all the sarcastic remarks this time."

Remo felt the Master Emeritus watching him. The old man was just standing there. Remo hated it when Chiun acted all quiet, as if pondering weighty matters—such as the magnificence of the ignorance of the man who was now Reigning Master.

"Well, like it or not, here we are," Remo announced finally. "So why don't you humor me and see if you can find anything suspicious."

"Very well," Chiun replied quite agreeably.

For the next ten minutes they ransacked the customized touring bus and went through the two bedrooms in the rear. They found prescription bottles, several stocked liquor cabinets and a plastic bag of Mary Jane's Delight Brand Legal Pipe-Blend. Even in a sealed plastic bag Remo could tell it was only catnip and oregano.

"I do not believe we will find what you are seeking, my son," Chiun said as they finished their rounds.

Remo said nothing, just stood in the small dining area with a realistic-looking electric-log fireplace. His freakishly thick wrists twisted absently.

"Any bombs?" asked the driver with a smile as he strolled through the curtains that partitioned off the driving area. He made for the kitchenette, where he refilled his insulated mug.

"Can't be too careful," Remo replied as his wrists stopped twisting.

"I 'preciate your thoroughness."

As soon as the driver left, Remo went to the kitchenette. He snatched open the doors of the golden oak cabinets.

"I have already searched the kitchenette," Chiun said.

"Maybe it's in the coffee. They used to try to hide cocaine in coffee shipments because the drug dogs couldn't sniff it out that way."

"My sense of smell is superior to that of any drug-sniffing dog. If there were drugs in the coffee I would have found it."

"I know you would, Little Father," Remo said through gritted teeth—as he opened a five-pound can of Folgers and plunged his fingers into it. He scooped up several handfuls of coffee.

Just coffee.

16

"All right, let me have it," Remo said after an hour of excruciating silent treatment.

"Let you have what?" Chiun asked.

"You're mad at me, and you're dying to tell me about it."

Sitting with legs crossed, Chiun modestly adjusted the skirts of his kimono. Every loose bit of silk fluttered in the wind. "I do not know what you are talking about."

"Overpass," Remo announced, nodding his head low on his chest. The big tour bus rumbled at sixty-five miles per hour under the concrete supports of a county highway that had been routed over the interstate. There was just an inch of clearance between the wind-whipped tips of his close-cropped dark hair and the underside of the overpass. Chiun didn't even bother to bow his head. At about five feet tall, he was already as low as his adopted son was ducking.

The overpass was left behind in a flurry of rushing air.

"I didn't trust you or I second-guessed you or something when we were in the bus. You told me the drugs were not in the coffee and I went and looked in the coffee anyway. You're mad about that."

Chiun said nothing. The white tufts of hair decorating each of his shell-like ears looked as if they would fly off any second.

"Well, I guess I can understand why you'd be mad. I don't know why I checked the coffee. Even I could smell that it was just coffee. Aw, crap."

A state trooper, lying in wait behind the viaduct, was now speeding up behind the tour bus.

"Why couldn't he be sleeping?" Remo complained.

"You did not expect to ride half the morning atop this vehicle without being noticed," Chiun said. "Besides, the first two police *were* sleeping."

They stood and walked to the front of the bus, which alarmed the trooper into sounding his siren. They stepped off at a point near the front where they would be unseen by the trooper and bus passengers, then jogged alongside as the bus slowed. Finally they veered off into the wildflower field that encroached on the two westbound lanes.

"I guess I really wanted to find the stuff in the damn bus," Remo continued as the two of them stepped up into a comfortable looking tree and watched the trooper clamber all over the tour bus. They heard the derision cast on the trooper by the bus driver and several of the occupants, who had debarked to watch the entertainment. The trooper's face was bright pink by the time he crawled onto the roof himself and searched it, expecting to find a trapdoor or a hiding place.

"Is that why we are staying with the bus? Because you cannot stand the thought of being mistaken?"

"No, because I don't think I am mistaken," Remo said. "I've got a strong intuition that there's a link between this entourage and the outbreaks of violence. Like when I was in Boston putting the screws to Jorge Moroza. The TV was on in the restaurant to a Spanish language station, and they showed one of the news items with Greg Grom. Then we saw him on the news again in Nashville. And I think I saw him at the Big Stomp—remember the limo that pulled in right after we got there? I saw half a face inside it. Just the eyes. And it was through the dark glass. But I think it was him. Grom."

Chiun looked at him as if waiting for a punchline.

"I had this sort of feeling that I was missing something, you know. I couldn't put my finger on it, but for some reason I kept smelling pork tamales in my head."

Chiun looked more interested, and slightly pitying.

"Crazy, maybe, but I couldn't shake it out. Then I was just sitting there on the plane, not even trying to think about it, and that's when I remembered smelling pork tamales. It was when I questioned Jorge Moroza. He must have eaten thirty of them. That was when I remembered that I had seen Grom on the TV when I was with Moroza. Everything clicked into place."

"You equate an obsession with pork tamales with investigative insight?" Chiun pondered. "Pork tamales no less, Remo. Pig fat and corn. There must be no more appealing food on the planet to one with your bizarre and degraded pedigree."

"Chiun, I guarantee I will never eat a pork tamale, especially not after watching what they did to Moroza. And I must have been onto something. I had Prince Junior check into it, and he figured out that this bus has been within strike range of all the outbreaks of violence."

"Was anyone else?"

"Well, yeah, a few hundred people, according to the flight schedules."

The trooper was standing outside his car having an animated exchange with whoever was on the other end of his radio. Someone was reading the trooper the riot act for harassing a politically sensitive elected official.

The trooper's face was as red and hot as a freshly murdered lobster being lifted out of the boiling pot. "Go!" He shouted at the bus crew. "Get out of my state!"

The occupants joked and tittered at the expense of the trooper as they filed back inside and the bus pulled off the shoulder. The trooper kept his lights on until the bus was getting up to speed, then he zoomed ahead. Remo and Chiun ran up behind the bus, keeping themselves in the blind spots of the windows, and leaped aboard. By the time they had seated themselves again, they could see the trooper up ahead in a U-turn lane reserved for emergency vehicles.

Remo waved. The trooper snatched off his mirrored sunglasses, uttered a handful of profanities, then slammed his car into Reverse.

"Not again, you don't." Remo tossed one of the rocks he had gathered during their stop. The little stone sped through the air too fast to be visible and tore through the sidewall of one of the trooper's rear tires. A second rock deflated a front tire. The trooper jumped out of his car and danced in frustration.

"So why are we again on this bus?" Chiun asked.

"To see if my lead pans out."

"Did you not admit that the lead already panned in? We are wasting time. Let us look for an eastbound bus. Perhaps we'll find one that will even allow us to take passage on the inside. I understand this part of the nation has loosened its bus travel restrictions."

"Look, this is my gig. I thought it up. I'm doing what I think I ought to do."

"And I have warned you that thinking is not always your best skill, my son."

"Cram it, Chiun."

"This advice I offer with the best intentions...."

"If you mean your intention is to be a first-class son of a bitch then you pull it off with flying colors."

The youthful eyes seemed to withdraw into the eggshell skull. "Why do you insult me with bitter words?"

"Me? Insult you? I'm so freaking stupid I don't know that you just called me a moron. And you know what? Now that I think about it, you called me moron the very first time we met. And, wait a second, unless I'm a total moron, you've called me a moron every day in between!"

"Control yourself."

"Smith thinks I'm an idiot, the Little Prince thinks I'm a dull-witted playground bully and every President whose life I every saved thought I was a dumb bouncer. You know what, they even thought I was a dim bulb back when I was on the force. Hell, when I was in the freaking Marines they used to say behind my back that I could fight my way out of a steel cage, but I couldn't think my way out of a wet paper bag. And you know where it started? The nuns used to whack me on the shoulder blades when I'd get it wrong and say, 'Think, Remo. Why won't you just think?'"

"Is that the cause of this outburst?" Chiun demanded. "Have you been carrying around this anger toward the Virgins of the Carpenter sect for so long that it has finally boiled to the surface?"

"What brought it to the surface was you treating me the same damn way as the Sisters," Remo said hotly.

Chiun gasped and shot to his feet. The wind turned his kimono into a furiously flapping flag, like a hundred silk fingers wagging disdainfully at Remo Williams.

"You compare me to the foolish nuns of the Christian cult?" Chiun challenged.

"If the habit fits, wear it."

"I will not stay and be insulted!" Chiun warned.

"Don't let the overpass hit you in the ass on the way out."

Chiun stamped his foot in impotent fury, creating a foot-deep crater in the aluminum roof of the bus, then turned and jumped up. It looked like a light hop, but the leap carried him twelve feet into the sky and his feet settled perfectly on the rail of an overpass.

He walked along the steel rail, then leaped down again, alighting atop a moving van heading east, and sat with his back to Remo Williams as the distance grew rapidly between them.

Remo had not even bothered to watch where his mentor went. Right now, just the fact that Chiun was gone was good enough.

17

The elected president of the United States Protectorate
of Union Island was sporting a bad case of bed head and
rubbing the sleep gunk out of his eyes when he emerged
from his bedroom into the outer cubicle occupied by his
secretary.

"You missed the excitement." Amelia Powlik made
a sound like a small dog choking on a chicken bone.

"What's so funny?" Grom asked.

"We got pulled over by one of North Carolina's
finest. He said we had people riding on the roof."

"What?"

"When he looks on the roof and can't find anybody,
he says there must be a trapdoor on the roof to let people get up top from the inside. You know what I think?"
She pantomimed drinking out of a flask and then rolled
her eyes like a drunk. Amelia thought she was im-
mensely humorous and hacked at her own hilarity.

"So what happened?" Grom demanded.

"He wanted to get into your private room to look for

this trapdoor, and that's when I called and got the Feds involved. By the time he goes to his car to radio for backup he's got his CO on the other end telling him to back off."

Grom felt like he was missing a piece of information. "But did he really smell like he'd been drinking?"

"Naw, but he was out of it. Wacko." She barked delightedly. "By the way, we're twenty minutes from the photo-op stop."

Grom retreated into his room to get washed up in his phone-booth-sized shower. Funny how talking to his secretary made him feel strangely unclean. In fact, every woman on board the Union Island Freedom Tour Bus was less than attractive. This was one of the attributes that got them their high-ranking positions on the president's staff.

President Greg Grom didn't have much say in the matter. At some point the personnel responsibility had been usurped by his minister of tourism, although Grom couldn't quite explain how or when it had happened. Somehow Dawn Summens had wiggled her way into the role as personnel manager, and Grom's access to women was curtailed. That was fine so long as he had access to Dawn Summens. There wasn't a straight guy on the planet who wouldn't trade his own mother for a taste of Dawn Summens's goodies.

But pretty soon that well had all but dried up, too.

It hadn't always been like this. Before Dawn Summens came onto the scene, Greg Grom had been awash in women. There had been women by the boatloads, women of every color. Shy ones and bold ones. Fresh-faced college girls on spring break and sophisticated aristocrats. Even royalty. It didn't matter to Greg Grom as long as they were attractive. He scored with just about every woman he went after.

Greg Grom, once upon a time, had made a very important discovery.

THE DARK AND FOREBODING shadows of the pile of rubble would have frightened your run-of-the-mill, superstitious rabble. Greg Grom was highly educated superstitious rabble, and he was scared out of his socks.

Even in daylight the overgrown ruins were ominous. At night, the shadows held primordial demons that disregarded all the education and sensibility of a twenty-first-century man.

Greg Grom stood in the open area that had once been the town center. Around him the earth swarmed at knee level with weeds and shrubs. All around the periphery of the buildings waited the dark, huge malevolence of the rain forest trees, silent minions of the long-gone inhabitants. Once this was home to Miytec, which, as far as anyone could tell, was a little-known Mayan-Toltec breakaway group that thrived on Union Island briefly in the fourteenth and fifteenth centuries. By the time Columbus landed in the New World, Union Island was empty.

Grom still felt the Miytec. They were all around him, and they weren't happy to have a grave robber in their midst. He was quivering with fear. A mosquito flew up his left nostril, and he slapped at his face and snorted for fifteen seconds. The moon peeked cautiously over a nearby tree.

Forget this! Grom thought. I'll do it in daylight!

But he stayed where he was. There was no way to do this during daylight, when the ruins were full of excavators. Grom was himself part of a team of students from all over the U.S. doing an internship on Union Island. It wasn't a prestigious dig site, but it was mostly unexplored, and all the enthusiastic young people came with high hopes of making a major find.

Greg Grom actually made a major find—and he wasn't telling a soul. He wouldn't share this with anyone, which was why he had to do his excavating in the dark of night.

The second level of the massive stone building had collapsed in on itself during the five centuries since the mysterious disappearance of the Miytec. It was on the ground-floor level that the real finds were being made. Some of the rooms had become sealed by earth or by flora, preserving their contents.

One of the lower-level rooms had been opened just two days earlier, and there the team discovered its first human remains. It was a middle-aged man slumped against a wall. In his hand was a paintbrush. On the floor was a pot of dried, cracked paint. On the walls were painted his final words.

They were in Miytec, which was tough enough to translate. But they were in such crudely penned Miytec as to be almost illegible. None of the others could make sense of it. Not even Burnt Haller, the professor in charge of the group.

But Central American languages were Greg Grom's specialty. And what he read there made his feet perspire with excitement. He took some snapshots to study. He translated them carefully in the hotel bar, when none of the other team members were around.

If true, it was an amazing find.

The dead man and author claimed to be the last Miytec holy man, imprisoned in the tomb by attackers from other islands and from the mainland. The small allied army that had come and wiped out the Miytec on Union Island had been afraid even to touch a Miytec holy man, let alone risk the wrath of the Miytec gods by striking him dead. They had satisfied themselves with sealing him alive in his precious storeroom.

"Here I tell the secret of the Miytec power to rule," the holy man wrote. "With this rite, a man loyal to the pantheon of Miytec deities will gain control of the will of all men."

When Greg Grom read this he thought, Interesting. Something persuaded him to keep it to himself. On some strange impulse he tapped the cracked pouch in the skeletal fingers of the long dead Miytec priest and was surprised when a bit of coarse powder trickled out.

The powder was the source of the Miytec's strange ability to "control the will of all men." It had to be a myth. It couldn't be true. Could it?

Greg Grom knew he had to test it. He had to know.

His test was a big success.

Now he was coming back to get the powder—all of it.

In the black of night the old corpse was a hideous specter. It stared up at Grom with gaping eye sockets, and laughed at him with yellow teeth. Grom couldn't stop thinking about how the man died.

The old Miytec holy man was trapped underground.

The oil in his lamp was nearly exhausted. "I taste of the powder. I descend into death. I perform the ritual of resurrection upon myself."

Grom knew what that meant. Too much powder worked like Haitian zombie powder. The metabolism slowed and the body seemed to die. Pulse and respiration slowed until they were virtually undetectable. The subject appeared dead. Days later, the subject's metabolism sped up again. The subject, to all appearances, died and came back from the dead.

The holy man took the powder in hopes of extending his life in the unlikely chance that the tomb would be opened up again.

In the irrational, superstitious part of his brain Grom was convinced that now, finally, after seven centuries, the Miytec holy man would resurrect.

It took hours for Grom to get up the nerve to move the holy man. He had to move him—the old Miytec had inconveniently laid himself on top of the stone slab that led into the storage chamber. Using a wide broom, Grom gingerly shifted the body off the stone, only to have it crumble into pieces. After that he felt less anxiety. The old Miytec wasn't a body any longer, just a pile of bones. Grom swept him into a corner, then pried up the big flat stone. Underneath was blackness.

Grom poked his flashlight inside and looked around, and had to clamp a hand over his own mouth to keep from laughing out loud.

There were dozens of stone jars. Dozens of them.

Grom worked hard that night, carrying jar after jar

out of the storeroom to his rental car. He checked every single jar, and every single jar was brimming with powder. An hour before dawn saw him replacing the stone entrance and shoving the crumbling bones back into place. He drove back to the hotel and used the luggage cart to move the stone jars to his room.

Heidi Fenstermaker was there waiting for him. She helped him pile the jars in the closet, then gave him a nice long back rub. In fact, she did whatever Greg wanted.

Heidi, after all, had been the subject of the very first test.

THE MORNING BEFORE, Greg had waited under a vine-covered arch that had grown shaggy from neglect. It was the only entrance to the hotel's dismal patio restaurant where the crew of archaeology interns took their meals. Heidi Fenstermaker couldn't avoid him.

"Morning, Heidi," Grom greeted her cheerfully. "Join me for breakfast?"

Heidi's eyes flitted around the empty tables as she tried to come up with an excuse to have breakfast with anyone else. However, Grom's bold and overtly friendly invitation gave a polite girl like Heidi no way out.

Grom led her to a tiny round table for two. A surly waiter appeared long enough to deposit two cups of coffee.

"You're heading back to the States in a couple of weeks?" Grom asked conversationally.

"Yes, finally." Heidi sighed.

"I wish you wouldn't go."

"Why not?"

"I like having you around."

She was taken aback. "Greg, you haven't said ten words to me since I got here."

He lifted the cup of coffee out of her hands. "Ugh. A bug just flew in it," Grom said. "I'll get you a fresh cup."

He stood and tossed the coffee over the patio rail into the weeds, then got her a clean cup at the waiter's station. He sprinkled in the precious, tiny bits of powder and added fresh coffee.

"Dash of cream, no sugar, no bugs—just the way you like it," he announced as he placed the coffee before the lovely Heidi Fenstermaker.

"Thanks."

Grom tried not to stare as she lifted the white porcelain to her full, beautiful lips. The moment of truth. What did dried, ground-up, poisonous octopus powder taste like, anyway? It couldn't be good. He half expected Heidi to spew java all over him.

Instead, she rewarded him with a faint smile.

"It's okay?" he asked.

"As good as it gets around here."

He nodded. Now the next big test.

Would it work?

It couldn't work. How could it work? The Miytec story had to be just a myth.

Well, he would know soon enough.

"I was saying, anyway, I was hoping we might get to know each other," Grom suggested.

"So why'd it take you three months to talk to me?"

Grom tried to look self-effacing. "I'm shy around women." He drank his own coffee, hoping to encourage her by example.

"You're not acting shy now." She sipped.

"You know, for once this is pretty good coffee," Grom said.

Heidi Fenstermaker nodded. "It's not bad at all, really."

"You'd like a little sugar." He said it simply. Not a question. Not a command. He just said it.

Heidi started to say something, then stopped. "I would like some sugar," she said.

Grom poured it in for her.

"It was nice of me to pour your sugar," Grom suggested.

"It's very sweet of you to sweeten my coffee," Heidi said with a wide smile. She sipped it.

"Great joe they have here," Grom observed.

"It is wonderful!"

"I'm attracted to you Heidi. And you are extremely attracted to me."

"I am, Greg. I guess I never really admitted it to myself until this very minute."

"You are in love with me, passionately. You want me. You'd do anything for me, Heidi."

"Yes, Greg, anything." She leaned over the table, her eyes drinking him in lustily and giving him a fine view down the front of her light cotton shirt. She looked around and surreptitiously opened a couple more of the shirt buttons. Grom's view got even better.

Heidi pulled the rubber band out of her hair, transforming her tight ponytail into a bountiful spill of corn-silk. "Let's skip breakfast and go back to my room," she suggested.

Grom leaned back, brimming with satisfaction. His future was assured. His success would know no bounds. And what better way to celebrate it all than with a morning romp with Heidi Fenstermaker? He said, "Finish your coffee for me first, will you, honey bunch?"

The cup was drained before he reached the "unch" part.

GREG GROM FONDLY recalled those first heady days spent testing the capabilities of the powder. It worked just as well as the translations promised. In fact, it seemed too good to be true. Grom kept waiting for his test subject to develop horrific medical problems or dementia or, well, something.

There were a few glitches along the way. When Heidi Fenstermaker discovered that Grom was regularly bedding nine of the fourteen female interns, she became hysterically jealous. Grom calmed her down and gave her a cup of coffee. He suggested to Heidi that she was *not* angry with him for sleeping with every other attractive woman in the group. As a matter of fact, Grom suggested that...

Well, that opened up whole new vistas of opportunity.

Even after Grom began using his powder for other purposes he still enjoyed many and various sexual exploits. He learned from his mistakes and soon developed a very effective set of suggestions. He took his women, enjoyed them, then discarded them with a code word. They went away just as happily as they had come to him.

Grom could have gone on like that for a lifetime had it not been for the arrival of Dawn Summens. She was just some bikini model hired for a commercial. By then Grom had engineered for himself a rapid rise through the ranks of the tiny Union Island government bureaucracy and was already chief of staff to the island administrator. Grom invited Summens to dinner after the commercial shoot and, somehow, in just one evening, everything changed.

It was as if Summens had used his own powder against him, captivating him entirely. That wouldn't have been such a bad thing if she had not outsmarted him at the same time. She learned about the powder, somehow, and threatened to expose him. She had documented evidence hidden somewhere. She blackmailed him at the same time she was giving him the best sex he had ever had. He never quite got around giving her the Miytec powder until it was too late.

He had to admit that it had all turned out for the best. Summens had assumed control of his ambitious strategies and pushed them further. He rarely let her touch the powder, but she strategized how he used it. Pretty soon Grom found himself elected administrator of Union Island. He changed the office to president, and the islanders loved him for it. His tourism initiative succeeded wildly. Union Island prospered and Greg Grom got rich fast.

Could he sustain this pace? Maybe. Maybe not.

There had been a lot of dried-up octopus powder in the stone jars from the Miytec ruins, but those jars emptied fast when he began sprinkling it on the hotel breakfast buffets. The supply was virtually exhausted. The synthetic version of dried-up octopus powder seemed prone to triggering side effects.

Grom was getting nervous. They were at a crucial stage. Union Island had to break away from the United States of America. U.S. restrictions were hindering his income potential. When he was the one and only rule of law on the island, he could tax tourism as much as he wanted.

But independence would come only with strong federal-level support. Since no elected official in his right mind would support Union Island independence, Grom needed the powder to make it happen.

But the powder was almost gone.

18

The Union Island Freedom Tour bus was nearing its stop at a restaurant at one of the highest points in the Great Smoky Mountains National Park. President Grom was scheduled to partake of the restaurant's famous down-home pie and fresh-brewed coffee, then make a brief speech.

Remo thought it was odd. Why here? It was picturesque, sure, but he couldn't see what connection it had with Greg Grom's independence movement.

Remo stepped off the roof and jogged easily along the hiking trail for the last few miles. The bus was straining against the incline, and it didn't take much effort for Remo to beat it to its destination. He entered the restaurant and found it to have a large two-tiered interior, giving all patrons an unobstructed view of the mountains through the glass wall. He took a table on the top tier and watched Greg Grom perform below, at the best seat in the house.

"What'll it be?" The waitress didn't even look in his

direction. She was watching Greg Grom. Remo asked for steamed rice and fresh fish, only to be told there was no rice on the menu. Did he want his fish deep-fried or pan-fried?

"Steam the fish, too, would you?" Remo asked.

The waitress took all of six minutes to return with a plate of smoked ham, candied carrots and mashed potatoes under a vast, gelatinous pool of auburn gravy. By then Greg Grom had finished his public pie-eating and was delivering a brief speech on the indomitable spirit on the Smoky Mountain folk. Somehow his compliments dovetailed into an exhortation for the freedom of Union Island. Remo didn't try to follow the logic. Grom made his excuses and headed for the men's room.

"Second helpin's on the house," Remo informed the old man in the next booth, handing over his own untouched and inedible plate of country victuals. The old man looked as if he'd won the lottery.

Remo slipped from the restaurant without being noticed by the wait staff, who were busy discussing their brush with a world leader.

With a little fast footwork Remo got outside and under the exterior window to the men's room, but he kept on moving. Union Island staff were wandering the grounds casting their suspicious gaze on any and all patrons. Two of the agents had clearly had U.S. Secret Service training in how to blend into a crowd. The others were regular staff drafted into security duty and spent most of their time actually watching the suit-and-sunglasses twins, imitating their behavior strategies for looking natural. Remo passed through them unseen, but he wasn't sure a passle of teenagers doing a Big Stomp line dance couldn't have passed unnoticed through this self-absorbed bunch.

Still, Remo was interested in some quality alone time in the men's room, and he didn't want to be bothered. He sought a distraction.

The wide, manicured lawn was dotted with wooden lounge chairs inhabited by relaxing guests of the hotel that was attached to the restaurant. Most were elderly widows reading sleazy hack romance novels and occasionally looking up to admire the view. The lawn went down the mountainside for a quarter mile, then ended at a white picket fence. Beyond that stretched a mile-deep canyon. Even in the late-morning sunshine the verdant crevices and mountainsides were caressed by the clinging veils of mists that gave the Smokies their name.

Beautiful, Remo thought. Not the scenery, but the nifty diversion that just popped into his head. As he walked, he reached out with one foot and gave a nudge to one of the lounge chairs.

The chairs were outfitted with large wooden wheels, which were functional enough when it came to moving the heavy chairs from one place to another but were not designed for locomotion. Despite the long decline of the lawn, the hotel management had never worried about one of their chairs rolling off with one of their patrons.

Maybe they should have.

The chair shot across the lawn like a rocket, the front legs sheering off so that the front end flattened on the neatly mown grass. One of the federal-trained Union Island security agents was scooped off his feet. He collapsed onto the chair and then just kept going, zipping down the hill at a speed that should have been impossible.

The security detail responded with raised eyebrows, and the other tall agent, the one with the darkest sunglasses of all, showed real concern.

Remo was mildly impressed when the man in the fleeing lounge chair had the wherewithal to operate his radio. "This is Samson—I'm under attack!"

"Oh, shit!" said the agent in charge, snatching at his two-way radio. "Samson, this is Hercules—maintain radio silence! We've got journalists in the vicinity."

"Did you hear me?" squawked the panicking agent. "I'm under attack!"

The Union Islanders ran off in pursuit. The speeding lounge chair lost its wooden wheels a few yards short of the end of the lawn, spun sideways and slammed into the white picket fence. Wood splinters flew in all directions. The chair and its occupant vanished into the brush-filled drop-off beyond. The running bodyguards tried to slow down but realized the slope of the lawn wasn't as gentle as it looked. They tried to stop, but they just kept on going....

"Thought they'd never leave," Remo muttered, entering the men's room. He moved with inhuman silence, and Greg Grom, president of Union Island, never knew the Master of Sinanju was with him.

It was a while before Remo emerged again, breathing for the first time in minutes. "Well, that was a lot of work for nothing," he said to no one in particular. He had been convinced he was going to catch Greg Grom red-handed accepting a pickup of whatever poison he was using, but all that happened in the men's room was what was supposed to happen in the men's room.

Dammit, he wanted to be right about this.

He hadn't seen that minivan that parked out front. There were lots of cars coming and going and this one wasn't unusual, except that the driver wore a navy-blue jumpsuit with a logo on the pocket. He checked his clipboard and jumped from the van, yanking on the sliding door and rummaging in the back. He found a heavy, square box with several Warning! tags, skull-and-crossbones labels and the occasional Danger—Poison label.

"I'm looking for the United States Protectorate of Union Island tour bus," he asked the bus driver.

"You found it."

"I'm the SIC man." His eye twitched involuntarily.

"Sorry to hear that."

"I'm from Ship It Carefully. We have a package."

"Hello!" Grom said, wiping his hands on his pants as he came from the restaurant. He had no idea where his security team had got to, but that was just as well. With a minimum of fuss he showed his ID to the deliveryman, and then practically ran inside the bus with the package.

The SIC man wished people would treat their deliveries with a little more respect. The company slogan was Special Shipment? Ship SIC!, but special was euphemistic. They delivered dangerous chemicals, flammables, other specialty items that UPS and FedEx and those other wussies wouldn't touch. SIC had all the hazardous-materials transport permits, federal and state.

They were as expensive as hell. So you would think that people who accepted a package from SIC would treat it with a little dignity. Not go running up the bus steps like a kid with a box of candy.

The side of the SIC man's face spasmed nervously. He returned to his minivan and closed the door—gently. He checked all his rearview mirrors and turned in his seat twice before backing out of the parking place. He drove five miles under the speed limit all the way down the mountains and back into North Carolina, face twitching all the way, but the angry honking of other drivers never bothered him in the slightest. It took a special kind of man to be a SIC man.

AS THE SCRATCHED and tattered army of security agents clambered up the hill, Remo walked away, finding the hiking trail and feeling disconsolate.

He had expected Greg Grom to accept delivery of a package in the men's room at the restaurant. It would have made sense. It would have solved his dilemma. It would have answered a lot of questions. And for once it would have been Remo Williams who did the solving. Sure, it was a long shot. Mark Howard thought so. Chiun had been so sure Remo was wrong he hadn't even bothered to wait around to see the facts prove Remo wrong.

Distantly he heard the tour bus start up and minutes later it low-geared down the Blue Ridge Park past him. Over the fragrance of pine needles and mountain ferns Remo tried not to breathe the diesel smell and just as unsuccessfully tried to come to a decision about what to do next.

He would not rejoin the Union Island entourage. What was the point?

He kind of liked the woods. Maybe he'd just hike his way through the Smoky Mountains for a few weeks, catch his dinner out of the cold freshwater mountain streams, maybe nab any abortion-clinic arsonists he happened to cross paths with along the way.

It wasn't like he'd be missed by Upstairs. He hadn't exactly been doing them a lot of good in recent days.

Two things made him stop where he was, on a small rock overlooking a vast space between the mountains. The first thing was the thought that he was feeling awfully effing sorry for himself.

The second was the smell.

It wasn't a smell that belonged in the mountain woods. And it wasn't the diesel smell from the bus, but it had come with the diesel smell and was fading with it. It was chemical and vaguely familiar.

"Mother of crap!" Remo Williams exclaimed when he recognized the smell.

"Crap crap crap," the mountains echoed.

"I was right!"

There was silence.

"I said I was *right!*" Remo shouted, making it very loud.

"Right right right right," the mountains echoed.

"That's better," Remo said. "This doesn't happen often, and I want credit for it."

HE JOGGED BACK to the mountaintop restaurant and grabbed a pay phone in the hotel lobby, leaning on the

1 button until the phone system connected him. The voice that answered was not a voice he knew.

"Aloo?"

"Who's this?" Remo demanded.

"Why, it's Beatrice, luv."

"This is Agnes up the street."

"Agnes, my dear, how are—?"

"Give me Smitty, would you?"

A moment later the familiar voice of the director of CURE came on the line. "Where are you, Remo?"

"Hey, Smitty, your new receptionist sounds hot."

"She's not real, Remo. It's the new voice verification system."

"Save it for later, Smitty. I've got news. I've tracked down the source of the run-amokers down south."

"What? Where are you?"

"Uh." Good question, actually, Remo thought. "Some big hill. Don't have time to explain. I've got a bus to catch. Go ask Junior."

"Mark knows about this?"

"Sort of."

"What about Chiun?"

"Departed. Vamoosed."

"I don't think I understand...."

Remo could feel the bus getting farther away, and his patience getting shorter with every passing second and every particle of misgiving transmitting through the line. "Here's the situation in a nutshell—and I know it's gonna be a real mindblower, Smitty. The truth is, I figured it out. I homed in on the clues, I followed up on 'em. I solved it."

"So where is Chiun?" Smith asked.

"Dammit, Smitty, I did it. Just me. Chiun had nothing to do with it. Truth is, he was tagging along until he got fed up and went home."

"Did what, exactly?" Smith probed.

The stainless-steel cable snapped apart like button thread when Remo yanked on it, then he hung up the receiver and left the restaurant, sputtering obscenities like an inconvenienced Teamster.

NATIONAL PARK RANGER Ricardo Wegman hated traffic detail. As far as he was concerned, catching speeders was the state's job. Not the National Park Service. But up here on the Blue Ridge Parkway the access was limited. North Carolina ended and Tennessee began halfway through the park. All this made it difficult to persuade the troopers to come in for an occasional look-see.

Tourists in the Smoky Mountains ignored the warning signs as a matter of course. They thought they could get all the way to the bottom riding their brakes, never mind the burning smell. Some flatland geniuses even turned off their engines and tried to coast all the way down, just for yuks. The real laughs started when their heat-stressed brake rotors and pads disintegrated, then there would be a bunch of frantic swerving and grinding of gears as the panicking motorists struggled to bring the car to a halt with a mixture of low-gearing and hard praying. Neither worked too well when you were on a steep downhill grade that wound from an elevation of four thousand feet down to an elevation of two thousand feet in a matter of a couple of miles.

Wegman had to admit that there was something amusing about the speeders—the idiots who got going as fast as they could at the top of the hill before the long slalom down.

When the radar beeped, Wegman was lounging in his seat with his eyes closed. By the time he opened his eyes the speeder had disappeared around the curve. The radar display said fifty-three miles per hour. It took a special machine to get going that fast on this short stretch of mountain blacktop. Of course, the guy had probably gone straight over the lip at the next curve.

Ranger Wegman drove down the road to the guardrail, which was unmangled. The speeder had managed to make the curve. Had to have hit the brakes hard, although there were no skid marks.

He accelerated his Jeep until he was pushing his own safety limits, and only then did he spot the speeder. The speeder wasn't a car.

It was a man.

Ranger Wegman brought his jeep up behind the running man, then pulled alongside him.

"What the hell are you doing?" he asked as he paced the runner.

"Jogging," said the runner. "Nice day for it, but the altitude slows me down a little."

Wegman tried to make sense of what he was seeing and decided there was no sense to be made of it. "Son, you're going fifty-three miles per hour."

"Well, I gotta admit the incline makes up for the thin air."

Wegman steered himself around a curve in the road, tires squealing in protest, and tried to figure out what he was missing in this little scenario. The man looked awfully normal. Maybe thirty-something or maybe not. No stringy marathon-runner muscles. No bulging weight-lifter muscles. Nothing abnormal about the guy except a pair of extrathick wrists.

"You bionic or something like that?" Wegman asked.

"Something like that. Sharp curve ahead."

Wegman knew this road like the back of his hand and of course he knew there was a sharp curve ahead, but the world wasn't real to him right now. He slowed just enough to take the curve with his tires sliding on stones. Somewhere in the back of his head he was thinking that he was driving like the idiot flatlander tourists who didn't quite understand that a slide onto the shoulder at this height meant a slide into oblivion.

Of course, the running guy had no troubles at all navigating the curve.

"You stop now, son," Ranger Wegman called, head protruding from the window as he floored his vehicle to catch up again. "You're speeding and breaking the law!"

"Better reread your rule books, Ranger Rick," the running man said. "I'm not operating a vehicle, and I can run as fast as I want."

"Son, I don't know if that's true or not, but I'm telling you to pull yourself over and stop, *now*."

"This next curve's a doozy, Ranger," said the running man.

"Son, you— Shit!"

Ranger Ricardo Wegman suddenly felt the strong

strands of reality take hold when he found himself barreling headlong into the Two-Mile Hairpin at better than fifty miles per hour.

Just the kind of fool stunt one of those idiot flatlanders would pull.

Wegman stood on the brakes and steered the Jeep into a sideways skid, maximizing the friction on all four tires in a desperate attempt to slow the car before it hit the retaining wall. It was a hopeless gesture, and he knew it. He also knew they would be shaking their heads and calling him a damn fool for pulling a flatlander stunt like this. They'd be saying it even while they were dragging his broken car and his banged-up remains off the mountainside.

The rubber screamed for a lifetime, and the stench of scorched radials was the smell of humiliation in his nostrils. The big Jeep didn't feel like it had slowed at all before it slammed broadside into the safety barrier. The SUV flipped neatly over the barrier and plummeted into the underbrush that clung to the steep-sided mountain.

The crashing went on and on as if it would never stop, like it would go on for an eternity.

Then it faded away.

Ranger Ricardo Wegman opened his eyes. He was floating in thin air, looking down on the path of ruin created by the tumbling SUV. Then he knew—he was dead. His soul had left his body, which had to still be inside the jeep getting pounded to pulp.

"I'm discorporated!" Wegman gasped.

"You're a dipshit," the skinny guy said.

Wegman craned his neck back and down and up,

and found that he was in actuality hanging over the sheer mountainside drop. The skinny running man held him by his belt, in one hand.

"What happened?" Wegman asked.

"You drove off the road. Like fifteen seconds ago. Remember—squealing tires, crunching body panels and all that? I pulled you out through the window when your National Park-issue transport went on its gravity-verifying fit."

Wegman looked flabbergasted—then stricken. "You should have let me go with the car!"

"Huh?"

"Go ahead!" he pleaded. "Throw me in! I'll never live down the humiliation!" Wegman didn't even feel the fantastic agony of his shorts and trousers practically splitting his crotch in what had to be a world-record wedgie. All he felt was the disdain that was yet to come. "You don't understand! It was the kind of thing a flat-lander would do!"

"It's just a car. So what. You should see some of the stuff I've wrecked. Whole villages and shit."

"Please! End it for me! I'm begging you!" Wegman started twisting and clawing at the iron-hard fist that clung to his trousers, but it was like scratching his fingernails on steel girders. To his mortification, the skinny young man carried him to the shoulder of the road and put him safely on his own two feet.

"If the department of agriculture makes a higher moron classification than Grade A, then you rate it," Remo Williams said. "Listen, just tell everybody you were chasing some guy who was running fifty miles per hour and you got so caught up in it you didn't pay attention to the road."

Ranger Ricardo Wegman gave Remo a disdainful look. "They'll think I'm crazy on top of being stupid. I'd rather be dead."

"Fine. You want to end it, you go ahead. I've got a bus to catch."

Remo ran off. In a matter of seconds Wegman was alone. If it weren't for the obvious signs of the crash, he would have doubted the entire event had really even happened.

Now that the shock was wearing off, he started thinking—who was that guy and how the hell had he managed to pace a jeep at fifty miles per hour anyway?

The enigma was so distracting he entirely forgot about throwing himself off the mountainside before the first emergency vehicle arrived on the scene—and by then it was too late. Killing yourself right there, in front of your peers? It just wasn't done.

19

Remo wondered if the fates were aligning against him. Here he was trying to do something good, trying to prove himself, for crying out loud, and he was getting nothing but misery for all his trouble. Chiun throwing a hissy fit, Smitty giving him the third degree and then Ranger Rick driving his car off the hill so Remo had to stop and yank his ass to safety. Only to get a lecture in the strict codes of National Park ranger machismo for his effort.

But the big hill was finally starting to cooperate, and he spotted the tour bus below him on the twisting, curving Blue Ridge Parkway.

"Time for a shortcut," Remo announced to no one and vaulted off the road into the underbrush, slipping soundlessly as a shadow through the bushes and wildflowers that clung to the steep grade. A hundred feet lower the ground leveled out enough to afford purchase to a few deep-rooted trees, and Remo scampered up the trunks into the upper limbs, then vaulted from tree to tree. His hand-sewn Italian loafers, already ruined from the downhill run, landed perfectly every time, supporting him for a second before he was flying on to the next tree. Moments later he landed on the road just a few hundred paces behind the Union Island Freedom Tour Bus, and he caught up at the next curve.

He climbed on the roof and glared at Chiun, who was arranging the fluttering silk of his kimono as if he had not moved from his seat in hours.

"That didn't take long," Remo grumbled.

"It certainly did," Chiun retorted. "The bus has been on the road for nearly twenty minutes."

"I'm not talking about me. I'm talking about you."

"I, however, am talking about you. Then, lo! what do I see but the Reigning Master of Sinanju flinging himself through the trees like some ungainly combination of Strong Man Jack and Lord Greystoke."

Remo pondered. "Lord Greystoke is Tarzan, right?"

Chiun rolled his eyes and sighed to the crisp blue sky.

Remo shrugged. "I give up. Who's Strong Man Jack?"

"Another character from twentieth-century American fiction or folklore or whatever passes for literature in this part of the world." Chiun waved his hand at the sky above, implying that "this part of the world" included the mountains and all the rest of the planet that was west of Pyongyang.

"So you're saying I'm sort of like Jethro Clampett meets George of the Jungle."

"I wouldn't have brought it up at all had I known I would be forced to explain it during the entirety of our downhill journey."

"Just trying to get a handle on the insults that keep getting hurled my way," Remo said.

"Maybe if you had an inkling about the written word, even the florid clutter that passes for literature in the Western world, you would understand what I say and why I say it."

Remo grinned without humor. "Hey, I'm getting smarter already—you just told me my culture is stupid and I'm stupider."

Chiun sniffed. "If the oversize novelty T-shirt fits..."

"Now that we understand each other on that point, let's move on to the next bit of trivia. How'd you get back here so fast? I just got off the phone with Smitty and next thing I know you're back in the saddle. So, what, are you carrying a mobile phone these days that you're not telling me about."

"I would not carry such a device. The waves emanating from them cook the tiny cells of the brain and addle the thoughts." Chiun looked suspicious. "Have you been using one behind my back all these years? It would explain much."

"So what *are* you doing here? Last I saw you transferred to the eastbound train, bound for Hoboken."

Chiun nodded, as if the question was a perfectly reasonable one, and one that he had no intention of answering.

"Well?"

"I am here. Is that not enough?"

"You've got something up your sleeve you don't want to talk about."

"You are mistaken."

"You lie like a rug. Spit it out, Chiun—you realized I was on to something."

"What do you mean? On drugs?"

"The truth. My lead was panning out and you knew it and you came back because you had to be in on it when I solved this mystery."

Chiun, for a moment, looked genuinely surprised. Then he shook his head pityingly. "My son, that is not why I came back."

"Bulldookey. Then why?"

With a reluctant, graceful sweep of his arm the ancient Korean Master waved one hand at the billboard awaiting them on the very boundary of the national park.

"There is your answer."

It was a magnificent, tawdry sign that put a blemish on the natural beauty of the mountain scenery the way a slash with garden shears would have blemished the Mona Lisa.

The billboard letters were multicolored, metallic and sparkling, and they spelled out: Mollywood U.S.A.! Just 15 Miles to the Entertainment Hub of the Smokies! Ms. Molly Pardon's Smoky Mountain Theme Park.

Remo groaned. "Molly Pardon as in country music singer Molly Pardon?"

"The same," Chiun enthused.

"Mountainous mammaries, big blond bogus bouffant, that Molly Pardon?"

"I have it on good authority that her hair is not bogus. Her silky tresses are naturally pale and golden."

"As natural as the boobs, anyway." Remo shrugged. "I've heard her sing."

"She has an angel's voice," Chiun enthused.

"Wolverines defending a carrion stash sound more angelic."

"She's no Wylander Jugg," Chiun admitted, "but she sings with the same sincerity and passion. It is the music of real people, music that flows from the heart and soars from the lips, Remo."

"You say soars, I say hurls."

Chiun beamed. "You are an admirer of the beauteous Molly Pardon? I never knew this, my son."

"I wouldn't call it admiration so much as fascination," Remo said when the second billboard followed just minutes after the first. Molly Pardon herself was pictured, a fifty-year-old bleached-blond giantess rendered in thermoset plastic. Her ruby-red lips, open in a wide Southern-girl smile, could have swallowed a minivan. Her famous mass of hair had been constructed with the not-found-in-nature fluorescent yellow of plastic lemons. Her face had been re-created with a photo-realistic transfer technique so accurate that a layer of fleshy-colored enamel was added to blot out the crow's-feet around the eyes and surgical scars around the scalp, lips, temple and chin. Not that anyone even saw her face. Remo found it impossible to focus his attention beyond the swell of her re-created cleavage, which reflected the daylight like patent leather.

"That is one immense Molly," Remo said.

Chiun was mildly stunned at the spectacle. "It is large."

"Large? I'll bet they recycled five or six thousand soda bottles into each one of those knockers."

"Pah! You see only her womanly charms," Chiun said.

"How could I see anything else? Those things should have telescopes sticking out of them."

"She is well endowed, granted, and yet her attraction is in her voice, not her bosom."

"On anybody else you'd have called them 'udders.'"

"They would be so if she flaunted them in the same way the women you cavort with parade their milk-producing organs."

Remo laughed. "Come on! You're not seriously trying to tell me that Molly Pardon doesn't trade on her boobs."

"She does not!"

"You're wrong and you know it, but far be it from the Wise and All-Knowing Master Chiun to own up to a mistake."

"Someday I might make a mistake. Then I would indeed be the first to acknowledge it."

"And someday monkeys will fly out of my butt."

Chiun nodded seriously. "Such a feat would certainly be unique among all the Masters who have come before you. Is this the type of outrageous anecdote you plan as your legacy in the scrolls of the Masters?"

Remo was about to respond when he caught it again. The whiff in the air, so faint, so fleeting, he was almost not sure of it. Then he saw Chiun lift his head and draw air into his nostrils. Chiun smelled it, too. It was here. Whatever it was that was making people go violently bonkers, it was right here in this bus.

20

Frank Curtis always did what he was told. As long as it was Greg Grom who told him what to do.

Frank Curtis had infinite respect and measureless affection for Grom. Every word President Grom uttered resonated with ageless wisdom. Every action Grom took was purposeful and correct. Doing Grom's bidding was so *gratifying*.

Not everybody understood that, including his best friend since college, Randall Switzer, who would say, "I don't get it. You used to hate that guy, Frank."

"I never hated Greg!"

"Yeah, you did. You told me you did. You said he was the biggest moron ever to belong to Mensa."

"I never said that!"

"You called him an ambitionless, egoist jerk-off."

"Never," Frank Curtis had protested.

"The point is, you used to despise this little schmuck, and now all of a sudden you think he's God's gift to you."

"Don't call him a schmuck, Switz," Frank warned.

"I won't call him a schmuck if you admit that you used to say he was indolent as a sloth but with less personality."

Switz had been Frank's best friend for twenty years, but not anymore.

Frank's wife wasn't much better. "Frank, tell me the honest truth, honey," she demanded finally. "Are you gay? Are you having relations with this young man?"

Frank shook his head sadly. "Pauline, you know I am not gay."

"But Frank, I don't understand this obsession," Pauline wailed. "You're missing work, you're constantly away from home. Whatever this boy wants is your top priority, and everything else comes second. Where did this come from, Frank? You've never acted this way before—it's an infatuation!"

"Pauline, it is simply my respect and admiration for an important and powerful man."

"Powerful?" Pauline snorted.

"He's the elected president of Union Island!"

"It's just a small town that happens to be surrounded by water. If the place didn't make so much money on tourism, the mayor's position wouldn't even be a paying job."

Frank had not cared to continue that discussion. If Pauline Curtis couldn't show a proper level of respect for President Grom, then she could just go to hell.

Just that morning his boss had turned against him, too.

"Professor Curtis, is this young man blackmailing you?" asked University Director Jack Holdsworth.

"Of course not! A ridiculous suggestion."

"I cannot think how else a rather unimpressive graduate student—a student you once fervently disliked—could turn you into his errand boy," the university director observed. "He's got you jumping through hoops. You've spent all your vacation days and personal days in his service—not just this year's, but next year's, as well. Hear me out—a few years ago, when Mr. Grom was our student, you disciplined him in a way that he may have found humiliating, although you were perfectly justified. It seems to me that he may have been angry enough to dig up some sort of dirt on you and use it against you."

"Nothing could be further from the truth," Professor Curtis insisted.

The university director sighed. "Well, I'm not going to pressure you on this, Professor, but I am also not going to authorize another day off so you can go propitiate this young hoodlum."

"Hoodlum—?"

"Go to your classroom, Professor."

Professor Frank Curtis left the office of the director of the university, but he didn't go to his classroom. He got in his car and he drove away. Out of town. Out of Virginia. Maybe he'd never go back.

His wife, his friends, his fourteen years of tenure in the department, all those things could wait. Right now he had an important job to do. It was important because Greg Grom said so.

He had been driving for hours when he spotted the tour bus a couple of miles ahead of him on the interstate. He closed to within a half mile and set the cruise control to pace the bus at sixty-six miles per hour, then opened the window and held the digital camera outside to avoid the windshield glare. With one hand he fumbled to get the tiny display adjusted so he could see it, then to max out the digital zoom. It was difficult getting the extreme close-up of the bus into the viewfinder while keeping the car from veering off the road.

When he finally got the tour bus in the shot, he snapped of few dozen high-resolution images and put the camera on the dashboard to see his results.

It was the latest top-of-the line digital camera for use by professional wildlife photographers, and had all kinds of bells and whistles that were beyond the understanding of a professor of anthropological studies. Somehow, though, he managed to take several high-quality shots. There were close-ups of the shoulder of the road that were crisp enough you could count the stones. Quite a few images of the surface of the highway showed contrast so vivid you could practically feel the texture of the concrete.

Only the last few shots finally managed to get the bus in the frame. A fender with some mud spots. The back window with a brilliant reflection of the late-morning sun. And finally, the top of the bus—and two people sitting there.

"Well, I'll be!" Curtis exclaimed. Then he squinted into the display. "Dammit!"

He tried shooting another round of photos. His aim got better but his frustration mounted. The third time he managed to get a total of six shots of the roof of the bus, but he was so irritated with the result he felt like ripping out his comb-over.

He plugged the camera into the data port on his phone and E-mailed the best of the photos while hitting the speed dial for a voice call. "This is Professor Curtis, Mr. President."

Greg Grom sounded tense. "Took you long enough, Frank," his former student said. "I expected you an hour ago. Did you get the camera?"

"Yes, sir."

"Did you get good shots of the bus?"

"Yes, sir."

"Well, come on, Frank, were they there or not?"

"Yes, sir," Curtis said. "A white man and an old Asian. You can see them plain as day relaxing on the roof, as comfortable as you please."

"Oh shit, Frank!"

Professor Frank Curtis, Ph.D., *always* followed President Grom's orders without question. This time was no exception. Still, he couldn't stifle the grunt that accompanied the sudden but successful effort.

"What's the matter with you?" Grom demanded.

"Nothing, sir. Excuse me, sir. It's just a habit, I guess."

"What's a habit?"

"When I—you know," Curtis stammered.

"Frank, I haven't got the foggiest clue what you're talking about."

"Just following instructions, sir," the professor said, embarrassment mixing with disgust at the smell and the squishiness. "I sent you the shots, sir."

GREG GROM DOWNLOADED the files onto his laptop. They were so big they seemed to take forever, but the high quality was worth the wait. It was amusing to think how much the professional-grade digital camera had to have cost the old fart.

When the first image filled the screen, Grom wasn't amused anymore.

There they were, sitting on the roof. It was weird; it was eerie. Except for his strangely thick wrists, the white guy could be any one of fifty million Caucasian adult males in North America. The senior citizen from the Far East was another story. He looked too frail to get across the sunroom at the nursing home without a walker. He looked underfed, and it seemed as if the billowing silks of his geisha outfit should have taken him into the air like a kite. And yet he sat cross-legged and relaxed. He looked like he was meditating, for crying out loud.

Grom magnified the image, muttered an insult at the old fart on the phone and moved on to the next image. Then the next.

"You moron, there's not a single good shot of their faces!" he said into the phone.

"I know, Mr. President. But it is very strange. Everything else is perfectly in focus."

What the hell was the old loser talking about? Grom magnified the next shot until the lounging white guy filled the screen. The dark blue T-shirt was perfectly in focus. Grom could count the neat stitches on the expensive Italian loafers with the ruined soles. But the face was unidentifiable, as if his features had been moving too fast for the camera to focus on.

The ancient Asian was the same. Grom could see the

perfect stitching in the embroidery, but the face was just an expressionistic mess of colors.

Every photo was the same way. In the last shot, the white guy was shown giving the camera a friendly wave.

"Oh, shit!" gasped the President of the United States Protectorate of Union Island.

"I'll try my best, sir," the old professor replied mournfully. He grunted again.

"Stop it, you moron. Get closer and get me some better shots. I gotta have face shots! And patch me in to the camera feed."

The real-time, frame-a-second images from the old fart's new toy fed into his laptop in low resolution, but the camera electronics stabilized them pretty well. As the professor closed in on the bus, the images of the pair on the roof became vivid.

Grom was squinting at the screen and barking at Curtis whenever he lost the bus from the frame.

"Hold it there!" Grom ordered. He was as close as he could get and still have the top half of the white guy in the frame.

The white guy was just staring into the camera.

"Take some more high-res shots but keep me on the feed."

"I'll do my best, sir," Curtis said.

"Get one now!"

"Got it, sir."

"Now zoom in on that asshole."

"Yes, sir." The image moved up on the white guy.

"Take another one."

"Okay."

The face. The damn face was still not coming into focus! Even the low-res feed showed the guy's torso in crisp detail, but the face was a blurred mess.

Were they human?

Grom's fear mounted.

"Keep shooting!"

"Yes, sir."

The guy bent down, and in the next frame he was standing again. He had something in his hand.

"Uh, sir," Curtis said uncertainly.

"Keep shooting!"

The man raised one hand, holding an unidentifiable object, and he waved with the other hand. This time it was a goodbye wave.

The next frame showed the object as large as life, hanging in the air a few feet above the hood of Professor Frank Curtis's Lincoln Continental.

Damn good camera, thought Greg Grom. The three-foot steel tube looked frozen in place, and the crisp detail showed the jagged end where it had been pulled off the roof of the bus. Amazing that you could get such detail when you consider that the metal spear had to have been thrown with tremendous force.

Alone in his little private room, Greg Grom was thinking these things as the muffled sounds of the violently self-destructing Lincoln Continental reached him and then receded.

Then came the screaming. Well, it was more like the hacking of a hyena trying to vomit out rotten meat. It was Amelia Powlik, of course.

The bus was slowing, and there were shouts of alarm

and pounding on his door. "Mr. President, there's been an accident," Amelia screeched. "A horrible accident!"

Greg Grom was sure it was quite horrible. Shattered wreckage and a mutilated body inside. But somehow that wasn't as horrible as the image on his screen. The last photograph relayed by the camera was still there, waiting to be refreshed for a follow-up image that would never come.

That damn piece of metal tubing, hanging in midair, was coming almost straight at the camera—but not quite. It went just a little bit higher and a little bit to the left, which meant it was targeted directly at the old professor himself. When they finally extracted the corpse from the wreckage, they would discover the old man had a piece of metal skewering his skull—not to mention a pants load of poop.

Well, the old professor had been a total asshole. Grom would have enjoyed Curtis's final touch of humiliation if he wasn't terrified.

He didn't know who these two guys were, where they came from, how they had tracked him down. He only knew that they were ruthless killers, with some sort of Special-Forces training like Grom had never heard of.

And they were onto him. And the bus, it occurred to him now, was stopping.

"Oh, shit!" he shouted, bounding to the door just as the air brakes brought the bus to a halt on the shoulder of the highway.

He burst out the door of his private room. Amelia Powlik was babbling tearfully while the rest of his staff jostled for the exit.

"Get back in here!" Grom shouted. "Get this bus moving now!"

The bus driver, pulling the first-aid kit from its wall mountings, gave him a look of disbelief. "Mr. President, there's a horrible accident and we have to help."

"Help?" Grom's laugh was morbid and humorless. "He's dead! That's why he crashed! And whoever got him is trying to get me!"

"What's going on here, Mr. President?" demanded the ex-Secret Service agent in charge Grom's security detail. His voice always dropped deeper when he became annoyed, and right now the words were rumbling out like the big tumbling boulders.

"How about we discuss it after we get out of range, you idiot!"

"Oh. Yeah." The agent turned on the openmouthed driver and boomed, "What's your problem, driver? Get this vehicle moving now!"

Greg Grom collapsed in a leather couch, his body drained of energy but his mind a riot of conflicting emotions. And none of them were good. He laid his head on the back of the couch and stared straight up.

He expected that any second the ceiling of the bus might begin showing a small round opening to the daylight. Once the killers realized they had failed to flush out their prey, it seemed logical that they would simply start firing into the vehicle at random. Eventually they'd get Grom. Or they'd kill enough people that the bus driver would surrender and the killers would come in and get their intended victim. Isn't that the kind of thing hard-core killers did?

"You feeling okay. Mr. President?"

Grom realized that the two warm bodies pressed up against him on either side were the pair of Justice Department rejects hired for his protection.

"How about some space?"

The bodyguards scooted to the ends of the couch but stayed close, 9 mm semiautomatic handguns held at the ready. The agent in charge touched a hand to his earpiece and nodded. "State and local emergency services are on the scene of the accident. One car. They've got the fire out and they can see one victim inside, but the wreck's still too hot to pry open. You want to pass on your information, Mr. President?"

"I got a phone call," Grom lied absently. "A stranger. He said I was about to be ambushed by a group of trained snipers. They'd cause an accident, hoping we would stop to help, then gun down me and my staff."

"I'll have a Justice forensics team called to the scene," the bodyguard said without hesitation. "I'll need your phone to trace the call."

Two exciting ideas came to him at that moment, and Greg Grom stifled his enthusiasm. He scowled at the bodyguard and said, "No way in hell."

21

Eileen Mikulka knocked, waited a moment, then pushed open the door to Harold W. Smith's office. She entered with a tray. Tea and prune whip yogurt for the Folcroft director, coffee for Associate Director Mark Howard.

She took one step inside and stopped, feeling something in the air that wasn't pleasant. Dr. Smith was as emotionless a man as Mrs. Mikulka had ever known, but right now he was angry. It was there in his hard eyes, his locked jaw. He was actually gripping the edge of his desk. There was a vein, emerging from the sallow flesh of his right temple, that Mrs. Mikulka had never seen before.

Mark Howard was sitting stiff and uncomfortable in the ancient, creaking chair in front of the desk.

She set down the tray. The air in the room was poisonous.

"Will there be anything—?"

"No, thank you."

Mrs. Mikulka left as fast as her arthritic knees would carry her. When she collapsed at her desk, she felt like crying.

Whatever was wrong, Dr. Smith was clearly not happy with his assistant. Whatever could Mark have done that would make Dr. Smith so angry? Dr. Smith never got that angry.

"Oh, dear." She bit her lower lip to stop its quivering. She couldn't bear to think of that nice young man losing his job. Mark Howard had brought life back into Folcroft's executive wing. A little sparkle. A little humor. The years before Mark came seemed so gray and bland by comparison. To lose him would be awful.

AFTER THE DOOR CLICKED shut, Dr. Harold W. Smith said, "Mark, I want to know why you did this."

"I understand, Dr. Smith," Mark Howard replied tentatively, as if he felt remorse but also felt unsure of how to proceed. "First of all, when I give you my full report you'll see that there was no real urgency. Remo did not have anything to go on."

"Obviously he did," Dr. Smith replied. "He went after the Union Island tour group and now there's been an assassination attempt on the Union Island president. Remo is up to something."

"He didn't come across as having any agenda other than tracking down the source of the violent outbreaks," Mark insisted. "When he came to my office, he asked me to trace the movements of the Union Islanders. They happened to have an itinerary that meant one of them could cause the poisonings. I tried telling him we had a long list of people whose known movements gave them the opportunity."

"So what made him suspect the Union Islanders?"

"He had no reason, not that he would tell me about."

Harold W. Smith frowned, and some of the anger was evaporating. "So why did he suspect them?"

"He mentioned seeing the island president on TV, on a talk show, and placed him at the first set of poisonings. But that was all he had. We tried to brainstorm on a motive and couldn't come up with anything. There's nothing that connects the Union Island group to anybody involved in the mayhem. Nothing. We couldn't see any way the island independence movement could benefit from the killings. And that was about it."

Dr. Smith had his assistant start from the beginning and report, word for word, the conversation between Mark and Remo. It didn't take long.

Smith looked drained then. Paler than his typical gray. "Remo either mislead you about what he knew, or else he was simply getting into this avenue of the investigation impulsively."

Mark Howard shifted uncomfortably in his chair. Smith seemed to have lost his quiet anger, but it had been so startling and out of character that Mark simply didn't know where he stood now. He didn't have experience with this aspect of the director of CURE. "Sir, I don't think either of those characterizations is accurate."

Smith had been regarding his hands, folded on the desktop, but he raised his eyebrows and his rock-steady gaze met Mark's.

"Explain."

"I got the feeling there was a lot going on with Remo when he came in. I mean, that was unprecedented in itself. Since when does he come to me for help? I got the impression he was in a sort of strange place."

"You got an impression," Smith repeated evenly. "What kind of impression?"

Suddenly Mark was even more uncomfortable. He had long ago come clean to Dr. Smith on the subject of his special abilities. Abilities Mark himself didn't understand. These abilities manifested as impressions, intuitions, sudden burst of knowledge that came to him out of nowhere. There were times when he would be writing words on a page or entering data into the computer and suddenly realize he had written something unexpected, something that had not come from his own conscious thought.

Those brief riddles had more than once been unraveled and led CURE to the answers it needed.

But Howard's unique mental abilities had proved a great bane to CURE, too, when they opened the door to the reawakening of one of the great enemies of the Master of Sinanju, and the world. This bastard son of Sinanju, Jeremiah Purcell, had been locked away at Folcroft and maintained in a comatose state. For years his bloodstream was perpetually saturated with drugs that kept him unconscious. Purcell had used his own unique mental powers to find purchase in the conscious world, but his reach was limited. There were special minds in the world that Purcell could use, could bend, could manipulate, but none of those had come within the range of his clawing psychic fingers in all those years.

Until Mark Howard was assigned to be the associate director of CURE and, for cover, of Folcroft Sanitarium.

Jeremiah Purcell's malevolent influence on Mark Howard was tentative, but in time he coerced Mark into ordering the termination of the pharmaceutical regimen that kept Purcell comatose. Harold Smith learned of this only when it was too late—after Jeremiah Purcell, the one called the Dutchman, had escaped. Mark Howard nearly died.

Nobody expected Purcell to fade quietly away, but when he inevitably made his move against the Masters of Sinanju he brought with him, or was brought by, an even greater foe.

For months Mark Howard carried a heavy sack of guilt for his responsibility in those events.

"Mark," Dr. Smith asked, "are you saying Remo had some sort of psychic intuition that led him to the Union Islanders?"

"No. Dr. Smith, you remember what you told me the first time I told you about my, well, foreknowledge events. You suggested that they might simply be a heightened level of intuition. My subconscious putting the clues together in ways my conscious mind couldn't."

Dr. Smith looked uneasy. "Yes, I remember saying that." The truth was, he still preferred to cling to that notion, despite the evidence that proved there was much more to it.

"That's what happened here. Remo's investigative skills were kicking in. Maybe he picked up some subtle clues along the way. Maybe his heightened awareness of everything in his environment gave him an idea of who was responsible. He was going with his gut feeling."

Smith nodded. "I see."

"There's more," Mark added, less confidently. "I think Remo's got something to prove, and I think he's trying to do it by tracking down the people responsible for this violence."

Smith twitched his lip. "I find that hard to believe. You heard Remo's last tirade about being sent to do detective work."

"Yeah. He said something like, 'Smitty, we both know I'm not the sharpest tool in the shed.' And you didn't disagree with him. And Master Chiun would have called it a mild understatement."

"So this is all an attempt to throw mud in our eyes?" Smith demanded.

"I think he wants to prove to himself that he's more than just hired muscle," Mark said. "Maybe he wants to show that he's got what it takes to be Reigning Master—that he's got what it takes up here."

Howard tapped his temple with one finger. Smith nodded, considering that.

Mark was on a roll. "You know what they say in business and government and the military, that a talented man will rise through the ranks until he reaches one level *above* his level of competence. A man who knows his own capabilities knows when to refuse a promotion. Could Remo be trying to prove to himself and all of us that he has not been promoted beyond his skill level?"

Smith's mouth became a hard line. "That aphorism was a cliché when I was in military intelligence. In the middle ranks we used to make our own estimation of who would get the next advancement-into-inadequacy promotion. But there's something more to consider. A man who is a success, who finds himself in a new environment where success eludes him, will remake himself into a man who can succeed. If Remo Williams feels he needs to rise to the occasion to be worthy of the title Reigning Master, then I believe he'll do it."

Mark Howard screwed up his face. "I don't know if I've seen Remo show much genuine determination."

Smith turned to his keyboard and began typing rapid-fire, saying, "Then you need to look harder."

"REMO," CHIUN SAID excitedly, "we are just minutes from Dixie's Answer to Disney World!"

"Can't wait," Remo muttered insincerely. He'd be glad when this bus-top ride was done with, though.

He had hoped to solve the problem on the highway when he put a stop to the picture taker. The bus had actually come to a halt, and Remo had planned to simply take a stroll among the occupants until he literally sniffed out the guilty party. Somebody inside was going to have a sharp smell like fishy poison clinging to him or her, and that man or woman would have some serious explaining to do.

Then they took off again.

The bus stopped for fuel at a truck stop, but security was high. Nobody got on or off. A gathering of local law-enforcement officials was on hand for added security.

"Why do we sit here doing nothing?" Chiun demanded. They were waiting in the trees a hundred yards behind the truck stop. "Let us simply enter the traveling palace and gather up the guilty parties."

"'Cause there's maybe thirty parties that ain't guilty, and some of them will end up dead."

"You imply that I would slaughter innocent civilians indiscriminately? I am an assassin, not a berserker."

"Yeah. Maybe. But I'm more worried about Agents Anal and Retentive. They've got that shoot-first, file-a-report-later approach to security work. Not to mention that half the staff is probably armed and incompetent."

"Why should that worry us?" Chiun scoffed.

"Come on, Little Father, you know it's not me and you I'm worried about. It's everybody else inside this Playboy Mansion on wheels. There's no way we can protect the whole entourage if the bullets start flying."

"Pah!" Chiun scowled and observed the refueling of the bus and the patrols of the local law enforcement with disdain.

Then, without warning, he vanished.

Remo Williams was the only witness as the Tennessee Highway Patrol Special Response Unit entirely failed to detect the intruder in their midst. They never realized that the very thing they were looking for—a highly suspicious individual—slipped through their perimeter on his way to the truck-stop store. They would have been especially chagrined if they had known he returned a minute later and passed through their midst without their ever noticing him or his brilliant kimono.

"Remo, see what I have!"

"If I know you, Chiun, it's Slim Jims and a Vanilla Coke."

Chiun tried to frown, but he was too excited. What he pulled from the sleeves of his kimono was an inch-thick stack of glossy travel brochures. His eyes sparkled with boyish glee. He felt inclined to share his enthusiasm as they retook their rooftop seats and continued their drive.

"The town of Pigeon Fudge is a veritable country music paradise."

"Who says?" Remo demanded.

"I do, after reading the words in this handbill."

"I wouldn't believe everything I read."

"Remo, it is as if they transformed an entire Southern town into a wonderful magic kingdom. Mollywood is only one corner of this city of delights—there are hundreds of attractions, each more exciting than the next."

"Chiun, you've already got a lifetime pass to Disney World, and when's the last time you used it?"

"Ah, but this is different, Remo. I have learned to love the heartfelt ballads of the South."

"Wylander Jugg's, anyway."

"Jugg. And my tastes are not so limited as you would believe. Look!"

Remo turned to face into the wind and found the bus coming up on the exit for Pigeon Fudge, Tennessee, where the sign promised Mollywood Is Just the Beginning of the Wonders You'll See.

Next to the sign was Molly Pardon herself, re-created as a forty-foot fiberglass automaton. Her upper torso moved from side to side, allowing the nylon ropes of hair to flop this way, then that. Some developer's marketing inspiration had resulted in the Molly-bot getting a genuine red flannel shirt, which was tucked into her disproportionately narrow waist and left entirely unbuttoned. Remo happened to glance over at the exact moment the giant robotic country music star tipped to one side in a strategically programmed manner that allowed her shirt to flap open and provide arriving vacationers a voyeuristic glimpse inside.

"Well, you sure wouldn't get to see nipples as big as beer kegs at the Magic Kingdom," Remo observed.

Chiun sniffed. "It is a cheap display. Perhaps Molly Pardon does not possess the same sincerity as the beauteous Wylander Jugg."

"Yeah, but Wylander doesn't have jugs nearly as bodacious as Molly Pardon."

"We can only hope this monstrosity does not represent what we will find throughout Pigeon Fudge."

Remo didn't have time to answer when they merged from the exit ramp onto the thoroughfare that headed directly into the heart of town.

22

Remo Williams had seen it all—or thought he had. The long years as the chief enforcement arm of CURE had exposed him to things too bizarre to be explained by science, too incredible to be chalked up to the supernatural. Now, with that wealth of experience under his belt, the Reigning Master of Sinanju was a tough guy to amaze.

But right at that minute he was pretty much stupefied.

Even his mentor and trainer, the illustrious Chiun, with his decades of life experience and a breadth of wisdom handed down from all the past Masters, had never seen anything quite like Pigeon Fudge, Tennessee.

Remo observed, "Like it or not, I've heard every Wylander Jugg song that ever was, and not one of them is about dinosaurs."

"For once your feeble mind remembers truthfully. The soulful Wylander does not sing about dinosaurs," Chiun replied.

"Does Molly Pardon?"

"No. She has no dinosaur songs."

The bus stopped at a traffic light near a strip mall with a cigarette store, a pizza place and a purple velociraptor. "So how come that's the fourth dinosaur we've seen so far?"

The next block was dominated by a miniature golf center crowded with people who putted fluorescent orange and pink golf balls through a tropical rain forest. The trees and rocks were plastic. The robotic hippos, elephants and monkeys guffawed, trumpeted and screeched at the players. On the final hole they watched a young boy putt his ball into the hole, which brought an automatronic tyrannosaurus out from the plastic green ferns. The thunder lizard bent at the waist, made a roar like an air horn, stood erect again and slid back into the ferns.

There was a stegosaurus in an enclosed playground at the fast-food restaurant next door. Then came a candy shop with a triceratops holding a giant lollipop in its beaklike mouth.

"I thought this place was about country music," Remo said.

"I, too," Chiun replied. "And what sort of a dinosaur is that?"

Remo blinked and craned his neck at the eight-story pink monstrosity that loomed up out in front of a sprawling hotel. "Flamingosaurus, I guess."

From the beak of the flamingo dangled a twenty-foot sign made to look like driftwood with artificially fading white paint that read Jimmy Jack Jordan's Theater And Water Park.

"Hey, that's one of the guys you listen to," Remo said.

"Absolutely not," Chiun responded as the bus carried

them past Jimmy Jack Jordan's complex of low-rise hotel wings with fake thatched roofs.

"Yeah, that one Wylander duet. 'Where the Bayou Meets the Gulf' or something like that."

"You are mistaken," Chiun announced. The water slides were painted brown to simulate logs, and the swimming pools were surrounded with aluminum palm trees.

"No way I'm wrong about this one, Chiun. Thanks to you I know that ugly croaker's repertoire backward and forward."

"And yet you are wrong," Chiun insisted.

Remo wasn't listening. "Holy crap—look at that!" It was a Paul Bunyan figure, complete with blue ox, standing knee-deep in a forest of trees. The entire construction was made of steel-reinforced concrete, and Paul himself was more than fifty feet high. Remo watched a glass elevator rise up and disappear into Paul's gigantic crotch. "It's a hotel."

"It is unsightly."

"Hey, Chiun, look at that! Wailing Mining's Paul Bunyan Resort and Showplace. You listen to Wailing Mining, don't you? Boy, *all* your favorites are here."

"Wailing Mining never performed with Wylander." Chiun was on the defensive.

"Yeah, he was on that special on pay-per-view— *Wylander's Winter Wonderland* or something."

"I never heard of it."

"You tried to get me to watch the damn thing last December. You said it would snap me out of my Christmas depression."

"But you did not watch it—"

"I saw enough of it to get more depressed. And that's the guy who sang the chestnuts-roasting song with Wylander."

"Remo, you are speaking nonsense. You have never paid attention to the music I enjoy and you do not know what you're talking about."

"Hey, I'd be in denial, too, Little Father. This place is sleazier than Las Vegas."

"I am not in denial! The powers behind these monstrosities are not in the same league as the beauteous Wylander. This is trash!"

"White trash?" Remo clarified.

"Exactly!" Chiun exclaimed. "More precisely, American trash."

"Does it get any trashier than that?" Remo asked hypothetically, then answered his own question. "Oh. French trash."

Chiun nodded seriously. "Although that phrase is redundant."

It seemed as if every block contained a resort more extravagant and tasteless than the next. A rotating ice-cream sundae with picture windows turned out to be the revolving restaurant atop Clarabelle Escalande's Candy Castle and Performing Arts Center, Theatrical Home to the Reigning Queen of Country. All Our Rooms Are Sweets! exclaimed the signboard, which wasn't garish enough to compete with the oddly shaped mass of neon across the street.

The neon lit up one letter at a time until it had spelled the word "Arkansas." The billboard below it exhorted them to stay at the Arkansas Hotel, home to the million-selling band State of Arkansas. Experience All the Thrills of Arkansas—Right Here in Tennessee.

Between every resort were gift shops, T-shirt shops, candy shops, refreshment stands and fast-food restaurants. They all had some extravagant sculpture representing them. Purple elephants and flashing aliens. Even the local dive bar sported a human-sized neon bottle tilting to pour neon beer into a neon mug. When they couldn't think of anything better, they resorted to dinosaurs.

"This place is a joke. Or a nightmare," Remo commented. "I'm not exactly sure which."

"Molly Pardon's Magic Country Kingdom will be a welcome relief to this excess," Chiun remarked. "I am surprised that you are not enamored by it all, Remo. There are many bright colors."

"I get my fill from your wardrobe," Remo said. "Don't set your hopes too high for Mollywood, Little Father. Somehow I doubt her standards are head-and-boobs above the rest of this place. And I was hoping you'd give me a hand with the Caribbean king."

"You need help persecuting the freedom fighter?"

Remo sighed. "You know I'm on the right track this time."

"I know no such thing."

"You're full of it. You know the stuff is on board this bus. You know I'm the one who figured it out. Me. Remo the Pale Piece of Pigs Ear Piece of Crap Reigning Lazy Ass Master of Sinanju. But your friggin' ego is so friggin' huge because you're Chiun, Chiun the

Wise, Chiun the Patient, Chiun the I'm Never Wrong and Remo Is Never Right."

"Are you through?"

"No, but you are. There's Molly Pardon and her high-class Magic freaking Country Kingdom. Go have a ball."

Chiun examined the distant spectacle of Molly, her inhuman upper-body proportions digitally recreated on a vast screen made from hundreds of lights.

Come On In, Y'All! the sign proclaimed, and several hundred cars were obeying her command, creeping at a snail's pace through the front entrance and into vast parking lots. In the distance they could see the ticket gates, towered over by a roller coaster with several loops, a water ride that tried to replicate a river in the Smoky Mountains and a single ravenous-looking dinosaur.

"You are right," Chiun said.

"Huh?"

"Mollywood. It looks to be as tacky and low-brow as the rest of this Pigeon Fudge place."

"Yeah."

Chiun sighed. "And you are right."

This time Remo said nothing.

"I have detected the smell on this bus. The poison used on the people to make them into killers. It was not here before and now it is. I found it hard to believe."

"You didn't have faith in me."

"You were suffering from the arrogance that comes of being a newly appointed Reigning Master. Your pride tainted your judgment."

"Not enough to make me wrong."

"This is so."

"So?"

"So I will not hold your unseemly outburst against you."

"Thanks a whole lot."

Chiun nodded magnanimously. "You are welcome."

23

Just because you were a biker didn't mean you were a bad guy. Some bikers repaired PCs or sold advertising for the local newspaper and restricted their biker activities to a few hours on a Friday night. Then there were the beer-drinkers and hell-raisers. The kind who got arrested every once in a while and maybe had a few turf wars and maybe sold a few drugs.

And then there were the serious hard-case bikers. The true one-percenters. They hated the world because, for whatever reason, the world hated them.

But there were some hard-ass bikers that even the one-percenter subculture thought were beneath its dignity.

They called themselves the Smoking Hogs, but other gangs called them Mollyriders, or Hell's Pigeons, or Pigeon Fudge-Packers. From Louisville to Charlotte the Hogs were a laughingstock.

Donald Deemeyer had heard the laughter. It hurt your feelings to be laughed at like that, you know? Some of his gang actually moved away from Pigeon

Fudge and tried to integrate into a more respected motorcycle social club. It never worked out. They always found out where you came from, and then you got laughed out of town—in fact, you got laughed all the way back to Pigeon Fudge, Tennessee.

And that kind of ridicule, year after year, it got to you, you know? If made you feel bad. Made you kind of bitter.

Donald Deemeyer found a useful outlet for that anger. It happened one night when the Smoking Hogs attended a biker festival at a roadside motel in the Smokies. It was an annual event, with motorcycle social clubs from all over the region.

The taunting started early this year. The new leader of the Raleigh Rampagers seemed to think the Smoking Hogs came just for his entertainment.

Donald Deemeyer finally got fed up and called the Raleigh Rampager leader a pussy. The Smoking Hogs jumped on their bikes and the Rampagers roared out after them, pursuing them on the twisting mountain roads. When the Rampagers closed in, the Hogs let them have it.

Eight quarts of motor oil.

The Rampagers slipped and slid and piled up on the mountain road. It was a mess, and a miracle that not one of them careened off the mountain. They were still trying to get back on their bikes when the Smoking Hogs reappeared.

"You Pigeon fuckers are dead! Dead!" the commanding Rampager shouted.

But he was incorrect. One too many times Donald

Deemeyer had been ridiculed. He dumped the contents of a red plastic gasoline container at his feet. It trickled downhill, mixing with the oil. The other Smoking Hogs had gasoline cans, too. Donald Deemeyer lit a match and the Rampagers burned alive.

When the flames sputtered out, the Smoking Hogs returned to the biker party. It was curious how the raucous, drunken revel became deadly quiet.

"The Smoking Hogs and the Raleigh Rampagers have patched things up," Donald Deemeyer announced. "Haven't we, old buddy?" He dragged a fire-blackened corpse into the light of the bonfire.

"See? No more nasty comments about the Smoking Hogs!"

The bikers knew how to deal with a knifing or a brawl or a shooting, but this one had them stunned.

"Does anybody else want to say anything about the Smoking Hogs?" Donald demanded.

Nobody did.

Needless to say, the party was over. And the Smoking Hogs were no longer welcome at regional biker gatherings. They were never charged with the mass murder of the Raleigh Rampagers, but the truth became known. The chief of police of the Town of Pigeon Fudge, Incorporated, let Donald Deemeyer know what he knew. He brought it up several times. He brought it up again that afternoon right about lunchtime.

"Yeah, so arrest me."

"I don't want to arrest you, D.D.," the chief said, ordering himself a beer from Belle, owner and proprietor of the Watering Whole. It was the closest thing Pigeon

Fudge had to an honest-to-god biker bar, although the truth was it was way too clean and well-maintained for a biker bar. The place had ferns. It had old-fashioned advertisements for bars of soap framed on the walls.

It had a kids' menu, for God's sake.

"So what the hell do you want?" Deemeyer demanded.

"I want you to do a favor for a friend of a friend," the chief of police said.

"A favor."

"Yeah."

"Something illegal, I assume?"

"I don't know and I don't want to know. But I know you'll get paid for the job."

"You're trying to set me up, pig," Deemeyer growled. He tried to sound gruff but, to his humiliation, the wait staff had gathered around a nearby table, presenting the diners with a cupcake stuck with a burning sparkler.

The waiters and waitresses began clapping and singing. "Hap! Hap! Hap! Hap! Happy happy birthday! We! Hope! You! Have-A! Happy happy birthday!"

Everybody applauded the birthday girl. Even the chief clapped. Deemeyer was horrified to glimpse a few of his own Smoking Hogs in a back booth clapping, too.

Deemeyer tried to ignore it all and took a chug from his too-clean beer mug.

"I give you my word this ain't no setup, D.D.," the Chief added.

"Don't call me D.D. Makes me sound like a damn cheerleader."

"Watch your mouth!" snapped the owner as she strolled by with a tray full of her namesake Belle Burgers. "That ain't the kind of talk we tolerate in a family place. This is your last warning, Deemeyer. I hear you cussin' in my place one more time, and you're outta here. Got it?"

Deemeyer glared into the beer.

"You wanna go back to drinkin' your beers at the Applebees?"

"I got it!" Deemeyer snapped.

"Don't you take that tone with me, biker boy. I know your momma!"

Belle stalked off. The chief was chuckling. "Life just ain't fair to a hard-ass like yerself sometimes, is it, D.D.?"

"Got that right."

"I think you need a little hell-raising. Get back to your roots."

"I don't need to get back to my roots."

"Then do it for the boys." The chief nodded at a back booth where several of the Smoking Hogs were using complimentary crayons on the placemats Belle had printed up for her twelve-and-under patrons. Cocker was coloring an elephant bright orange, his tongue sticking out of the corner of his mouth. Could that actually be the same Jake "Shit-Kicker" Cocker who had run his bike over the smoking skull of a North Carolina biker just to see the steaming brain porridge squirt out? Damn, those were the good old days.

"Okay." Deemeyer sighed. "I'll do it."

Even if the chief was setting them up, Deemeyer thought, some quality jail time could do the Smoking Hogs nothing but good.

24

"It's a little something for your trouble," said the nervous woman in the ugly orange dress jacket.

"The agreement was for cash," Deemeyer said testily.

"Oh, yes, that is correct. The beer is just a, you know, a bonus." The woman laughed like a coyote. Deemeyer wanted to clap his hands over his ears. Better yet, over her ears. He forgot about that when she pulled out the envelope.

"Here you go."

Deemeyer snatched it, ripped it open and counted the contents.

"And here are your instructions." Timidly, the woman placed a small boom box on the floor of the garage.

"What the hell?"

"They're on the tape," she explained nervously. "Please listen to the entire first side."

Deemeyer shrugged. "Whatever."

The nervous woman practically ran to her little rental car and tore off.

"Man, this is weird," Blackeye Bierce complained.

"The cash is real," Deemeyer said, examining the bills. He counted off fifteen Smoking Hogs. Then he recounted the $4,500 in cash. That came out to, how much again? Was it two hundred each? No, wait...

"The beer's real, too," said Jake Cocker, downing most of his plastic cup in a few swallows.

They gathered around the kegger and listened to the tape. It was a man's voice, and he took a long time to come to the point. First he described in detail the tour bus that was on its way to them. They were not to enter the bus. No one inside the bus was to be harmed. The voice then described two men who would be riding atop the bus.

"Did he say on top of the bus?" Cocker belched.

One man would be Caucasian. The other would be an elderly Asian.

"Why we supposed to beat up some old guy?"

"Why the hell would an old guy be riding on top of a bus?"

"This is too weird."

Deemeyer had been thinking the same thing. He poured another beer as he thought about it.

"You like this beer very much," said the man on the boom box. "It is the best beer you ever tasted."

"Weirder and weirder," said a Hog.

"He's right, though," Deemeyer grunted. "I never knew brew this good."

All the Smoking Hogs agreed it really was the best beer they had ever tasted—and they drank a lot of beer.

"You hate the two men riding on top of the tour bus," said the voice on the boom box.

"Yeah, what the hell is with those assholes!" Cocker exploded.

"You hate them! They are the ones to blame!"

Deemeyer saw it all. Suddenly it was clear as crystal. All the ridicule. All the jokes. "He's right. It's those two guys on the bus!"

"They're pricks!"

"They're lower than slime! They're lower than the Raleigh Rampagers!"

Yeah, Deemeyer thought. They two guys on the bus had to know pain. They had to pay hugely. They had to suffer agony like the Rampagers never suffered.

The man on the tape said, "Those two men on top of the bus—those are really bad guys. You want to kill them. You want them annihilated. You'll do whatever it takes to wipe them out."

"Wipe them out," Blackeye Bierce said.

"Wipe them out," Shit-Kicker Cocker echoed.

"Yeah," Deemeyer said. "Wipe them *out*."

25

Greg Grom snatched up the phone on the first beep. "Yeah?"

"It's Amelia, Mr. President," said his secretary. "I did what you said."

"You gave them the beer?"

"Yes, Mr. President."

"And the money and the tape player?"

"Yes, sir, but I don't know if I feel good about this. They seemed like an unsavory bunch of characters."

"Never mind, Amelia. I'll call you soon."

Grom made his way to the front of the bus and stood at the driver's shoulder, nervously scanning the hideous extravagance that was Pigeon Fudge, Tennessee. After dropping Amelia at the car-rental agency, he had kept the bus circling for a half hour without a complaint.

"Horrible-lookin' place, ain't it?" the driver said conversationally. "You know why they call it Pigeon Fudge, don't ya?"

"Not really," Grom answered, not really listening.

"It ain't from all the fudge shops."

"You don't say."

"Used to be a certain kind of pigeon that stopped by here from Canada in the summertime. But the original settlers came in the fall and set up their village and didn't suspect a thing. Then come summertime, and they had near to six hundred thousand pigeons congregating in the trees overhead. Made a terrible mess of the place."

"I can imagine."

"Word spread that the entire village was covered in pigeon shit, but for purposes of politeness the euphemism started getting used more frequently. And that's a story you won't find in the brochures." The driver chuckled. "In the brochures they say the name comes from all the fudge shops."

Grom pointed. "See that entrance?"

"Uh, yes, sir."

"We're going to pull in there."

The bus driver started to protest, but Grom was already making his announcement to the entourage. "Listen up, people! This is a security alert! Everybody take cover!"

Mayhem followed as men and women pushed and shoved to get under bunks and tables.

"What's going on, Mr. President?" one of the security agents demanded.

"We've got hijackers on board the bus," Grom said acidly. "If you people had provided me with adequate protection, you would know this by now."

The agents were flabbergasted. "Where are the hijackers?"

"On the roof."

"What?" the lead agent almost squealed. "Prepare to apprehend," he commanded his partner.

"Too little and too late," Grom declared. "I've got my own enforcement team ready to handle the situation."

"That's unacceptable! We will handle this."

Grom snorted in the agent's face. "Listen, dim bulb, you leave this bus and you'll be a target. The people I've hired won't care who you are or what branch of the federal bureaucracy you crawled out of."

The former Secret Service agent gave Greg Grom a haughty twitch of the lip. "We'll see about that."

26

"Olly Outlander's Old Tyme Opry," Remo Williams read. "Temporarily Closed for Remodeling—Open Again Soon Folks. What are we doing here?"

"I believe the signage is misleading," Chiun observed.

"Yeah, this place looks like it's been locked up since Dubya's daddy was running things," Remo said. The bus nevertheless rolled across the weed-grown parking lot and headed around the dilapidated lobby entrance. "You know, I have a feeling they're not really remodeling this place, either."

"There you are mistaken, my son. Here are the carpenters now."

The bus came to a halt in the middle of the empty lot. The brakes squeaked and the engine idled.

"You know, Little Father, I don't see any trucks. Just motorcycles. I don't think a real carpenter could carry all his tools on a motorcycle."

Chiun stroked his wisp of a beard thoughtfully. "You have a point, my son."

Remo shrugged. "Let's ask 'em. I think they're coming over for a chat."

Chiun nodded. "We will put on our friendliest faces."

The Masters of Sinanju stepped from the bus and plummeted fourteen feet, but their feet touched down almost without a sound and neither of them stumbled.

The bikers didn't seem impressed.

"How y'all doin'?" the Reigning Master said with a friendly wave.

"Wipe them out. Wipe them out," came the menacing chant.

"Wipe who out?" Remo asked.

"You're to blame," accused the barrel-chested giant at the head of the pack. "It's your fault!"

"What's my fault?" Remo asked.

"Everything!" The man had a heavy length of chain, which he whirled faster.

"You've been listening to the old Korean fart."

"We'll wipe you out!"

The bikers formed a half circle. Remo and Chiun were in the middle, backs to the bus.

"You are trapped," the leader growled. "Now you die."

"Maybe it's the leather jackets," Remo observed. "Nice warm day like this, they must be making you all hot and cranky."

The biker with the huge chest broke from the circle and bore down on Remo and Chiun, then with a roar he aimed the chain at his two victims. The massive weapon damaged only the side of the bus—Remo and Chiun were no longer there.

"It is your fault," Chiun said. The two Masters were

now standing on the opposite side of the bus. Not a biker in sight. "You are to blame. Even strangers sense this."

"They're bonkers," Remo replied. "Whatever they say is obviously the opposite of reality."

"The deranged often possess their own vivid wisdom," Chiun noted.

"Or claim to."

The old Korean gave his protégé a look hot enough to cause sunburn.

"Here they are! Wipe them out!" There was a chorus of boot steps coming around both ends of the bus. The Masters retreated across the parking lot.

"Why are you guys called the Smoking Hogs?" Remo called, reading sloppy jacket decals. "Is that like a Dixie version of a Sweat Hog?"

"Wipe you out!"

"Because the Sweat Hogs has been over for, like, decades."

"Sweating does appear to be their only talent," Chiun noted.

The bus lurched to life and spun in a circle. Remo wasn't about to let it escape. He led the herd of Hogs into position to block the bus's exit.

"You run like a dog!" the barrel-chested biker taunted them.

"This is as good a place as any to get wiped out, I guess," Remo said. The Masters were suddenly at a standstill, and the bikers bore down on them with amazing speed.

Remo watched the leader come at him with the

chain. The man moved fast. Too fast for an overweight, beer-sodden thug in a restrictive leather jacket.

Not that he had anything to worry about. As the mass of metal careened at his head, he simply ducked beneath it, then reached up, grabbed it at precisely the right point and gave it a nudge for added momentum. Donald Deemeyer saw it coming at him and dropped his mouth wide in surprise. The chain hit. There was a liquid crunch, and then his jaw was all that remained intact of D.D.'s head.

Another biker howled and brought together a pair of crowbars, intending for Remo to be between them. Remo allowed the crowbars to clang together, then he gave them a hard shove. The bars drove forcefully into the guts of the man holding them.

More of them came, their rage spurring them to greater speed. Remo sidestepped a red-eyed, cross-eyed machete wielder and sent the big blade rocketing skyward with a quick kick. The maniac stumbled and looked around wildly for his lost weapon.

"Little to the right," Remo said, stepping in close and giving him a small shove. "Hey, look!"

Remo pointed up. The maniac looked. The machete was falling with tremendous velocity when it went in his mouth, out the bottom of his jaw and into his chest.

Two more stabbed at Remo from either side with more conventional cutlery, but the knives disappeared from their hands, and he inserted a finger into an eye on the left, then the right.

There was a gunshot. Remo stepped around the bullet, then ran at the shooter. Only one more shot slid past him before he had taken possession of the handgun and bent it into a horseshoe. He did the same thing to the shooter until he heard vertebrae crunching.

"Weapons are for amateurs, Remo. Have I taught you nothing?" Chiun grumbled. He had finished off his fair share of leather-clad Smoking Hogs.

It was the machete wielder he was referring to. The man had somehow extracted the weapon from his face and neck and was bearing down on Remo, the howls of outrage bubbling out of his neck. Remo stepped around him and whacked him hard on the back of the head. The machete wielder became airborne, dead already.

Chiun tsked over the body when it fell. "Very messy."

"I was just playing around," Remo protested.

"Are you prepared yet to enter the bus? Or should we take our rooftop perch again and see what other surprises they have in store for us?"

Remo sighed. "I guess we go in. But let's try not to kill everybody, Little Father."

Chiun sniffed. "Don't insult me."

27

"Why is everybody screaming?" Amelia demanded.

"Shut up and listen!" Grom barked. "We're going with emergency Plan B."

"But why, Mr. President?"

"Just come get me!"

"Okay—two minutes!"

Grom couldn't believe he was putting his life in the hands of Amelia Powlik.

He strapped on the gas mask. Nobody noticed. Half the staff was cowering under tables while half found it impossible to tear themselves away from the horrors outside.

The ex-Secret Service agent turned and was about to make some sort of a pronouncement. Instead he said, "What's that for?"

Grom brandished a stainless-steel canister. It had been a part of the special package delivered for him just that afternoon at the mountaintop restaurant. It looked like a can of Pledge without the label. He shot the agent in the face.

Hope this works, Greg Grom thought. Before long he was spritzing everybody on the bus and issuing orders. He had never used the stuff in aerosol form before, and he wasn't one hundred percent sure it would work. Also, he had never used this specific formula. Who knew what it would do?

Soon twenty-three employees and hirelings of the United States Protectorate of Union Island piled from the bus and ran screaming in different directions. All the security agents jumped off with a hooded figure held hostage, their guns pointed at the figure's head. The bus jerked into motion, heedlessly rolling over dead Hogs.

CHIUN STOOD with his hands inside the sleeves of his kimono, which fluttered in the diesel fumes coming from the tour bus's tailpipe. "It is the prerogative of the Reigning Master of Sinanju to determine our next course of action."

"Of course it is," Remo said in exasperation. "You go after the bus, I'll get the hostage. Then we both go round up the civilians. Unless you have a better plan."

"I will do as you ask," Chiun said agreeably.

Remo bolted after the Feds, muttering. "Why am I not surprised that this is the one time you're going to let me make up strategy?"

He stooped as he ran and picked up a pair of rocks, then let them fly after the trio of agents. They never saw the rocks coming, and they never got the chance to fire their guns at their captive. Both awoke hours later in the Pigeon Fudge Lutheran Hospital with huge headaches and no memory of what had happened after lunch at that nice restaurant up in the mountains.

Remo pulled the hood off their hostage and found himself staring at a young woman named Betsy Shak, assistant in the Union Island budgeting department. She kept walking until Remo pulled her to a stop. Then she just stood there, smiling slightly, eyes closed and snoring.

"Ah, crap!" Remo exploded.

Even that didn't wake up Betsy Shak.

REMO AND CHIUN INTERSECTED seconds later, both sprinting at speeds that would have broken Olympic records.

"Any luck, Little Father?"

"No one was on the bus except the driver, who was under the delusion that he was hauling a trailer filled with ripe hogs to a sausage factory in Wauconda, Illinois. He called me Good Buddy Mao."

Remo's heart sank. "Oh, no."

"I did not kill him," Chiun said. "But he will not make such a mistake a second time."

"The hostage was a ruse. Let's assemble the civilians," Remo said. "Any one of them could be our guilty party."

"A lunatic round-up. I am honored to be a part of your great undertaking." Chiun sped away like an arrow shot.

Remo went in the other direction, muttering. "Two dozen maniacs running loose in a city designed by nutcases, and my only help comes from the sun source of all oddballs," he complained to no one in particular. "I need a vacation."

It was at about that moment that he jumped the ten-foot security fence around Olly Outlander's Old Tyme Opry hotel and found himself face-to-face with a billboard that said, Why Not Take ALL Your Vacations in Pigeon Fudge, Tennessee? See Our Luxurious Condominiums—Models Now Open!

The realty office had a pink-and-purple seismosaurus, bigger than a toolshed, squatting in one corner of the parking lot.

A handful of the bus people had run pell-mell in this direction, but Remo couldn't see any of them anywhere.

The seismosaurus grinned inanely.

Remo Williams, the man who was created the Destroyer, felt his blood boil. "I have had just about enough of you." He snatched the thing off the ground and brought it down. Hard.

He felt better, but as he raced down the street in search of bus people there were more grinning dinosaurs everywhere he looked. Remo knew they were laughing at him.

28

Eileen Mikulka had made up her mind about something. She was up until the wee hours of the morning mulling it over, but when she finally came to a decision she felt such a surge of joy and relief that she knew it was the right thing to do.

Eileen Mikulka was going to confront Dr. Harold W. Smith and give him a piece of her mind.

She had never done such a thing, but there was a time for everything. She couldn't stand by and let Dr. Smith fire Mark Howard, no matter how serious his transgression.

And how bad could it be, whatever Mark had done? There hadn't been any sign of trouble. Mrs. Mikulka considered herself as intimately involved in the operations of the place as Director Smith himself. Even if he made the decisions and set the procedures, Mrs. Mikulka communicated his edicts and collected feedback. Over the years she become increasingly responsible for reading the piles of reports that came to the director from every department, distilling them into the briefs that Dr. Smith preferred. Deciding what details did and did not get passed on to Dr. Smith made her, in reality, a very powerful figure in the sanitarium hierarchy. It also meant she thought she knew everything about *everything* at Folcroft.

That's exactly what she intended to tell Dr. Harold W. Smith. She would follow it up with this concluding and irrefutable argument. "Whatever mistake Associate Director Howard made, I have not heard a word about it. Therefore it can't be as significant as you believe it is, and it is most certainly not worth terminating the boy over."

Dr. Smith would likely say something like, "I've never seen you so determined about anything, Mrs. Mikulka."

She knew exactly how to answer that, too. "Because, in all my years as your secretary, this is the first time I thought you were making a serious error in judgment."

There were other things she could have said, but she didn't dare. Like she knew that whatever Mark had done that was so horrible, it was probably just a minor and accidental deviation in the painfully rigid procedures Dr. Smith insisted upon for his tiny executive staff. She would not point out that it took almost superhuman patience and self-discipline to work in his environment.

She would also not point out that Mark was good for Dr. Smith. Mark's easygoing nature had rubbed off in subtle ways.

Finally, she would never bring up the fact that Dr. Smith was as old as the hills and his life spent behind a desk had left him with a frail constitution and persistent digestive irritation. For the future of Folcroft it was a good idea to have an assistant on hand to take over day-to-day operations. Just in case.

Shame on you, Eileen, for even thinking such morbid thoughts.

But it was true. She wasn't a spring chicken herself, and lately the brevity of her remaining years had been much on her mind.

Maybe she should retire.

With her head of steam up, she didn't waste a moment. She knocked on the doctor's office door as soon as she walked in that morning.

When she entered, Mark Howard was lounging in the creaky chair in front of Dr. Smith's desk. Dr. Smith was doing something strange with his mouth.

He was—what? At first she assumed he was on the verge of being sick.

"Dr. Smith, are you feeling ill?"

"What? No, I am just fine, Mrs. Mikulka. Would you bring us tea, please."

"Yes. Of course."

Mrs. Mikulka left the office feeling flustered. Dr. Harold W. Smith had been suppressing amusement. Not a laugh, certainly, and probably not even a chuckle. But as close to it as she might have seen in years. Why, Dr. Smith and Mark were sharing a joke.

You could have knocked over Mrs. Mikulka with a feather.

She felt like a silly old biddy for having wasted all those hours worrying that Mark was in Dr. Smith's doghouse. At the same time she was fervently curious.

What in the world could have been so funny to an old sourpuss like Dr. Smith?

What she wouldn't give to know.

"OH YEAH, REAL FUNNY, Junior," said the disgruntled voice out of the speakerphone.

"The Associated Press took a really nice photo, Remo," Mark Howard said, unfolding the newspaper when Mrs. Mikulka was gone. "The *Rye Record*'s got it right on the front page. 'Who Smashed Digger—And Why?' Listen to this—"

"No, thanks."

"No, just listen," Mark Howard insisted delightedly. "'Digger the Dinosaur never hurt a soul during his short life. In fact, the purple dinosaur with pink spots was only six weeks old. Yesterday, however, his brief existence was snuffed out when vandals smashed the two-ton fiberglass figure to pieces in the parking lot of the Carefree Vacation Condominiums development in Pigeon Fudge, Tennessee.'"

"Boo-hoo for the Carefree Vacation Condominiums," Remo said sourly out of the speakerphone.

"There's more. 'The vandalism occurred yesterday afternoon, but police say they do not know how the dinosaur was destroyed. "He was so new he was still shiny," said Max Scheaffer, president of Carefree. "Who would have thought somebody could do such a heinous act.""'"

"I know you think this is the most fun ever, but could we get on to business?" Remo grouched.

"This is business," Mark protested. "Your stunt turned out to be the curiosity-of-the-day in papers and newscasts around the country. You came pretty close to exposing the organization. Not to mention that it was just, well, a heinous thing to do."

Mark Howard stifled a chuckle.

One corner of Dr. Harold W. Smith's mouth twitched, very slightly.

"Hello?" Remo demanded. "Are there any adults in the room?"

"Remo, this could have been a real problem," Dr. Smith said, his voice almost, but not quite, as sour as ever.

"You're welcome. Thanks. No, really. Just doing my job."

"What are you referring to?"

"Tracking down the source of the poisoners? Remember? The job you couldn't do?"

"Yes, I assumed you would be able to do so," Smith replied. "But the little melee in Pigeon Fudge scared the islanders back home. A Union Island spokesperson claimed President Grom and his entourage were attacked by American ultranationalists. All the islanders were rounded up and flown out before they could be examined at the local hospital."

"They wouldn't let that happen because they've all have their brains melted, except maybe for the president himself," Remo said. "I think it's him, Smitty. That punk kid Grom. He's a sniveling, self-important little brat. I don't have to tell you about those kind."

"What evidence points to Grom?" Smith asked.

"The same evidence that led me to this can of nuts in the first place. None."

"So why do you think it is Greg Grom behind all the

outbreaks of violence?" Smith demanded. "We still don't know what he has to gain from any of it."

"You got me there," Remo said. "Maybe he's using some kind of mind-control potion. Maybe that's what got him where he is today."

Smith stared at the phone. "You mean, he drugged the people of Union Island to get himself elected? That's absurd."

"You wearing that butt-ugly green tie every day for forty years, that's absurd. Greg Grom spiking the coconut milk on Union Island, that makes perfect sense."

"If he did, then every resident of the island would be violently insane," Smith protested. "That's clearly not the case."

"Yeah. I don't have all the details worked out, but I do know Grom didn't get elected because of his charisma or his credibility. He doesn't have either."

"Maybe," Smith said. "We must consider the possibility that whoever is causing the poisonings had no connection to the islanders until he or she joined up with the group on the mainland. Which means we could see continued outbreaks in the South-Central U.S., even with the entourage back on their island."

"Nope," Remo said determinedly. "It won't happen. My gut says it's Grom."

Smith stared thoughtfully at the newspaper photo of fiberglass splinters. "I don't feel as confident, but going to Union Island is the logical next step until we have another occurrence. Mark?"

Mark Howard nodded. "I agree. Even without evidence it seems likely that whoever it was behind the poisonings, they were with the islanders."

"But we need hard evidence before we start assassinating the presidents of U.S. protectorates," Smith warned. "President Grom is off limits until proved guilty."

"Don't worry, I'll find proof," Remo said. "I won't snuff the punk until I have it."

"That would be heinous," Mark Howard said.

"Ha-ha-ha click," Remo said acidly.

Dr. Harold W. Smith suppressed a subtle spasm in both corners of his perpetually sour mouth.

29

The short buses were painted with parrots and palm trees. Tropical Transport was the name of the tour company. All the buses had a cardboard sign duct-taped to the front window with Chartered hand-lettered with a big black marker.

More cardboard—lots of it—had been used to cover the windows.

There was nobody inside yet. The four buses waited at the end of the Union Island International Airport's one and only runway. The bus lights were out. The runway lights were out. There were no flights scheduled to come in until the first morning tourist shuttle out of Miami at 6:00 a.m.

That was five hours away. Still, the lights of an aircraft appeared in the distance. They came closer, descending for a landing.

The runway lights blazed to life at the last minute, and the wheels of the chartered 747 touched down seconds later. It slowed fast, then came to a squeaking halt at the buses. The aircraft powered down at the same moment the runway lights faded to blackness, and there was nothing left except for a few yellow flashlight beams.

The Union Island Police Department wheeled the stairs into place and marched up to the aircraft doors. They had their billy clubs out. The doors opened and the police went in.

"Jesus Cheee-rist," Chief of Police Checker Spence grumbled. "It's a damn loony bin."

The aircraft was stuffed to the gills with lunatics. Most of them had the dead, sightless, unfocused eyes of a human vegetable. Their mouths hung slack, and when they turned to look at the police, their heads lolled from one side to the other, as if too heavy to control properly. A few of them were excited, yanking and pulling at their belts. Not one of them spoke.

Every man and woman had their hands cuffed behind their backs, which had to be a pretty uncomfortable way to fly. They all had their seat belts on. Otherwise the limp ones would have flopped to the floor.

"Hey, it's Alan from the tourism department!" One of the officers was aiming his billy club at a drooling, cadaverous figure in an aisle seat. The island government was tiny—everybody knew just about everybody.

"Hey, Alan, you feeling okay?" The officer leaned close.

Alan, from the tourism department, turned to face the officer. Spence could see the utter lack of vitality in the eyes, eyes that belonged in a corpse. He and his officer were both taken off guard when Alan from the tourism department bit a huge chunk of flesh out of the officer's neck. The officer went down screaming in the aisle.

"Jeesus!" Spence stormed down the aisle. He wasn't sure what he intended to do. For one thing, get the hunk of skin and muscle that was dangling from the teeth of Alan from the tourism department in hopes it could be reattached to the officer who was now pumping blood onto the aircraft floor.

Captain Spence didn't let his shock slow him. "Get the ambulance!" he shouted back to his other officers as he dropped to the floor beside the wounded man and applied heavy pressure to the wound. He felt the spurt of blood against his hand like water from a garden hose, and he knew he was feeling an open carotid artery. How many pints of blood had his man lost in just the past few seconds?

"Captain, watch out!"

The warning came almost too late. He felt someone leaning over him and he twisted fast. A pair of teeth chomped down, locking on to the material of his shirt. Captain Spence retreated up the aisle on all fours, dragging the shirt free. It wasn't Alan from tourism but a woman on the opposite side of the aisle. Agnes. From the island public relations administration. She was in her late sixties and her dentures fell out and bounced on the floor.

Spence grabbed his wounded officer's ankles and dragged him to the front, out of the reach of the passengers, but he couldn't tear his eyes away from the lunatic face of kindly old Agnes. She used to baby-sit

Captain Spence's kids. They called her Grandma Aggy.

She had just tried to chew out his liver.

DIRECTOR OF TOURISM Dawn Summens never went to sleep that night.

She got her first clue of looming catastrophe when she checked her voice mail. There was a message from Grom.

"It's me. We've had some problems at this end, and I think it's time to pull the plug on the tour. We'll be heading back tomorrow morning. Let's meet for breakfast and discuss our next move."

Summens had been taking off her earrings when the message started and she stood there now with one of them, a glimmering emerald stud, twirling in her fingers. Then she replayed the message.

No doubt in her mind. Grom was suppressing his excitement—or agitation. Had he achieved success? Or had everything blown up in his face?

Something told her it was bad news, not good. Grom was hiding something, which was a dangerous sign. Summens and Grom had an agreement. Greg was never, ever to hide anything from his right-hand man-bikini model—honesty was the key to their working and personal relationship.

Her apartment was a luxurious penthouse atop the Union Estates building. It was seven stories, the tallest structure on the island, and the surf rolled at its feet with a faint whisper. Summens strolled onto the balcony and regarded the moonlit waves carefully for a moment, looking for her answers there.

Something was afoot. She felt it in her gut. And she was going to find out what it was. Nobody screwed with Dawn Summens's well-laid plans and got away with it.

Especially not that pudgy jerk Greg Grom.

She wheeled and headed for the desk in her bedroom. It looked like a very feminine dressing table, complete with a small mirrored tray of the world's most expensive perfumes. Summens sat at the frilly vanity chair, moved the tray aside and swung up the top of the desk. The levers inside lifted the keyboard to working height. She slid the top of the desk out of sight into its wall recess, revealing a twenty-inch flat screen monitor.

She snatched up the phone as she began her on-line search for information. Her first call went to her airport contact. She had a lock on at least one employee on each shift of the airport security staff. Her call automatically went to whoever was currently on duty.

"Ashecroft," he announced.

"It's me."

Ashecroft's voice immediately lowered. "I was about to call you, Minister. We just got word about the president's flight coming in."

"What's their ETA?"

"Forty-five minutes," Ashecroft said.

That lying son of a—!

"The police are here already," Ashecroft added.

"Yes?" Summens said. Why police?

"They look ready to go to war," Ashecroft said. "But they said they'll enter the aircraft with billy clubs. The guns and stuff are for emergency use only—you know, in case of real trouble."

Summens's mind spun in several directions, but she exercised great control when she spoke. "What do they expect?"

"They haven't told us a thing." The way he said it made it clear he wished Dawn would fill him in.

"Phone the minute you learn anything more. I'll be in touch." She snapped off the phone.

She had just accessed the flight plan for the inbound chartered 747, which was three minutes ahead of schedule and expected to be on the ground at Union Island International Airport before midnight.

She found her next set of answers in the on-line edition of the *Knoxville News Sentinel*.

Rampage In Pigeon Fudge, the headline read.

She scanned the story and made a quick conclusion. Grom dosed his own tour-bus staff with synthesized GUTX. That was a desperate move even for an idiot like him. He'd been in bad trouble—or thought he was.

But what else had happened? Why was he keeping it a secret from her? When Grom got in trouble, she was usually the first one he turned to. She was the brains behind this outfit; they both knew that.

What was she missing?

She quickly jumped to another conclusion.

Grom was scheduled to take delivery today of a new batch of GUTX synthetic distillates. There was an upstart pharmaceutical specialties lab in Minneapolis. It claimed to have a molecular mapping and replicating technique. Their scientists had promised their synthesis would be as close as was possible to the real thing. But it took a little longer.

Grom was making all the arrangements with the labs. He never entrusted Dawn with the original GUTX except in very specific cases, like the senator who visited in his absence. He wasn't about to entrust her with the synthetic GUTX, either. She never even knew where the deliveries took place.

What if the Minneapolis lab did the job as good as it said it would? What if Grom had tested the Minneapolis GUTX samples and found one that worked without side effects? Crisis averted, he'd start feeling cocky. He'd start feeling like he didn't need a business partner—not one with a will of her own.

That betrayal would violate the terms of their agreement, but the beauty of GUTX was that he could dose her—maybe spike her wine or her bottled water—then simply suggest that she thought he had done the right thing. Then she *would* agree.

She'd be his little pet. His puppet. She'd follow his every suggestion. She'd perform whatever act he wished her to perform and she'd like it—if he wanted her to like it.

The thought repulsed her.

If only she could have found his stash of GUTX, she could dose him first. As stupid as he was, he somehow managed to keep that one secret from her for almost two years. She had never seen the full supply, so it had come as a complete surprise when Greg announced that his stores were running low.

For months they had contracted all kinds of marine biologists and less scrupulous rare-animal collectors to search the waters worldwide for surviving members of a subspecies of the Blue Ring Octopus that had once existed in small numbers off the shores of Union Island, and, as far as they knew, nowhere else.

The Blue Ring was a small, poisonous octopus today, but the Union Island Blue, as it was known, had been as much as a yard in length and with a greater girth. One preserved specimen was known by the scientific community to exist today—an intact, desiccated mummy found on the island by President Greg Grom himself, back when he was an archaeological student working the local sites on a summer internship.

The truth was, he had found hundreds of Union Island Blue Rings that day, but the specimen now on display at the Union Island Museum of Natural History had been the only one not crushed into powder.

As the sign at the museum explained, the Union Island Blue Ring was described in the surviving writings of the original island habitants. It had great ritual value to them, but was notoriously difficult to catch because of its lethal sting. The sting, the museum display said, contained a poison that was chemically similar to tetrodotoxin, one of the world's most deadly naturally occurring toxins. TTX was also found in several varieties of puffer fish and was famous for being the secret ingredient in Haitian zombie potions. Indeed, the Union Island Blue Ring Octopus appeared to have been used in rituals in which the priests would "kill," then "resurrect" a subject as a demonstration of supernatural power.

A chosen subject was fed a crumb of octopus flesh. The poison, dubbed guaneurotetrodotoxin, or GUTX, probably had an effect similar to TTX, slowing the metabolic rate to a point of near-death unconsciousness. Outward signs of life were suppressed until no heartbeat or respiration could be detected. Days later, the GUTX would wear off and the body's metabolism would speed up again. The benevolent priests would restore life to the "corpse."

Most of those who were exposed to TTX today, often through consuming puffer fish, received a dose far larger than what the Union Island priests used. Victims could die in as little as twenty minutes. From the written records found on the island, GUTX was just as dangerous.

"No Union Island Blue Ring Octopus has been seen in at least four centuries," the museum display concluded. "Have no fear of swimming in the beautiful waters of Union Island—this poisonous marine dweller is extinct!"

Their hunt confirmed that.

After months of failure, Grom and Summens had even risked a little publicity and offered a substantial reward for anyone locating a recent specimen. The word was circulated among fisherman throughout the Caribbean. The specimens that came in bore no resemblance to the Union Island Blue Ring. More than one marine biologist and rare-marine-animal collector shipped them hopeful-looking samples, but in all cases the pickled octopus were proved to be simply uncommonly large standard Blue Rings. DNA testing proved they weren't from the same subspecies as that of the mummy in the Union Island museum—and more tests showed that these standard twentieth century Blue Rings produced no GUTX.

Thus they embarked on the effort to analyze and create GUTX synthetically.

Easier said than done. Every lab they approached was able to make something very similar to GUTX and none had so far produced an identical molecule. The synthetic versions didn't work on the human metabolism in the same way, either. They found out the hard way when Grom tested a batch on a honeymooning couple from Portland.

The couple was flattered to have the island's president stopping by their restaurant table to chat. They were honored when he bought them a bottle of fine wine and decanted it himself. The never saw the extra ingredient he slipped into the wineglasses.

After drinking their wine, Grom suggested to the couple that they were having a fabulous honeymoon and they absolutely loved everything about Union Island.

The GUTX synthesis seemed to be working fine at first, then the newlyweds became agitated. Grom left, feeling the first twinges of alarm, and watched what happened next through the restaurant's front picture windows.

The couple began jumping around, boisterously conversing with other diners. Grom learned later that one of the other patrons mentioned that, while Union Island was indeed wonderful, the beaches could stand a little less litter.

That was all it took to set off the honeymooners.

"It's perfect!" the blushing bride screeched at the naysayer. "Do you hear me! Do you understand, bitch?"

The lady who had complained about the trashy seaside understood nothing except that she was being slashed to pieces by a maniac with a steak knife.

It wasn't easy downplaying the only murder in Union Island's recent memory. Reporters made much of the island's increased tensions resulting from its exploding tourism business. There were a few damaging "in-depth" investigations by reporters who had never even been to the island.

Summens knew how to take care of assholes like that. She hurt those reporters in the worst possible way—by compromising their credibility. She invited them to the island personally, turning on her feminine charms full blast. "All I ask is that you join the president and myself for a welcome dinner," she explained. "After that you can spend as much or as little time as you like on the island and really get to know what it has to offer."

"What's your angle?" a *Washington Post* reporter demanded warily.

"My angle is that I believe you will see that most of what you wrote about is untrue," she said matter-of-factly. These hard-nose reporter types liked you to be straight with them.

"What if I think I was exactly right?" he probed.

"Then you let your first article stand," she said simply.

"What if I think it's even more of a shit hole than I wrote about the first time?" the *Post* reporter said with a sneer.

"You write whatever you think is true," Summens said, putting a smile in her voice. "We'll trust your judgment."

It took a lot of persuasion, but persuasion was what

Dawn Summens did best. Once she got two high-profile yeses, the other reporters fell in line.

As promised, she and Grom hosted a private dinner party at the presidential beach house. Oh, how smug that bunch had been when they arrived, just brimming with journalistic integrity.

"Giving journalists a dinner with the president is not going to influence our reportage," said one black-haired woman from some big East Coast newspaper, then added, after an insulting pause, "Ms. Tourism Minister."

"Is 'reportage' a word?" Summens replied innocently.

The newspaper bitch and her colleagues left the dinner with a new frame of mind, thanks to a healthy dose of GUTX—real GUTX, not the synthesized junk. They all wrote retractions and self-condemnations for their irresponsible and inaccurate earlier reports on the problems at Union Island.

The black-haired bitch was writing for the police beat now, from what Summens heard. Good riddance. All the others had suffered similar career disasters.

But that was enough trouble at home. Summens and Grom decided to take the testing abroad and arranged a PR tour for the president that would take him to some of the hottest vacation spots in the U.S., where he could test the GUTX samples on unsuspecting tourists. If the subjects went amok, it wouldn't be Union Island's problem.

Grom had taken delivery of more than thirty sample types from eight labs, and surely one of them would do what original GUTX did. One of them *had* to work, because their original GUTX supply was down to the dregs. However, each and every formula had ended with the subjects running amok. Grom created a swath of violence and insanity across the south-central United States. Now, if Dawn Summens was reading the clues correctly, Greg had finally found a formula that worked.

Now he would betray her.

Summens's notebook computer was a sort of cybernetics nerve center for most of the systems on the island, and she tapped into the security cameras at the airport, witnessing the police preparations for the arriving 747. Grom and his dippy secretary were the first off. Even the small, grainy image from the security camera showed Greg looking haggard and nervous. His dippy secretary Amelia was a different story. Walking with confidence and a slight, assured smile, her eyes never left Greg Grom, and she never left her proper place—to his left and two steps behind him.

That was all the proof Dawn Summens needed. Before Dawn came along, he had dosed up hundreds of women, and he always made them subservient—and that meant walking two steps behind him, always. Now he was back to his old ways. He had given his secretary a fresh dose of the new GUTX and she was playing the part he wanted.

That would be Dawn if she wasn't careful.

She almost began doubting her conclusions when she witnessed what happened next. Police stormed the aircraft and retreated minutes later with a severely wounded man. The next time they went inside they had guns and riot gear.

They hauled out prisoners too numerous to count,

but enough of them were recognizable on the security video feed to assure Dawn that these were, in fact, island government employees. All appeared violently insane.

Why were they given the bad stuff and Amelia given the good stuff?

Dawn's system could tap into video signals from around the island. Hotels and department stores. Emergency vehicles and street-pole cameras. She was able to watch the convoy sneak across town, without emergency lights or sirens, and pull into the lot of the small police station.

She opened a line to the station cameras and audio feeds and saw the lunatics herded into the basement lockup.

She clicked over to her feed from the presidential beach house, finding Greg Grom in his bedroom. Grom didn't know she had tapped into his home security system. She had watched him perform some very vile deeds in that bedroom—deeds he never admitted to her.

There he was now, performing one of his favorite and most revolting acts with a screeching, sobbing Amelia Powlik. Oh, yes, he loved it when they cried in pain and begged for more in the same breath. Amelia didn't disappoint.

"Did it hurt?" he asked her afterward.

"I thought you'd rip me apart," Amelia whimpered. "How soon until we do it again?"

"I don't know. Maybe never. I have tastier fish to fry."

Amelia was clearly hurt by this, but she was an innovator. "I know what would get you interested again, Mr. President."

Dawn had no inclination to view another such display, but she was mesmerized when the plain, unattractive Amelia came out of the bathroom seconds later wearing one of Dawn's very own bikinis. She had to have left it there months ago.

"I am Union Island," Amelia said in a pouty imitation of a Dawn Summens commercial. "Come to me."

It was an unflattering imitation.

Greg Grom had not proved to be strong when it came to instant replays in the bedroom, but all of a sudden he was bolt upright and ready for more.

"Dawn!" he barked at Amelia Powlik. "Time for you to get what's coming to you."

"Will it hurt?" Amelia asked in a falsetto voice as she scampered to kneel at Grom's bedside.

"You better believe it will. It's been a long time coming."

Grom was true to his word. He made it painful, and he made it humiliating, and he made the fake Dawn sob. All the while he was violating her he was rattling off an endless litany of petty crimes that had been committed against him by Dawn Summens, and how she would endure endless nights of suffering and degradation as punishment.

When he was done, Amelia Powlik collapsed on the woven rug. "That was magnificent," she gasped finally.

"Wait until I get the real thing," Grom said. "I went easy on you compared to what I'm gonna do to her."

"Ooh, can I watch?"

Grom considered that. "Sure. Why not? Maybe I'll let you have a go at her, too. I'm bound to need a break sometime."

"And what would you like me to do to her?" Amelia asked, raising her head, eyes glinting in the darkness. "Maybe you should demonstrate."

Incredibly, Greg Grom rose to the occasion. Soon he was taking out his anger once again on the Dawn Summens stand-in.

The real Dawn Summens could not tear her eyes away. She had never seen Grom so confident, or so cruel, and she had certainly underestimated his anger.

What if she ended up in that role? One dose of GUTX and Grom would have her, body and mind. She would accept whatever he dished out, and she wouldn't stand a chance of escaping. She wouldn't *want* to escape.

She watched the performance for hours. By sunrise Amelia was a mess of small wounds and bruises, and she finally passed out from exhaustion. Grom finished off with her anyway and then fell into a dead sleep.

But Dawn watched him still, her plans ripening in her brilliant, devious mind.

It was a desperate plan with no small risk, but she never even considered taking the safest approach—getting off Union Island and never coming back.

This bikini model was fated for greatness, and she would not back down in the face of danger—no matter how terrible the consequences of failure.

30

Chiun stood outside the cab and slowly craned his ancient head to take in the entire facade of the faded pink Many Palms Resort. Clearly he wasn't pleased with what he saw.

"This," he said, turning to Remo, who was extracting chests from the overstuffed cab trunk, "is your fault."

"Huh? What?" Remo balanced the chests on his shoulders, "My fault? What is my fault and why is it my fault and why the hell can't it be some other guy's fault this one time?"

"This hotel," Chiun said evenly.

"Finest on the island," piped up the taxi driver.

"That's what you keep telling us," Remo muttered. "It's a frigging dump, but you know what, Chiun, it ain't my hotel."

"You brought us here," Chiun said reasonably.

"American Airlines brought us here."

"It was your investigation that led us to the Caribbean. Again."

"So you think I should have come up with different suspects or what?"

"It's a vacation paradise," the taxi driver enthused.

"Shut up," Remo told him. "You keep telling me to use my head and this time I used my head, and I'm getting nothing but grief for it. From you. From Smitty. From Junior. You think I'm any happier about coming back to the Caribbean? You think I want to spend time in this sleazy little junkyard with a beach?"

"Everybody says that at first," the taxi driver assured them. "I promise—by the time you leave, you'll love it!"

"Didn't I tell you to shut up?" Remo snarled. "You can't blame me for this, Chiun."

"I do."

"Stick it in your ear."

They passed through the front entrance into an open-air lobby with a stone floor and a freshly thatched roof. The walls were open to the beach.

"See?" Remo said. "Not so bad."

"It's ugly," Chiun pronounced with a dismissive wave. Remo went to the front desk, leaving Chiun standing there to wait.

"You wanna see ugly, go look in a mirror."

Chiun turned slowly to face the insulting party.

"I like your pretty dress." The comment dripped with sarcasm.

Chiun found himself face-to-face with a bird. A big one. It was a strange and vibrant bluish parrot with a huge beak. Its small, shining black eyes were set in big yellow patches. There were other parrots inhabiting the display of driftwood in the middle of the open air lobby, but they were green and tiny, dwarfed by the macaw.

"Don't make trouble," Remo called as he returned.

"Ringing its neck would be no trouble at all," Chiun commented.

"Not from Smitty's point of view."

"Old man wanna prune?" the parrot demanded.

"Who would teach a bird to be impolite?" Chiun asked.

"How should I know?" Remo said.

"I was not asking you." Chiun leaned close to the big parrot. Then leaned closer.

"Halitosis halitosis!" The bird squawked.

"Yellow and blue make a hideous color combination," Chiun told it, moving in even closer.

"Awk!" The bird tried to peck him, but Chiun held its beak in his fingers. The great black eyes rolled and the bird shifted on its driftwood perch.

"Not so long ago, in Rome, the Caesars considered parrots a delicacy," Chiun said.

He released it and the bird scrambled away, trembling. Chiun chuckled.

REMO WAS on the phone as soon as he had settled into the presidential suite at the Many Palms Resort. Settling in consisted of putting down the assortment of eight trunks Chiun had chosen for their short jaunt to the Caribbean, while the old Master himself plopped down in front of the television and began channel-surfing for Spanish-language soap operas.

"I think you sent us to the wrong island, Smitty," Remo declared.

"I doubt it," Harold W. Smith replied curtly.

"This place is a dump. And by place I mean the whole island, including this hotel."

"The Many Palms Resort is supposed to be the finest hotel—"

"Oh, Christ allmighty, not you, too," Remo said, cutting him off. "Okay, it's not so awful, but it's strictly two-star and that doesn't bode well for the rest of the island."

"You don't know that. The U.S. has invested a half billion to improve the island infrastructure."

"I'll believe it when I see it."

"You're not there to look for evidence of a public works embezzler," Smith reminded him. "You're there to put a stop to the killing."

"Yes, of course. I'll call you."

Remo replaced the phone as Chiun gave a disgusted sound, flicking off the TV and tossing the remote, which buried itself in the wall.

"No soaps?" Remo asked.

"None."

"My fault?"

"Of course."

Remo sighed. "I'm going for a walk."

31

Dawn Summens didn't move. Her face was blank, as if her emotions had been erased.

"I had to do it," Greg Grom apologized.

She just stood there.

"I had no choice," Grom insisted.

"Christ, Greg," Dawn said, turning away from the small barred window in the steel door. "It's horrible."

"They'll snap out of it. I'm sure they'll snap out of it," Greg Grom said worriedly, his own alarm growing. Dawn had been too shocked to react at first, but now her face was pale and she looked frightened. She leaned against the bare concrete wall.

"I had to do it," he whined. "The Feds were there. Those special agents I told you about? They were right there! The only way to get away was to cause such a big mess I could get lost in it. So I dosed everybody on the bus."

She looked at him with a stark eye. "Then what happened?"

"They went crazy. Just like all the others. They went on a rampage. It was just, just insanity."

"Rampaging?" she asked.

Greg nodded vigorously. "Yes. Not like they are now. This didn't happen until a few hours ago. They were still full of energy when we locked them up. Then this morning—this."

Dawn didn't want to look again, but she was drawn to the steel door. Through the bars she saw a large, low-ceilinged room containing fully half the administrative staff of the island government, maybe forty people in all, and not a word was spoken. Most of them simply stood in one spot, eyes wide, looking slowly around with bloodshot eyes. Several were pacing the cell slowly. One woman was putting her hand to the cold concrete wall again and again, and Dawn realized she was trying to flatten a spider. It wasn't fast, but the woman moved as if in slow motion and she kept missing it.

"Are they dying or what?" Grom whined.

"I don't know," Dawn Summens said slowly, although her thoughts were beginning to race. Schemes and strategies began to construct and collapse rapidly as she considered how she might use this development to her own advantage.

"What about the others on the mainland?"

"Some are normal and don't remember a thing," she said. "Some of them, if they weren't killed, are just like this."

Grom's jowls and baggy eyes drooped. He was worried. Dawn was delighted. Grom had intended to turn the tables against her, but the tables had lurched a little back in her direction.

"Greg, I'm scared," she said, putting a vulnerable lilt in her voice. "None of the ones on the mainland turned this fast. It took days and days. But it hasn't even been twenty-four hours since you dosed our people. What if they all die? We won't be able to cover it up. Not without GUTX."

"Yeah," he admitted, nodding and avoiding eye contact.

"What about Amelia?" she asked, and was satisfied to see him stiffen.

"What about her?"

"She's the only one missing from the lockup. Don't tell me she was killed?" Dawn pleaded.

"No. She was the only one who didn't get a dose. She's fine."

"Oh, thank God. How's she dealing with all of this?"

"She's fine," Grom said quickly. "Dawn, they're here."

"Who?"

"The agents. The two who've been after me. They were on the morning flight out of Miami. That's where I really need your help now."

"What can I do?"

Grom gave her a sick smirk. "You're Dawn Summens. You know what to do."

THE BEACH WAS rocky and dirty. The ocean wasn't so much turquoise blue as it was sea-slime green. The clientele were less attractive. Around the swimming pool, lounge chair after lounge chair strained under the massive pasty skin-sacks of American vacationers. Not one of them was flattered by the tiny straps and G-strings that were standard swimming attire.

The waiters, all local islanders, strolled among the vacationers and looked tiny by comparison.

Remo went the long way around the pool, but he could feel the eyes on him. There were a few catcalls and three drink offers. One woman jumped off her lounge chair—quite agile, considering her age—and started toward him with a gleam in her cataracts. Remo sped up.

"Not so fast, sweetums! Let's get to know each other over foreplay."

Remo often had problems with overamorous admirers, a side effect of Sinanju training. It had been fun for a week or two, but that was a long time ago. These days, his control over this animal magnetism was inconsistent. Right now he seemed to have lost his edge. He zipped around the side of one of the resort wings and leaped skyward, slipping over the rail of a second-story balcony. He sat there listening as his pursuer came around the corner and stopped below him, wheezing.

"Oh, shit," she said.

Somebody else was coming up behind her and making a lot of noise doing it. Through the narrow gaps in the balcony floor he saw a steel walker appear, followed by its owner, who made a deep frown out of her wrinkles.

"Where's the kid?"

"Got away. Sorry, Sally."

"Shit!" Sally thumped the walker in frustration.

"We still have Duncan and Buck in the suite across the hall. They're eager to please."

"I suppose, but they're so second rate," Sally complained. "The kid with the big wrists, now that was prime beefcake."

Remo was on a private balcony, and now he heard the faint swipe of a keycard and the door opened in the room behind him. The bleached blonde who entered could have been any over-the-hill waitress from any truck stop in the U.S.A. Her sunburned face brightened with happy surprise.

"Hiya, sweetie!" she called to Remo through the glass. She peeled off her I Came To Union Island T-shirt as she headed his way.

Beneath him Remo heard Sally and her friend turning back to the pool.

The bleached blonde had a one-piece bathing suit, and two steps later the bathing suit was wadded up in the corner.

Remo preferred not to make a miraculous disappearance that might get people talking, but Sally wasn't exactly moving at lightning speed and she'd see him if he just jumped down to the ground. If he escaped via the roof, the blonde might start asking around about the flying skinny guy. He was stuck be between a skank and a wrinkly place....

The peroxide waitress unlatched her door and at that moment Sally and her companion were gone around the corner. Remo jumped off the balcony—fast enough to escape the blonde but slow enough to look normal.

"Come back!" wailed the blonde, her voice muted behind the glass of the balcony door. "Look what I have!"

Remo tried not to look. He tried hard. But then he looked.

The blonde had pressed up against the patio glass, flattening and expanding her impressively large breasts into pale white circles of flesh that were big as dinner plates and, with a little mashing, getting bigger.

On the beach he marveled at the variety of skin shades. Some vacationers were pale as death. Several of the great quivering mounds of flab were pink turning to scarlet with nicely progressing burns.

Alice Aberwicz, however, was in a class by herself.

"Hello, Remo!"

The Reigning Master of Sinanju looked this way and that. There was nobody else in his vicinity who might possibly be named Remo.

"I'm talking to you, silly boy!" Alice Aberwicz waved and smiled from her beach chair. Remo approached cautiously and gazed down at a vast, glimmering, bronzed body.

"Do I know you?"

"I saw you check in last night and asked the front desk for your name. I'm Alice Aberwicz."

Alice Aberwicz wasn't pale or pink. She had a beautiful, bronze tone to her skin. Many hours of careful sunning, turning and basting had to have gone into achieving her perfect overall doneness. Her coating of coconut oil was so thick that it dripped from her elbow when she shielded her eyes from the sun. Being topless, the gesture also hoisted one massive breast off her lap and it, too, dripped oil.

"Nice tan," Remo said politely, trying not to stare. Alice was certainly—something.

"I thought you'd like it. Join me for a drink?"

"No, thanks."

"Want to just go to my room right now and get it on?"

"Maybe later," Remo said as he strolled off.

"I'll take that as a promise!" Alice called after him.

Remo kept seeing that great, golden, greasy image in his mind. He was turned off—probably for good.

And all at once he was turned on again.

She came out of the water not fifteen feet away. The late-morning sun shimmered around the figure in the emerald-green bikini, emerging with the natural grace of an auburn panther. Her skin was slightly dappled with the cutest freckles Remo had ever seen, and her tan had the depth of great art, rich and dark in some places but lighter in other places, as if inviting you to explore those places. Her hair was dark, swirling around her neck and shoulders, with a few dark strands clinging to the gentle swelling of her breasts as if they were directional arrows pointing the way.

Her features were strong, almost severe, but then she looked at Remo Williams and smiled a warm, provocative smile and she could not be more beautiful.

"You look hot," she said.

That wasn't what he had expected her to say, and for the life of him he couldn't think of a response that sounded intelligent, although he tried hard.

The girl in the emerald bikini added, "The long pants, I mean. They're too warm for the beach."

"Oh. Oh yeah. Well, I forgot my swimsuit."

"You're joking!" She laughed.

Remo was convinced at that moment that he was the funniest, wittiest man ever. "No, really, I did," he said. "I guess I should buy one at the gift shop."

"I'll have somebody get it for you," she volunteered.

"That's not..."

She gave a brief wave and three of the hotel staff came running. She gave them quick instructions and they were gone again. "Yes, Minister," one of them said as he went.

"So," Remo remarked, trying not to stare at her below-the-neck parts, "you're a man of God."

She laughed again, enchanted by his refined sense of humor. "Not that kind of minister," she explained. "I'm minister of tourism, here on Union Island."

"Really?"

"Really. Maybe you've seen some of our commercials?"

"I avoid TV, when possible."

"Ah, that is wonderful! Most people watch far too much television. It is nice to meet someone who doesn't recognize me."

There were heavy footsteps on the beach behind him. They came unhurriedly but they came in his direction, without question. He maintained an awareness of them, using the part of his brain not needed for ogling. "You mean you're in your own commercials?" he asked.

"That's how I started out, doing the commercials. The government jobs came later."

Remo had been really enjoying himself for thirty seconds or so, but now he was suspicious. How had he just happened to come upon this very, very attractive member of the island government when he was on the island trying to track down a guilty party who was part of the government?

But the funny thing was that this woman was not one of the government people he was looking for. She had not been among the passengers of the tour bus on the mainland—he would have remembered.

"Care for lunch?" she asked.

"Yes, Ms. Minister," he answered, "I do care very much."

The footsteps were close now. Somebody said, "Lunch is going to have to wait, wrists-for-brains."

"What's going on, Alice?" Remo asked as he turned to find Alice Aberwicz closing in. Now that she was standing up she was simply awe-inspiring—tall and proud, her giant body endless, her massive breasts swaying ponderously over her stomach, which cascaded in thick rolls of flesh that completely hid the bikini bottoms she may or may not have been wearing. She was like some goddess of prehistory, the Earth Mother herself, carved life-size by an ancient artisan from pure gold.

But the face was all wrong. Forget solemn or jolly, Remo thought. More like wrathful.

"You are a slimeball!" Alice spit foam in her fury.

"You should get out of the sun maybe," Remo suggested.

"Arrgh!"

"You know, if you're the Earth Mother, then I'm hitching a ride on the very next shuttle off the planet."

"I'm more than Earth Mother. I'm pure woman!"

"Several of them," Remo agreed.

"I've been cast aside by cheap pieces of meat like you for the very last time!"

"Didn't mean to hurt your feelings," Remo said insincerely. He couldn't help but notice the others coming. Five more women. All in swimwear. Every one of them had come on to him in the past half hour. Sally was in the rear but coming faster than seemed possible, her walker kicking up sand.

"I'm sick and tired of taking your crap!" Alice said.

"We just met."

"I mean you men! You fifth-limbers are all the same. Filthy, shallow ingrates!"

The spurned women were forming a half circle, and there wasn't a smiling face in the crowd. They had wild eyes. Sally was frothing.

Remo sighed. "Look, I'm really sorry. You're right, of course. I'm a male pig. I think with the wrong head. I treat women like crap."

"Unless they're women like that!" Alice jabbed one padded finger at the freckled beauty in the emerald bikini.

"Leave her out of it," Remo said. "In fact, just leave us both out of it. Go relax, have some drinks. Charge them to my room."

"Forget it! This time you face the consequences!" Alice Aberwicz put one arm behind her back and brought out a machete. It was two feet of curved gleaming steel—and there was only one place she could have been carrying it.

"Oh, God," said the minister of tourism, grabbing Remo's arm and hiding behind him. Remo glanced at her, reading stark terror on her face.

For some reason he had assumed this was a setup; the woman in the emerald bikini *had* to be in on it. But her fear was no act.

"Okay. Enough, Alice. Shoo."

"You pricks aren't getting away with it anymore— you will be the first to taste our vengeance."

"Scapegoated again."

"You are the symbol of the eternally evil penis!"

"And you're nuts."

With Remo's insult, Alice slipped the surly bonds of sanity and she thundered across the sand, the machete whistling in the hot air. The ranks of his spurned victims charged after her. The woman in the green bikini dug her fingers into Remo's arm and gasped, "Oh my—"

But by then the attack was already starting to be over.

Remo was no longer in her grip, but slipping up alongside the golden Earth Mother that was Alice Aberwicz, ignoring the slashing machete as if it were of no consequence, and pinching her by the scruff of the neck. Then he ran away, skimming fast over the sand to the next wild-eyed woman.

The woman in the green bikini wasn't even sure she was seeing what she thought she was seeing. Again Remo seemed to do no more than touch a woman's neck.

Alice Aberwicz had come to a stop and stood there for a long moment with a kind of contentment relaxing her anger. The fiery coals of the rage in her eyes were being doused as if by a heavy, cool fall of peaceful rain. She smiled crookedly and collapsed heavily on the sand. Her massive bottom flattened, her gargantuan

bosom flopped and by then Remo was giving the same
sort of neck adjustment to the last of the menacing
ladies.

Alice rolled onto her back and her eyes closed. She
was almost smiling. Like punctured water-filled bal-
loons, the others collapsed one by one into the sand and
went limp.

Dawn Summens was wide-eyed. "What happened?"

Remo found a green filmy wrap on a nearby beach
chair. "This must be yours."

"Did you kill them?"

At that moment Alice snored raucously.

"They're not hurt," Remo said. "Not by me, anyway.
As far as I know, they'll wake up just as pissed off as
before, so what say we take lunch off the property?"

She couldn't take her eyes of the unconscious women.
"Hello? Ms. Minister?"

Dawn looked at the man with the dark, cruel eyes.
"Dawn," she said. "Dawn Summens."

"Hale Jr. Remo Hale, Jr."

Summens nodded, forcing her mind to work as she
donned the wrap. This was the third major shock she
had received in just twelve hours—each unexpected,
each a red flag warning her that she was no longer in
control of this situation. There was nothing she de-
spised more than not being in control. First the enig-
matic sudden return of Greg Grom. Then his startling
revelation of this morning—when Grom found his impromptu detention camp for violent maniacs was instead full of emotionless, mute semihumans. Zombies.
Their minds erased.

Summens knew she had been told the secret of the prisoners only because Grom was desperate. He didn't know what to do. He had hoped she would have a solution. But she had nothing to offer. She wasn't helpful, and now Grom saw her as expendable.

Next Grom asked her to try getting close to the U.S. agents. That pair had to be dealt with, one way or another. Obviously, Grom had other plans he wasn't telling her about. He had tried to have this Remo Hale Jr. killed by these crazed women. Dawn knew that she was supposed to die, as well.

She grabbed the phone from her beach bag and called the island police, then forced a smile, determined to downplay the event. "The police will come and give your admirers a good talking to," she said to Remo. "You really should use more sensitivity when you reject amorous women."

Remo picked up the curved machete. "Now, where do you suppose...?"

"Beach bar," Dawn said, nodding at the thatched hut a hundred yards down. "They use it to chop the tops off coconuts. It wows the tourists."

Remo Williams snapped the blade off of the hilt and tossed the pieces away. "Bloody tourists," he muttered.

32

Greg Grom watched his secretary, Amelia Powlik, relaxing out on the deck of the presidential beach house. He smiled.

It all added up. Everything made sense. He knew what to do.

The synthesized GUTX, batch 42CD, was the batch—the Grail batch. The formula that worked. Amelia Powlik was living proof.

He had given her a dose that was tiny, just micrograms. But it was enough to work. Amelia was completely under his control. No uncontrolled fits of violence, no regression into a mute, zombielike state, nothing except a perfect adherence to his suggestion.

The synthesized GUTX samples had come in sealed containers of one kilogram each. Diluted for optimal dosage, Grom had enough to dose hundreds of people. And he would order more from the lab. He'd do it today.

He had some problems. That pair of bizarre federal

agents who were hounding him. Dawn Summens was getting suspicious. He'd take care of both those problems today. Maybe they were already taken care of. He had made some arrangements with the bartender at the hotel where Dawn was making her move on the agents. Grom honestly wasn't sure if he wanted Dawn to survive that encounter or not.

Then he remembered his night with Amelia. It had been fun pretending she was Dawn. It would be more fun with the real Dawn. Well, even if she did survive the beach brawl, she would no longer be a problem. Dinner would see to that.

GUTX-42CD was on the menu.

"IS THAT YOUR BIRD?" asked the black woman in the lightweight but formal-looking jacket. The pocket was embroidered with the words Manager Selena Teller.

"Certainly not," Chiun answered. "It is an impolite, arrogant brute of a bird."

"You seem to enjoy talking to him," she said. "You've been standing here for half an hour."

"You must understand," Chiun said. "I am alone most of the time."

"I thought you came here with your son?" Ms. Teller said, her voice softening.

"Yes, and now he is off somewhere without me. Seeing the sights, I suppose, while I am reduced to sitting in the room watching television, which I despise, or sharing my thoughts with a hideous chicken."

"Stuff it, slant eyes," the parrot squawked.

"And he is not the best company," Chiun concluded, his head drooping sadly.

"Full of it! Full of it!" the bird clucked.

"The thing is, the bird has never even talked to anybody else. We've all tried, ever since it showed up a few days ago. My assistant said it is a hyacinth macaw, worth maybe five thousand dollars. The way it took to you I thought maybe it was yours."

"I think it simply recognizes a figure worthy of its respect."

The bird blew a loud raspberry and made droppings.

"Well," the manager said, "let me know if it says anything that might be a clue to whoever owns it." Ms. Teller left them alone.

Chiun looked down his nose at the big blue bird. The sun was no longer shining directly into the lobby and the plumage had a purplish glow to it.

"You," Chiun announced, "are the color of something horrible that has been eaten and then regurgitated."

The bird glared at him.

"Heh heh heh."

The bird turned its back to him.

"Heh heh heh."

Chiun crossed the lobby and waited for Remo, who was coming up the quarry tile sidewalk. The ancient Korean in the bright robes attracted stares from the vacationers in their resort wear. He ignored them all.

"You smell of cow!" Chiun said by way of greeting. "Oh, Remo, has your uncontrollable lust for bovine flesh finally overcome your self-control?"

"You mean, did I eat a steak?"

"It was inevitable. You are a beef addict. The lure of cattle flesh was bound to overcome your meager self-discipline."

"I'm not a beef addict," Remo responded. "I haven't had a burger in decades. What's with the staff?"

The hotel manager was nodding meaningfully at Remo and Chiun. The other clerks glared at Remo and/or cast sympathetic glances at Chiun.

"You've been telling the story about the lonely old man and his negligent son, haven't you?" Remo demanded.

"Don't change the subject. Did you eat a cow?"

"Of course not. I had a lunch date and she ate a cow. *Some* cow. A steak."

As they walked by the bird display, the hyacinth macaw bobbed its head in greeting.

"Hi, bird," Remo said.

"Hello."

"Shall I tell you what I told the bird?" Chiun said. "Heh heh heh."

The macaw turned its back on them.

"Glad to see somebody here likes me instead of you," Remo said. "Okay, tell me."

Chiun repeated his regurgitation insult, then laughed uproariously—as uproariously as he ever laughed. "Heh heh heh."

"You need to get out more often, Chiun," Remo said. "It's not even really an ugly bird."

"I have seen more attractive vultures," Chiun said dismissively.

Far behind them the macaw squawked, "Prettier than you! Prettier than you!"

REMO GOT ON THE PHONE in the room, got an outside line, then held down the 1 button.

Chiun heard him argue briefly with whoever it was that answered the phone and then say, "Smitty, it's me."

Remo went on to detail his unproductive lunch date with the island minister of tourism. Chiun walked to the glass doors that opened onto a large balcony. He and Remo shared a spacious suite with a deck large enough for a dinner party. He slid open the door and stepped outside.

He was the Master of Sinanju Emeritus, and he felt restless.

At the time when Remo assumed the title of Reigning Master, in all the chaos that accompanied that event, Chiun had experienced something phenomenal. Amid a battle against horrific foes of Chiun's own making, he had been visited by Wang, greatest of all Sinanju Masters.

To meet with Wang while one was earning the title Master, undergoing Attainment, was a great honor. To meet with the great Wang at any other time in the career of a Master of Sinanju was unique in the annals of the Masters.

Wang told Chiun that his own future would be unprecedented in the history of Sinanju, but what Wang foretold was also less than crystal clear. Chiun's future would be magnificent, Wang said, but he hinted that a magnificent price would be paid.

But what price?

Chiun had slowed down in recent months, dwelling endlessly on the words of Wang, on the histories of Sinanju. He had sought to resolve in meditation the mysteries of Wang's prophecy, but had come away with only speculation. He had no clearer picture of his future now than he had when he was in the village of Sinanju, after the Time of Succession, after the final obliteration of Nuihc and the Dutchman.

Chiun didn't even have a path to follow. But he knew he needed to be more active again, escape the thrall of inactivity. Distantly he heard a familiar voice coming from the open-air lobby a few hundred feet from the balcony. "Prettier than you! Prettier than you!"

He allowed himself a slight smile. He did thoroughly enjoy berating that unbeautiful bird. But it was idle entertainment. He needed to clear away the cobwebs of his months of idleness.

There was a meaningless squawk, and then the bird spoke again.

"WHAT THE HELL?" Remo exhorted.

"What?" Smith said.

Remo hung up the phone and went onto the balcony, where Chiun stood with a shocked tightness to his face, as if his parchment skin were being stretched.

"Little Father?"

"Listen!" Chiun hissed.

Remo probed the grounds of the resort with his ears. Lots of air-conditioning noises. Vacuums from rooms being cleaned. The hush of the surf and laughter from the swimming pool. All the noises expected from a beach resort. Cutting through it all was the big macaw calling out from inside the lobby, "Prettier than you! Prettier than you!"

"What am I—?"

"Be still and listen!"

Remo shut up and listened. He knew Chiun well, and he knew something was wrong. But all he heard was the piercing squawk of that idiot parrot. Then even the parrot shut up.

"It is gone," Chiun said finally.

"What is gone?"

"Something strange," Chiun said ambiguously, looking out over the resort to the sea.

"That tells me a lot. Why'd you get so excited?"

"I was not excited," Chiun said, but without vehemence.

"Then why did you get so alarmed?"

"You may be assured I was not alarmed."

"Whatever! You were not your usually sunny self for a second there, so how come?"

"If you were ever to focus your attention away from Remo Williams, you would notice that I go through a range of emotions in any given day that we are in each other's company," Chiun said. "Sometimes I am aggravated, sometimes I am frustrated and sometimes I am irritated. There are times when I am exacerbated, disgusted, offended, sickened, shocked, galled, annoyed and appalled."

"Okay—"

"There are times when I am disturbed, or perturbed, or distraught, and sometimes I am just sadly amused."

"Well, whatever it was, you're sure back to normal now," Remo snapped and retreated inside the suite to call back Smith.

Chiun stayed on the balcony, watching the Caribbean glimmering in the sun but not seeing it. His concentration was on the sounds.

He did not hear it again.

Had he been mistaken? Could his ears have fooled him? Could he have been so engrossed in his momentous thoughts that his mind tricked him into thinking that he heard something that wasn't there?

Was his hearing starting to fail? He furled his brow and probed the sprawling resort. Down on the beach an obese and hirsute man was walking to the small shack where intoxicating beverages were dispensed, and Chiun concentrated on it.

"Can you make me a Singapore Sling?" the hairy one asked.

"Of course, sir," the bartender said with a habitual smile.

Chiun felt satisfied. He heard every word perfectly, despite the distance and despite the slurred speech of the hairy one. His hearing was still as good as ever— that is, well beyond the capabilities of every other human on the planet except for Remo.

But his moment of relief turned to worry. If not his ears, had it been his mind?

Losing his senses would be terrible; losing his mind would be worse. It would be humiliating.

No, by Sinanju standards he was far too young for senility or the infirmities of the elderly. A spring duck.

Bloody Tourists

But that meant what he heard was genuine. What could that mean? For his own peace of mind he would need to prove it. To himself.

DR. HAROLD W. SMITH HAD a pallid gray complexion on his best days. When he grew pale, he looked like nothing less than a days-dead corpse.

"Mark?"

"Yes, Dr. Smith?" Mark Howard was hunched over his keyboard, oblivious to the display on his screen. Smith had come halfway behind the desk to get a look at his associate's progress.

"What are you doing?" Smith asked.

Mark Howard stopped and looked up at Smith. "Researching. You asked me to create a profile on that minister of tourism."

"So instead you are downloading pornography?"

Mark Howard's mouth dropped open, then he followed Smith's gaze to the monitor. In one corner was a looping video window showing a woman in a bikini.

"That's not exactly pornography," Howard said, grinning. "I mean, she's not even naked."

"That is very close to naked," Smith said, lips pinching together.

"Well, that's her. The minister of tourism."

"Where? In the bikini?"

"It's a commercial," Howard said.

"That's the one Remo ran into?" Smith asked incredulously. "Dawn Summens?"

"Yeah. Lucky SOB."

Smith stared at the image for a moment and then turned away with a sort of painted-on shock. "I'll wait for your profile."

Mark grinned. The profile was just about complete, and he sent the batch of electronic files across the network to Smith's office.

He included the commercial.

"WHAT DID YOU MAKE of her," Smith asked Remo.

"Huh? Oh, Summens?"

"That is who we were discussing," Smith reminded him. "Are you sure you are feeling well, Remo?"

"I'm fine," Remo said, pulling his thoughts away from the strange behavior of Chiun, who was still standing on the balcony and was abnormally alert. Something had spooked him. That worried Remo. Chiun was his mentor, his father, his friend. Remo loved the old man more than any human being on this Earth.

Chiun was also one of the most powerful human beings on the planet by virtually any measure. He was a Master of Sinanju, for crying out loud. Masters of Sinanju don't spook easy.

So what just happened out on the balcony? What had Chiun heard, or thought he heard?

"So?" Smitty asked.

"Huh?"

"Minister Summens?" Mark Howard prodded.

"Where'd you come from?" Remo asked.

"I've been on the line since you called back," Howard said. "Remember, about ninety seconds ago when you said, 'Hiya Beav.' You were just now telling us about Minister Summens."

"Yeah. She's a strange one. You know she started as a bikini model?"

"We know," Smith said icily.

"We found some of the commercials that are traded on-line," Mark Howard announced. "She has her own fan clubs."

"I'd believe it," Remo said. "But she may be a part of whatever badness is going on. I don't know yet. She's about the most guarded person I've ever talked to. I had lunch with her and got nowhere."

Silence.

"I mean I learned nothing," Remo clarified.

"So what leads you to think she could be tied into the mainland troubles?" Smith asked. "She was not on the U.S. bus tour."

"My background checks show she does have strong ties to President Grom," Howard said. "They were romantically linked at one time. She's heavily involved in the proindependence lobbying effort, and with an uncanny degree of success. Senator Sam Switzer visited Union a few days ago, and today he came out in favor of granting the island independence and providing it an aid package to help it start a national government."

"Brainwashed?" Remo asked.

"I doubt that," Smith said.

"So he was already in favor of this little hot rock getting a free ride?"

"Actually, he was on record as being opposed to it," Smith admitted.

"There's more to it than that," Mark added. "Switzer was calling for federal corruption charges to be brought against President Grom. He flip-flopped on that issue, as well."

"So why do you think he's not brainwashed?" Remo asked.

"The newspapers have charged the senator with caving into the womanly wiles of the minister of tourism," Howard said.

"He was on the island for less than twenty-four hours," Smith added. "It takes quite a bit longer than that to brainwash someone."

"Depends on how you go about it," Remo replied. "I do think that's what's going on around here, Smitty. I think that's the key to all of it."

"Are we back to the poison smell again?"

"Yeah. I thought you were coming around to my way of thinking on the subject."

"Only to a point," Smith protested. "Remo, we know the substance is responsible for the acts of violence and the ensuing degradation of mental dynamics."

"You also know that there was somebody on the UI tour bus that was doing the poisoning," Remo added.

"Maybe somebody wanted us to think that," Smith said. "Even more important is the lack of motivation. Why would somebody on the tour bus set out to cause that kind of havoc?"

"Why would anybody do any of this?" Remo demanded.

"I do not know."

"So we can't rule out the UI president," Remo declared flatly. "We can't rule out brainwashing of visitors."

Smith sighed. "I fail to see the causal link between the poisoning and the ambitions of the Union Island leaders."

"So how long was Senator Shitzer here? A day?" Remo observed. "I bet he's just the latest victim. I'll bet there have been others. In fact, I have a feeling that just about everybody who comes to this place gets a quick cranial fix."

Smith made a sound then stopped. "Remo, I will not believe Union Island is brainwashing public officials and visiting tourists. It's outlandish."

"Yeah," Remo said. "Maybe."

33

Few people knew about Café Amore.

Café Amore wasn't listed in the travel brochures. The *Official Visitors Guide to the Caribbean Paradise of Union Island* made no mention of the restaurant. Often tourists would spot the unassuming little beachfront establishment and try to get in. Usually they were denied reservations. Most days the Closed for Private Party sign was propped up in the front window.

Dawn Summens ate most of her dinners here. It was the only safe place. There were actually few other restaurants on the island that weren't a part of one of the resorts, and anything you ate in any of the resorts had a chance of being, well, poisoned.

When Greg Grom originally embarked on his campaign to control the island, he had not been careful. As a demonstration of her usefulness when she wriggled her way into his confidence, Dawn Summens had mapped out a plan for a zone of noncontamination. "Are you going to trust that some minimum-wage fry cook at the Centauri Beach Resort isn't going to use some of the contaminated breakfast supplies in the dinner entrée?" she asked him.

"I told them not to," Grom had protested. "So they won't."

"So they won't *deliberately*," Summens said. "Who knows what they'll do *accidentally*. Greg, if they were smart they wouldn't be fry cooks."

Grom saw her point and agreed to make one restaurant entirely off-limits to their special brand of generalized GUTX contamination. They chose Café Amore. It served swill, but it served a higher grade of swill than the other places. Some of the new island profits were funneled into its accounts, and the fare was upgraded even as the clientele was reduced to a select handful. It was here that visiting dignitaries were entertained. If necessary, their dinners were salted with GUTX carefully, on an individual basis. The Café Amore staff had been carefully programmed to follow a strict regimen of safety rules developed by Dawn herself to reduce any chance of cross contamination.

When she and Grom arrived for dinner, they found the tables mostly empty. Just a few minor dignitaries and ranking locals. Grom shook hands and patted shoulders.

"Join us, please," said the mayor of a large Midwestern U.S. city. He had been dragged on this vacation by his insistent wife, on the advice of her sister Rosie. The mayor hated his wife's sister. Somehow, Rosie's obstinate opinions had a way of making their way into his political policy making. For once, though, Rosie was right. This place was wonderful. The mayor was already planning to retire here. Maybe he'd even opt out of the next election and move here that much sooner....

"Sorry, can't tonight," Grom begged off, smiling and holding up his briefcase.

"This is a working dinner for the president," Dawn Summens added. "You know how it piles up while you're away."

"Oh, sure!" the mayor agreed. He, for one, had no work piling up while he was away. He prided himself on his skills as a master of complete delegation. His workday consisted mainly of listening to his secretary read the summary conclusions of various city committee inquires and issuing decisions based on those reports. Some days he was on the job for less than an hour. That left time for golf.

Grom and Summens took the president's private booth and laid out piles of paperwork. Summens booted her government-issue notebook computer and they ordered without looking at the menus.

"Well?" Grom asked when the waiter was gone. "How was lunch?"

"Difficult to say," Dawn Summens admitted. "He's a strange one. He was wary."

"Suspicious?" Grom asked.

"Not as far as I could tell. But definitely slow to become interested."

"You mean interested in you?"

Summens nodded, thinking over her lunchtime encounter.

"Did you pull out all the tricks?"

"No," she replied quickly. "No tricks. He would have seen through them."

"He didn't look all that sharp to me," Grom said.

"Maybe not sharp exactly, but insightful."

"Hmm."

"I felt I had to be quite careful," she added. "I kept my questions neutral."

"You mean you learned nothing."

Summens nodded. "Nothing."

"Didn't you show him your tits?"

"Yes, Mr. President, I showed him my tits. He seemed to like them very much, but there was some trouble on the beach. He got distracted."

Grom's eyes flickered from side to side. They were beady little rat eyes. "What kind of trouble?"

"Woman trouble," Summens said. "Our friend had apparently spurned the advances of another tourist, and she took offense. There was some shouting."

"Really?" Grom said insincerely.

"I think he's very careful," Summens observed.

"Maybe gay."

She considered that. "I don't think so."

"Whatever," Grom declared, sitting back and tapping his Mont Blanc pen against the edge of the table. "Is he or is he not a federal agent?"

"Too early to tell," Dawn Summens said, and her voice reflected none of her rampaging thoughts. Greg Grom was acting differently. He was a little too confident. He was a little too belligerent. Dawn Summens was a student of human relationships, and she had made a point of studying this man especially carefully. She knew all his moods, and she knew when he had something to hide.

He intended to turn against her. Finally. Tonight. The betrayal was oozing from him, and she could almost taste the reek of it in the air.

"You struck out, Dawn," Grom said brusquely.

"I gained some measure of his confidence. We have another date planned for tomorrow."

"A lot could happen before tomorrow. Did you happen to notice that we're in a bad fix? We need some damage control, and we need it now. If those misfits really are federal agents—and I know they are—they're going to make things even worse."

"Maybe you shouldn't have led them here."

It was the kind of tart remark that would make Greg Grom fly off at the handle—or at least break out in an uncomfortable sweat that would start him scratching his itching palms and shifting in his seat.

He just sat there, looking at her.

"I don't appreciate you speaking to me in that way," he said finally in a low voice.

"And I don't appreciate you screwing things up for us," she said even more quietly, and she saw the anger blossom in his eyes. Had she overdone it? She couldn't be acquiescent. She couldn't risk letting on that she knew what he was about to do.

She and Greg Grom had been a team in a high-stakes poker game, but they were about to play the most important hand of all, and it was against each other. He knew it. She knew it. But he didn't know she knew it.

Martin came to the table. He was the only waiter who

worked Café Amore, ever. The less staff, the better the quality control. He flourished a small tray and placed their drinks before them. Stoli and tonic with a twist for President Grom. White wine for Summens.

"Minister Summens," Martin said apologetically, "Gerhard has suggested a change of entree. The mahimahi is off."

Of course it is, Dawn Summens thought. Steamed white fish would not disguise the taste. "What does he suggest, Martin?"

"A flavorful pasta Puttanesca, Minister."

"A little spicier than I am in the mood for tonight," Summens said thoughtfully, and out of the corner of her eye she saw Grom fidget. "But sure. I'll have the Puttanesca."

Martin nodded and left. Grom's shoulders slumped slightly with relief.

"Back in a flash," she announced to Grom. She strolled to the ladies' room, carrying her purse.

Locking the door behind her, she stared into the mirror and considered the huge risk she was about to take.

She could let her guard down when she was alone, and what she saw in the mirror was the face of a young woman. Smart. Pretty. Ambitious. The young woman in the mirror had a long life left ahead of her. The only way she could guarantee that long life was to leave now. Climb out the bathroom window and get off the island fast. Get away from Greg Grom and start fresh elsewhere.

Or she could go through with this, and take the huge risk. If she gambled, and she lost, then the woman in the mirror would be gone forever. Dawn Summens would no longer exist. There would be only a soulless puppet in the hands of puppet master Greg Grom.

But if she gambled and won...

Then she would hold the strings to Greg Grom and to all of Union Island. And Union Island was only the launch pad.

She had her sights set high.

Without further contemplation she opened her clutch purse and yanked out the black inner liner, then opened the small protective case hidden there. She snapped it open and twisted the lid off the bottle of charcoal capsules, upended the bottle into her mouth. She swallowed them all, washing them down with cupped handfuls of water from the faucet. That was a total of thirty-five charcoal capsules, each 260 milligrams, for a total of 8.32 grams or double a normal maximum supplemental dose. But would it be enough to absorb the GUTX that would surely contaminate the pasta Puttanesca she was about to eat?

Next she withdrew three prepared, sealed syringes and packets of alcohol wipes. She pulled up her skirt and swabbed a spot on her thigh, then jabbed in the first needle.

She was too preoccupied to even feel it. Would this work? Would it save her? She yanked out the needle, sterilized a second skin patch, and jabbed in the second syringe, squirting the contents into her leg. The first two syringes contained neostigmine and edrophonium, both of which were used to restore muscular strength in victims of intoxication by tetrodotoxin.

Hopefully she wouldn't even need it. Hopefully the charcoal would absorb most or all of it before it got into her system. But she just didn't know.

The third syringe contained 4-aminopyridine, a non-depolarizing neuromuscular blocking agent. It was used in the treatment of multiple sclerosis, and it had been shown to reverse tetrodotoxin toxicity in some animal experiments. She shot it into her thigh, then put the empty syringes away, snapped the case shut and tucked it back in her purse.

She left the ladies' room without even a backward glance at the girl in the mirror.

34

Martin, the waiter, cleared their plates. The president had hardly touched the big chunk of pork loin but he didn't seem displeased. In fact, President Grom wore an ear-to-ear smile.

Minister Summens had made thorough work of her Puttanesca, though. Not a scrap of a noodle remained.

"I'm glad to see you smiling, Greg," the minister said.

"You will be spending the night with me tonight," Grom announced. "That makes me happy."

"I'm glad it makes you happy."

They packed up the paperwork and left Café Amore.

They had walked just a few steps along the wide Bay Street walkway when Grom halted and turned on Summens. He smiled condescendingly. "Dawn, you know better than that. Tsk tsk."

They started down Bay Street again, but now, instead of side by side, Dawn Summens walked a few steps behind him.

It was a pleasant five-minute stroll to the presidential beach house, and Greg Grom was cheerful. He whistled. He tipped an imaginary hat at the waving police officers.

The cops waved to the tourism minister, too, who waved back, her nose crinkling in its delightful way, and the cops couldn't tell that inside she was screaming.

THERE WAS ALSO a policeman stationed at the beach house every night from dusk to dawn. The President of the United States had to worry about assassination attempts, but the president of Union Island had to worry about drunks who had a tendency to wander in thinking it was their hotel, or any hotel where they could spend the night. On average the officer on duty at the presidential beach house would taxi two drunks per night back to their resorts. Three on Saturdays and Sundays.

Tonight it was still early. The cop was pacing the grounds, just because he hated being locked up in his squad car. He had no problems serving as doorman for the leader of his island and soon, he was convinced, his country.

As they approached, Greg Grom gave Summens a suggestion, offhandedly and over his shoulder.

"Good evening, Mr. President," the officer said respectfully.

"It *is* a good evening, isn't it, Officer?"

"Yes, sir, Mr. President. Ms. Powlik has already arrived. Good evening to you, Minister Summens."

Like the damned she screamed. Like eternal agony the wails echoed inside her skull. She struggled to make the sound come from her lips. She had to let *someone* know this wasn't the real her.

"Good evening, Officer," she said. "Your tie is a little bit crooked."

She adjusted the police officer's uniform tie, her lips parted provocatively, and for a moment her slender, tanned fingers rested on his shoulder. The officer didn't know quite how to react, and before he could figure it out she was gone inside with the president.

He never guessed that, on the inside, she was howling like a rabid animal latched inside a steel cage.

AMELIA POWLIK WAS wearing nothing except a sparkle in her eye.

"Been waiting for you, Mr. President. Did everything go as planned?"

"It all went perfectly, Amelia."

Amelia Powlik barked happily. "I have more good news. Your federal friends just stopped by for a little dinner at the café."

"Oh, really?" Grom said.

"I was watching from the balcony. You just missed them."

"Pity," Grom said, wondering how the night could get any better, really. "Well, Martin knows just what specials to serve our honored friends from the federal government."

"Let's watch what happens!" Amelia bounded out the open balcony doors and put her eye to the telescope, which was angled down into the heart of Union Island's urban center, right at Café Amore.

"I'd much rather watch what happens in here than down there," Grom suggested.

Amelia jostled back inside, barking. And Grom was chuckling. And, on the inside, despite the smile on her face, Dawn Summens was screaming and screaming.

35

Chiun stood in the doorway of Café Amore and scowled at the decor, the potted plants and the hammered-tin ceiling. He scowled at Martin the waiter, who was coming at them in a smooth glide. Finally, he awarded his best scowl to the one who had brought him to this place.

"What's the matter with it?"

"It is someone's home," declared Chiun.

"Believe me, it's a restaurant."

"Excuse our intrusion," the ancient Korean declared to the entirely emotionless man in the tuxedo. "My ill-mannered son was under the impression that this is a restaurant."

"Hiya, Martin," Remo greeted the waiter. "Set him straight, would you?"

"This is indeed a restaurant, sir," Martin said stiffly. "Two will be dining, sir?"

"If this is a restaurant, why is there no garish advertisement on the street?" Chiun demanded.

"Relax, Little Father, it's a VIP place," Remo said.

"For visiting dignitaries, royalty, business tycoons. They don't want the regular street rabble coming in. Isn't that right, Martin?"

"This is an exclusive establishment," Martin agreed as he led them to a table.

"Maybe a little too exclusive," Remo commented as they took their seats. They had the place to themselves.

"Drink, sirs?"

"No, thanks."

"I shall fetch menus, sirs."

"No need, Martin. Just bring me whatever's the freshest fish you've got back there. Steamed, with steamed rice."

Martin pointed his utterly emotionless face at Remo for a long moment and was about to comment.

"Do you have duck?" Chiun squeaked.

"No, sir."

"Do you, perchance, serve parrot?"

"We do not, sir."

"Then bring me fish, as well," Chiun said offhandedly. "Whatever is more fresh than what you serve him. Prepared the same way."

Martin opened his mouth, closed it and left.

"The plastic guys who model flannel shirts at Sears, Roebuck emote more than that waiter," Remo commented.

"He is attempting some sort of deception," Chiun announced.

The kitchen doors swung open again.

"The fish is off," Martin declared in a monotone as he stood stiffly at their table.

"Give us the fish that is not off," Remo said.

Martin, finally, proved that he did have working facial muscles. He looked puzzled, as if he were trying to think through a brain teaser. "Um, *all* the fish is off, sir."

Chiun rolled his eyes.

"Let me get this straight," Remo said. "This is the most upscale restaurant on the island. There's an ocean so close I could probably toss you in it from here. And you're trying to tell me you're out of fresh fish?"

"Um," Martin said, "yes, sir."

"Um, bullshit. Okay, just bring us the rice. Steamed."

"We are out of rice, sir," Martin said finally.

"You served me rice not seven hours ago."

"That was the last of it, sir."

"Um," Remo grumbled. "I see."

"I see a man who is seconds away from death unless he ceases to tell falsehoods," Chiun said in Korean.

Remo nodded and asked Martin, "My father would like to know your recommendations."

"Your father would like to throttle the help," Chiun added in his native language, but he nodded agreeably.

"The chef has prepared an intriguing pasta Puttanesca," Martin orated.

Remo nodded. "We'll take it."

"And we'll force-feed you on it," Chiun added in Korean. But he smiled when he said it.

36

"Bon appétit," Martin declared, presenting plates of steaming, odoriferous pasta.

"Well?" Remo asked when the waiter departed.

Chiun looked distastefully at the platter before him. He sniffed very slightly. "Boiled gelatinous wheat flour," he stated. "Chemically solidified oil of corn."

"Yeah?"

"Tomato, smashed and burned for hours. Dehydrated pungencies added to mask the soot. Compressed anchovies to further confuse the flavor. Brine-cured olives mixed in because this is what American palates demand of their 'authentic' Roman cuisine."

"What else?" Remo asked.

"Various forms of curdled cow's milk and enough salt to taint a village well," Chiun said with a nose wrinkled in repulsion. "Also, poison."

"Mine, too," Remo agreed. "Oh, waiter!"

THE KITCHEN DOOR SWUNG open and Remo poked his head in.

"Oh, there you are, Martin."

"Is there something I can help you with, sir?"

"The name of whoever put you up to dosing the dinners."

The cook emerged from a walk-in cooler with a large fish held by the tail. He dropped it and charged Remo a second after Martin made his move. Both of them had large knives conveniently at hand.

Remo smacked Martin's knife away before the steel tips touched his T-shirt. Martin's butcher blade made a vibrating musical note as it embedded itself in an exposed wooden ceiling beam, and Martin looked at it in surprise. He missed seeing Remo's deft swat at the chef, whose scaling knife somehow ended up rocketing across the short space in Martin's direction. The scaling knife sliced thinly into the waiter's scalp before burying itself in the wall behind him. Frozen, Martin's eyes crossed to stare at the humming knife handle and then to watch the blood trickling down his nose and cheeks.

"Talk," Remo said, and he started squeezing earlobes.

"WELL?" Chiun asked.

Remo sat at the table. "They were lying. They did have fresh fish. It's in the steamer."

"I knew it."

"The whole bit about trying to poison our pasta is a mystery to them. They don't even remember doing it, or why or who told them to," Remo added.

"They were lying," Chiun said.

"I would have known if they were lying," Remo insisted.

A very shaky Martin emerged from the kitchen and came to the table. "I came to take away the unsatisfac-

tory entrées." He was whimpering, yet he still managed
to retain some of his condescending-waiter attitude.

"The unsatisfactory entrées are no longer here, obviously," Chiun pointed out.

Martin's eyeballs rolled in his head until they fo-
cused on two extremely valuable oil paintings adorning
a place of honor on a wall behind a velvet rope. They
were nineteenth-century Italian portraits, and their combined value was more than that of the restaurant itself.
Their value had been much reduced, however, when the
Italian duke and duchess were hit in the face with pasta
Puttanesca.

Chiun took Martin's wrist and applied pressure. "Did
you lie to my son?"

Martin's mouth opened and closed. He had been in
pain when Remo interrogated him. Now he was in *pain*.

"No!" he gasped like a suffocating carp.

Chiun frowned at him, then let go of the wrist. "You
have cut your scalp open, careless oaf," Chiun told the
man. "If you bleed on my fish, I'll throttle you with it."

Martin gulped. "Very good, sir."

Remo wasn't paying attention. "I'm sick of this tip-
toeing around," he announced. "I think we should go see
the president after dinner."

"Emperor Smith will be displeased."

"Smitty can stuff it."

"Good!"

"Good?" Remo asked. "Why good?"

"I have thought all along we should go interrogate
the whelp, despite Emperor Smith's dictates."

"So why didn't you say so?" Remo asked.

"I was waiting for you to make the decision. Now, if it becomes a political brew-a-ha-ha it will be your responsibility, not mine."

"If he's the guilty guy it won't matter," Remo said.

37

Dawn Summens was experiencing hell.

Greg Grom wasted no time in creating a repeat performance of the role-playing she had witnessed the night before. Only this time, instead of Amelia standing in as Dawn Summens, he had the real Dawn Summens to play with.

She had underestimated Greg Grom. The depths of his sadism and bitterness were far beyond what she had ever imagined. In the main bedroom of the presidential beach house, with Amelia Powlik cheering on the sidelines, Greg Grom took out months of pent-up anger and frustration on his minister of tourism in the most humiliating and painful methods he could engineer.

He suggested that she beg for more. She begged for more.

Her mouth made the words and her body acquiesced to his abuse, but inside she was fighting with every ounce of will. Some niggling sense told her that the chemical hold on her was weakening. Maybe her precautions had been somewhat effective. Maybe with a little more time...

Maybe it was just wishful thinking.

Greg Grom halted his entertainment and left her battered and bruised on the bed. He dressed, taking several plastic vials from the bedside table.

"I'm off! There are breakfast buffets to be spiced up!"

So he had enough supply of the good new GUTX synthesis to start dosing the tourists again. There was nothing to stop him now.

"We'll be waiting!" Amelia Powlik giggled.

"Amelia, feel free to entertain yourself while I'm gone."

"Thanks, Mr. President!"

"Just don't do any severe damage to the poor creature. That's my job."

"NOW IT'S JUST YOU and me!" Amelia Powlik exclaimed with a bark of joy. "Here, have a drink."

Dawn Summons, her head half-hanging over the edge of the bed, saw a bottle of tequila thrust in front of her. She hated tequila. But she took it and brought it to her lips.

"Take a nice big swig," Amelia said.

Dawn put it to her lips and then concentrated, with all her mental energies, on the act of closing her lips. As she upended the bottle, her lips did close. She felt the tequila burning against her mouth, but only a trickle got inside.

"That's right, honey!" Amelia said. "That'll get you going!"

Dawn sat up and held the bottle out to Amelia.

"No, you go ahead and take another."

"Yes, Amelia," Dawn said, and she pretended to take another big swig. Hope flared up inside of her—she was fighting it! She was disobeying!

Was she ready to take it to the next level, to try something really rebellious?

"We're gonna have fun while the prez is out on the town!" Amelia said. "Well, I'm gonna have fun. What'll we do for starters?"

"How about this?" Dawn asked as she held the tequila bottle by the neck and brought it down hard on Amelia Powlik's skull.

The bottle broke. Amelia grunted and staggered and sputtered to get the glass pieces and alcohol out of her mouth. She grabbed her eyes but forced glass splinters into her flesh. When she tried to blink her eyes open, the tequila burned her eyeballs.

Dawn gave Amelia a shove. Amelia staggered across the room. Another shove sent her onto the balcony. When Amelia's hip collided with the iron railing, she knew what was in store for her and she forced her eyes open. They were bloodred and burning. She managed to hold them open just long enough to see Dawn Summens coming at her again. Amelia tried to slap Dawn away and failed. Dawn grabbed her by the shins and lifted.

Amelia, with a bark of fear, flipped off the balcony and thumped against the beach twelve feet below.

Something snapped. It was her ankle. Despite the agony, she began a miserable turtle crawl.

"I found another bottle of tequila, Amelia," Dawn

called down. Amelia felt the liquid spattering on her back and buttocks.

"How about we heat this party up?" Summens asked.

Amelia once again forced her eyes open. Dawn was on the balcony with a tubular box of fireplace matches. She lit one and sent the slender flaming stick arching off the balcony. It landed in the sand and went out.

"Oops. Better try that again," Summens said.

Amelia whimpered. She watched another match arc through the air and land in the sand just a foot from her body. She tried to crawl away, backward, but her body was shaking and her leg was limp. The third match was on target. Amelia tried to dodge, but she simply could not move fast enough.

Then there was fire, a stench and contortions of agony.

IT DIDN'T LAST long enough, but burning Amelia Powlik was the most deeply satisfying thing Dawn Summens had ever done in her life. She even enjoyed the aroma. "Smells like victory!" she told the steaming human ruin happily.

She was getting more of her own will back every moment. She had to avoid people for a while. She had to get out of here, get things done. Not that Grom would be back anytime soon if he was really going on a full round of stops at all the resorts.

It was how he had done it for the past two years. He would go out one or two nights a week and sprinkle GUTX powder in the breakfast fare. He had tried coffee, eggs, pancake mix, whatever, before finding he had the best results with the breakfast potatoes, of all things.

Almost everybody ate them. The staff at the hotels had
received the suggestion that it was perfectly normal and
acceptable for him to sprinkle stuff on the breakfast
food. It was also standard operating procedure to broadcast Greg Grom's message to Union Island visitors over
the loudspeakers during breakfasts following his midnight visits. The tourists invariably complained when
the racket started, but soon they would be agreeing with
every suggestion Grom made.

It would take him a couple of hours to hit all the resorts. The longer the better, as far as Dawn Summens
was concerned.

38

"Yech," Remo Williams said. "Get a whiff of that."

"No, thank you," Chiun answered as he crinkled his nose into a hundred extra wrinkles and put his hands in his kimono sleeves as if to protect all possible flesh from exposure to the air in this place, which had to be toxic.

"Sex. Blood. Sweat. Somebody had a hell of an orgy, and it wasn't one of those nice orgies where everybody smiles. Looks like there was some beating and whipping involved."

"And burning," Chiun said, moving to the open doors of the balcony. Remo joined him a moment later and they gazed down at the horrid burned thing in the sand.

"These people like it pretty rough," Remo said.

Chiun glanced down at what Remo was holding. It was a small wooden drawer, empty.

"It's from the bedside table." Remo held it up and took a cautious sniff. His eyes widened.

"It is the poison."

"It is, but Grom is gone and he must have taken it with him."

"We must find him."

Remo looked down at the black thing. "Maybe she knows."

OUT OF THE DARKNESS came a souring song of agony. Her body flared to life with pain that burned and burned—

Until a hand touched her, on the neck, and the pain became as nothing.

"I was on fire," she said.

"Your skin is very burned," said a kind voice, a voice like someone old and young at once.

"Am I going to live?"

"Doubtful," said the kind, high voice.

"We need your help," said the voice of a younger man, deep and attractive.

"I'm going to die?"

"Where is Greg Grom?" the younger man's voice asked.

"President Grom is gone," she said, and she tried to smile.

HER EYES STARED into the heavens dreamily. Remo looked at Chiun, who was manipulating the woman's charred flesh, looking for the nerves underneath. "She is badly damaged and very heavily intoxicated with the poison," Chiun said. "Her body is fighting for life and fighting with itself."

"Can't you snap her out of it?"

"She is already much too snapped."

Remo wasn't sure what to think about the poor blackened thing on the sand. She was a victim. They were all victims. Even the pair at the restaurant who tried to poison their dinner. None acted with a will of their own. The list of responsible parties was really extremely small.

"We gotta find Grom," Remo said.

Chiun looked at him expectantly.

"I don't know how," Remo answered the unasked question. "I just know we have to."

"Why?" Chiun asked.

Remo made an exaggerated gesture at the sizzling woman. "Hello? Bad man up to no good?"

"Do not speak to me in that way, please. What kind of no good do you think he is up to?"

Remo fretted. "Who knows? Probably doing what he does—you know, poisoning all the tourists. Dosing them up."

"And he would do it in what way?"

"Same way they did us, I guess—put it in the pasta Puttanesca." Remo looked at the moon over the water. He looked suddenly at Chiun. "Or the scrambled eggs. What if he goes at night to the hotels and sprinkles his special seasoning in the food for the morning breakfast buffets? He'd get pretty good coverage."

"That would be effective," Chiun agreed.

"So we make the rounds of the hotels until we find him."

Amelia Powlik sat up. "Where you going?"

"Maybe you should keep from moving around too

much," Remo said as he watched part of her upper-arm skin slough off in a black crust.

"Wait, you. You sound kinda good-looking. Stay with me and let's get to know each other."

"You gotta be kidding me," Remo said to no one in particular.

"WE GOT A CALL for a paramedic backup," the dispatcher said.

"Take a message!" answered Chief of Police Checker Spence as another huge boom shook the police station, like a subterranean explosion. "Where's Weil and Lambert?"

"On their way," the dispatcher said.

There was another boom. This time it sounded different. Less resonant. The Coke on a nearby desk sloshed inside its bottle. "What about Fornes? Is he coming?"

"Fornes is dead, Chief," the dispatcher reminded him.

Spence stiffened, then nodded. Fornes had been killed by Alan from the tourism department, who bit a chunk out of his neck. The wound was huge. Fornes bled to death. And then Agnes, that nice old lady, had tried to do the same thing to Chief Spence.

The floor shook with another boom from below.

That would be Alan from the tourism department. And dear old Agnes. And the rest of the insane maniacs they had transported from the aircraft to the police lockup down below. They had been prone to violence, but at least they had quieted down eventually. Chief Checker Spence liked his maniacs quiet and cooperative.

So he became perturbed when the maniacs in the lockup started getting excited again an hour ago. Soon they were pounding the walls. Now they were pounding the doors. And Checker Spence had a sinking feeling...

Another boom, this time accompanied by a crunch. The steel door hadn't failed, but the concrete that held the bolts had crumbled.

Spence rushed to the top of the stairs. "Simone!"

"They're breaking through, Chief!" Officer Simone called up.

"Get the hell out of—"

Another boom and then a creaking sound, followed by a powerful crash.

"They're out!" shouted Officer Jacot from somewhere out of sight.

Spence shouted. "Simone! Jacot! Get out of there now!"

Simone came into view at the bottom of the stairs, but he was looking back the way he'd come. His handgun was drawn.

Spence hurried down the stairs. "Do not fire your weapons!"

He was almost drowned out by the thunderous gunfire and shouting. It wasn't Simone. Simone was just standing there.

Chief Checker Spence reached the bottom just in time to watch Officer Jacot die. The man was triggering his gun in every direction, shouting at the mob of bloody, battered, silent figures who encircled him. They moved ponderously, without speaking, ignoring those among them who fell from gunshot wounds. Jacot ran out of bullets and the mob closed in. They grabbed his arms and legs. They grabbed his head. They sank their fingers in the flesh of his torso. Jacot was lifted off the ground.

Jacot realized his fate then. He made an ungodly sound.

Then the eerily silent mob pulled his body apart.

"CALL THE MAINLAND!" Chief Spence barked at the dispatcher as he dragged Simone out and slammed the door, locking it with a dead bolt. "Call the army!"

The dispatcher ignored him and looking around worriedly. "Where's Jacot?"

Officer Simone giggled. "He's all over the place."

One glance told Captain Spence that Simone had gone out for lunch and might never come back. "Oh, great," he said. Then he heard the sodden clomp of heavy feet on the stairs.

"Are you calling for help?" he asked the dispatcher.

"Who you want me to call exactly?" she asked, getting worried now.

There was a crash against the door to the basement. They were throwing their whole bodies against it. The dead bolt was already buckling.

"Forget it," Chief Spence said. "It's too late. Let's go."

THE UNION ISLAND MUSEUM of Natural History had a sophisticated security system, but Dawn Summens had an override code. She punched in the code, commanding the alarm system to maintain a silent but active state. She didn't want the museum curator to notice that his little green LEDs had blinked off.

Curator Matthew Builder was just a nosy old busybody two years ago when he retired from the University of Florida at Miami. Greg Grom had been on his way to the top, laying the groundwork for his wild popularity spree, and had already moved into the Union Island Tourism Promotions Department. Grom rarely made intelligent decisions—it was sheer stupid luck that got him everything he had—but latching on to the old codger from Florida State had been a rare smart move.

When Professor Builder told Grom his dig sites on the island were of marginal value in terms of the greater archaeological research record, Greg Grom had suggested otherwise. Grom suggested, in fact, that it was the most important Native American site in the Caribbean islands.

"Why would I think that?" Professor Builder had asked as the GUTX laid his self-determination in Greg Grom's lap.

"You'll think of a reason," Grom told the prof.

And sure enough, Builder did. He claimed discovery of a series of hieroglyphics that showed the little-known Miytec of pre-Columbian Union Island had been rulers of far-reaching power, maybe for centuries. Newly translated Miytec hieroglyphics told how Miytec priests claimed to wield power over "all the kings of the earth." How the Miytec priests would receive the kings of all the lands. All rulers of power and influence were invited to drink the Miytec priests' sacred brew. The great secret was that, once the brew had been consumed, these men invariably became pliant to the suggestion of the Miytec priests.

Greg Grom had almost panicked when he heard the tale. It was too close for comfort. But even Professor Builder did not believe that the priests had ever had this power—he only claimed that this was what the priests themselves believed.

Professor Builder's reputation was rock solid. That's why Grom chose him. Despite a lack of archaeological verification, his theory was widely accepted. Even those who thought he was wrong still considered his claims worth investigating. Union Island became the subject of serious scientific inquiry, which boosted its prestige. Greg Grom got all the credit for it.

Professor Builder, at Grom's suggestion, returned to Union Island to serve as director of research for the Union Island Museum of Natural History, where a well-paid management staff took care of the day-to-day operations and Builder spent his days immersed in his research while the grant money, thanks to a few more well-placed suggestions, poured in too fast for the museum to spend it all.

Builder was always at the museum late into the evening. This was well-known among the Union Islanders. His car was also well-known—an electric golf cart with orange curling hot-rod flames painted on the doors. The cart was invariably parked in Builder's reserved spot at the private entrance in the rear of the museum. It was there now. From the third-floor research labs a single office blazed with light.

Dawn Summens knew the old professor would be buried in his research. She was pretty sure she could get in and out of the museum without attracting his attention.

But just in case... Well, she had brought a little something from President Grom's presidential beach house. It was a dagger of black obsidian, almost five hundred years old, and it had been one of Grom's first finds when he was a student intern on the island. It was incredible that something so fragile could have survived so many centuries, but it was intact.

If Professor Builder gave Dawn any trouble, she was going to see what kind of real damage it could do.

She found herself hoping she'd get the chance.

39

The phone beeped just as President Grom was pulling into the employee parking lot at the Turquoise Seas Beach Resort.

"Mr. President? It's Gaiman at the Miytec."

Grom switched off the engine and killed the stereo. Art Gaiman was the night manager at the Miytec Moon Village Resort. The old resort had recently been renovated and expanded with the addition of a new wing of three hundred hotel rooms. That made it one of the largest resorts on the island in terms of the sheer numbers of vacationers it could host. The Miytec was also the closest big resort to the town center, and it had been Grom's very first stop on his evening rounds.

"What's the problem, Art?"

"Well, Mr. President, it's about the hash brown potatoes."

Greg Grom felt his stomach tighten into a hard, knotted ball. "What about the hash brown potatoes?" he asked.

"Two men just came and stole 'em, Mr. President. All of them. Took every one of the tubs that you was working on tonight."

"Took them where?" Grom demanded.

"Down to the beach. That's the funny thing. They just heaved them out into the ocean. Never would have thought a man could send a plastic tub of hash browns that far. Splashed into the water so far out I couldn't see it and I could barely hear it."

"A white guy? With dead-man eyes? And a little Chinese grandpa?"

"Yeah! That's them!" Art exclaimed. "Asked for directions to the nearest resort and I told them because I wasn't going to say no to those two. Those two are crazy. I think they're gonna do the same fool thing over at Monte Carlo. What do those two have against perfectly good hash brown potatoes?"

Grom wasn't listening. His high spirits had fled like the breeze, when just a minute ago he thought everything was finally going his way, for once.

How come that pair of oddball agents wasn't dead? Grom had made sure that wherever those two showed up for dinner tonight they would get dosed with GUTX. A lot of it. Enough to send them into the deepest sleep of all.

That hadn't happened. The agents were alive, and they knew what Grom was doing. Which meant they knew why he was doing it. So they knew he had been using GUTX dosing to get him to where he was now.

Which meant they just might be able to bring it all to a screeching halt.

Unless, Grom thought determinedly, he screeching halted them first.

REMO HAD STOPPED explaining himself. At each resort they came to he simply barged in, headed for the kitchens and began looking for the tubs of thawing hash brown potatoes.

It was always the same. Big plastic ten-gallon or twenty-gallon tubs in the walk-in coolers filled with the same brand of spiced, shredded breakfast potatoes. The empty plastic bags would be in the trash can.

"You can't take the potatoes!" the night manager at the first resort had cried. "The visitors love our potatoes!"

Apparently Greg Grom knew that. He had a system in place that so far seemed to include every hotel and resort on the island. In the evening the food-service crew would start thawing as many bags of hash brown potatoes as would be needed for the morning breakfast crowd. Grom would stop by and stir in a little poison. Next morning the thawed spuds were served to the tourists.

"The president come often to inspect your hash brown potatoes?" he asked the night manager at the first resort.

"Coupla times a week. Why shouldn't he?"

That was the really weird thing about it—the resort staff went along with it all as if it were perfectly normal.

After Remo confiscated the tubs of spuds he would head for the ocean and shot-put them into it. Meanwhile, Chiun would be nosing around the kitchen looking for any other poisoned foodstuffs. But so far the poison was always in the hash browns.

The routine changed on their sixth stop, the Turquoise Seas Beach Resort. Remo wheeled the borrowed taxicab into the palm-lined front drive and found a throng of well-dressed vacationers in the lobby veranda.

"A reception line," Remo observed. "Think it's for us?"

"I think it's for you," Chiun said.

The crowd came down to greet them. Some still had drinks in their hands.

"Grom must've heard we were after him and he suggested the late-night partyers come welcome us."

"I can smell the stink of intoxicants already," Chiun agreed.

Remo pulled the car away just before it came within reach of the crowd. Driving on the grass, he took the shortcut to the service entrance, hidden behind some decorative tropical topiary.

"They have a lot of staff on the late-night shift at this place," Remo noted. There were about twenty of them. Cooks and cleanup crew, bellhops and janitors. Every one of them had a big knife of some kind.

"They must do their butchering overnight," Chiun remarked.

"Well, let's try not to do any ourselves, okay?" Remo said. "These people aren't murderers."

Chiun waved imperiously. "Then you take care of the problem."

Remo didn't have time to argue. Besides, it was probably the best option. He stepped from the cab and found the gang of staff bearing down on him. More of them were streaming out of the kitchen doors.

These weren't skilled fighters. And their hearts weren't in it. "Sorry about this, buddy," said the chef in a white paper hat as he swung a cleaver at Remo's neck.

"Sorry? Sorry isn't good enough." Remo stepped around the cleaver and pinched the chef's neck. He had to smack away the blade of a kitchen assistant who was aiming for Remo and would have chopped the throat of the slumping chef in the process. Then he put the kitchen assistant to sleep, too. For the next few seconds he became a whirlwind of motion among the confused, drugged night staff, who slumped to the ground one after another until only Remo remained standing, surrounded by unconscious bodies strewed around the service bay.

He jogged inside, grabbed the poison-smelling breakfast potatoes in the walk-in cooler and headed for the beachside dock. Here the resort tied up a boat used to take snorkelers to the nearby reef. Remo stopped at the end of the dock and sent the tubs flying hundreds of yards out into the night. He turned and sped off the dock before the last of them had even splashed into the water.

Chiun had vacated the cab and was standing by the darkened swimming pool.

"I assumed you wanted the rest of the rabble to remain unassassinated," he commented. Behind him approached the party crowd.

"You let them take the taxi?" Remo asked.

"And the knives from the sleeping staff," Chiun said. "It was either that or kill them all."

"You know, it's not like it was one extreme or the other."

The mob, armed with knives confiscated from the unconscious kitchen crew, fanned out to create a half circle around its prey. Remo and Chiun were trapped with the swimming pool to their backs.

"Let's finish this up! I wanna go dance!" complained a young woman in a pink halter top and a short pink skirt, accessorized with a gold navel ring and a stainless-steel boning blade.

"Can we assassinate them now?" Chiun asked.

"No. Forget it," Remo said. He nodded over his shoulder. "We'll go this way and hope we can find another car."

"We run like cowards?" Chiun squeaked.

"Annihilating this lot would be the courageous thing to do?" Remo demanded.

Chiun sniffed. It was his "I concede the point" sniff.

The first of many blades came slashing at the Masters of Sinanju, but the Masters of Sinanju were no longer there. They were speeding across the surface of the swimming-pool water in a blur of leather shoes and sandals, and then they had vanished into the blackness.

The party crowd looked at one another, silent and very, very confused.

"Can we go dance now?" demanded the woman in the pink halter top.

As a group, they decided that was the only alternative.

40

"Your shoes are wet," Chiun said accusingly when they reached the front of the hotel.

"They are not."

"They *are*."

Remo almost allowed himself to get dragged into the argument, but a distant sound distracted him. "Saved by the siren."

A moment later it had grown to a piercing wail. "A fast siren," Remo noted.

"Not as fast as your powers of deduction," Chiun remarked.

"Don't suppose the prez has got the cops out looking for us?" But Remo knew that wasn't the case when he caught the look in the eyes of the cop who was driving. A fraction of a second later the car was past them.

"I'm going to check this out," Remo said.

"Why?" Chiun demanded.

"Just because!" Remo said over his shoulder as he started running.

"Chief!" said Candice the dispatcher.

"What?"

Candice nodded at the chief's window.

The squad car was going about forty miles per hour. The guy running alongside it was making a circular motion with his hand to tell the driver to roll down his window.

Chief of Union Island Police Checker Spence had seen some crazy-ass shit today. He chose to ignore the absurdity of what he was seeing now. After all, if he admitted there was a guy running alongside his car at forty miles per hour, then he might as well resign himself to the same sort of insanity afflicting Officer Simone, who giggled in the back seat.

"Where's the fire?" the running man asked.

"No fire. Murder."

"Where's the murder?"

"Coming your way, son," Spence said. "There's a mob of vicious killers on the loose in the heart of Union Island City, and they're headed this way. Our civil control team is about five minutes behind me, sounding the alarm."

"So where are you hightailing to?" Remo demanded.

The chief barely slowed the squad car as he maneuvered through a curve in the road. The running man never fell behind. Not an inch.

"I got a crazy man and an innocent woman to protect, and I'm obliged to get our island president out of harm's way. I'm going to pick him up at the Seven Seas."

"You're putting Greg Grom's safety ahead of the safety of hundreds of sleeping tourists?" the running man demanded.

"Of course I am, fool! In times of danger the president's safety is always the top priority," the chief recited. "Under no circumstances will I allow harm to befall the Island president, regardless of the circumstances."

REMO WILLIAMS STOPPED running and watched the squad car disappear into the night.

"Well?" Chiun asked, arriving a moment later at his side.

"That son-of-a-bitch president has got *everybody* brainwashed. Every one of them. They've got some sort of murders happening in town, and the first thing the chief of police does is drive out to secure Greg Grom's safety."

"Why are we not going after the president, as well?" Chiun asked.

Remo shook his head. "He said something about a mob of murderers. I have a feeling the bunch from the tour bus broke out of their cage."

Chiun put his hands in his sleeves. "Are you insinuating we should once again chase that band of miscreants? I think one time is sufficient."

"I could use a hand. There's a lot of them."

"Why would they let them go free?" Chiun demanded.

"How should I know!" Remo exclaimed. "Why'd they go nuts in the first place? I don't have any answers here.

Everybody on the freaking island is crazy. That's your answer. Any more questions you have, that's the answer. Now there's crazy people that way and there's crazy people this way, but the ones that are this way may or may not be committing murder, depending on how much stock you put in the carload of crazy people who just went *from* that way *to* that way! Any more questions?"

Chiun, who had his mouth in a tight, pale little knot, said, "Yes, I do—"

"Stuff it! I'm going *that way*. You go wherever the hell you want."

And with that, Remo started running again.

"THIS IS AN EMERGENCY," boomed the PA system on top of the squad car. "Do not panic. Walk quickly to the street and proceed due east, away from the town. I repeat, proceed away from town."

The word had already gone out. Fire alarms were blaring in the hotels. Sleepy tourists were milling about, looking for an explanation.

"Proceed away from the town," the PA on the squad car blared as Remo jogged toward it. "No, no, *away* from the town!"

Remo stepped onto the hood and walked onto the roof, where he knelt and poked his head into the open window.

"Need your car."

"What?" the driver asked, and the word screeched out of the twin public-address horns mounted on the roof. Remo kicked off one horn and removed the other one with a twist, then handed it to the officer behind the wheel.

"Guess you're out of commission in the civil control department anyway," Remo observed. He opened the door and dragged out the driver, rolling him into the manicured grass on the roadside. Remo slipped into the driver's seat and grabbed the wheel before the car even swerved.

The cop in the passenger seat dropped his mouth open, then closed again. "Hey, you can't—"

Remo never learned what he couldn't do. The surprised-looking cop in the passenger seat was gone, replaced by a very old Korean man half his weight.

Remo gave him a grin.

Chiun didn't smile, but there was a little something at the corner of his lips as he pointed a thumb over his shoulder, back in the direction of town, and said, "That way."

41

With a quick tap on the security pad, Dawn Summens disabled all the exhibit alarms in the great hall of Union Island's Museum of Natural History.

The great hall was lit only by the glow of the floor-mounted aisle lights and the exit sign. That was all the light she needed. She crossed to the wood-and-glass case labeled Union Island Blue Ring Octopus.

There it was, carefully settled on a rubber-coated stand. It was an ugly, dried husk of gray matter no larger than a cat. It didn't look much like an octopus. The tentacles had adhered to its body during the drying process, which it had undergone some six hundred years ago.

As the sign explained, this was the one and only surviving specimen of the Union Island Blue Ring Octopus. That had been a lie up until very recently. But now, with Greg Grom's cache depleted, this really was the last one.

Dawn opened the case and took the exhibit. It weighed no more than a couple of pounds. She shoved it into her shoulder purse, pounding it and crushing it until it fit inside. Not that it mattered—she was just going to grind it up anyway.

As she closed the case, behind her she heard the buzz of a telephone, then the scrape of chair legs. It was old Professor Builder two floors up. For a moment Dawn wondered if somehow the phone call had alerted him to her presence.

But it was something else getting him all worked up.

"Oh, my God!" she heard him exclaim as he ran from here to there. "I see them!" he told his caller. "They're everywhere! Killing? Killing who? I don't understand."

What was that all about?

She went to the window to see for herself.

It took her just a moment to understand the slow-moving figures on the street. The drugged ones from the tour bus had escaped from police lockup. They were on a rampage, but it wasn't the same sort of rampage perpetrated on the mainland tourist town of Pigeon Fudge. There hadn't been time for much wholesale slaughter in Pigeon Fudge.

But there was now. The maniacs were carrying body parts like war trophies. The scattered, slow-moving, dull-witted mob was wandering through town and heading right for the museum.

It was time to go.

"Who's there?" came an urgent demand from the darkness. The rotund shape of Professor Builder was at the bottom of the stairs. Dawn hadn't even heard him coming down. Builder moved to the wall.

"Don't turn the lights on, idiot," Summens said sharply. "You'll attract them like bugs."

"Who are you? Show yourself."

"Professor, it's me. Dawn."

"Minister Summens?"

"Yes, Prof. Have you got your keys? We need to get away from here fast."

"Yes. But how did you get in?"

"There's no time, Professor! They're coming!"

Builder did a fast walk across the great hall, slowing just slightly to gape at the empty glass case where the last desiccated Union Island Blue Ring had been on display.

"Minister Summens, what is going on?" the old professor wheezed.

Dawn ignored him, opening the private entrance door. There were clomping figures wandering onto the museum parking lot. "We'll have to make a run for it."

"I can't run, Minister Summens," Builder panted. He wasn't a healthy man.

She nodded. "Give me the keys. I'll get the cart and we'll meet up at the bottom of the stairs."

"Yes. Yes," he panted. "I can get that far." He put the key ring in her hand. "The key with the black plastic handle."

"Thanks, Professor," Dawn Summens said, and she bolted out the door, attracting the attention of several dead-eyed figures in the vicinity. One young man in a very soiled shirt and tie was just twenty paces away. He came for her without a word, dangling a severed forearm from one hand.

She moved fast, feeling strangely calm but also oddly vibrant, and reached Builder's golf cart in seconds. She started the cart and stomped on the gas, yanking the wheel tight to the right and speeding across the lot to the young man with the extra limb. He was one of the PR logisticians brought to the mainland to help coordinate the president's busy tour schedule.

Dawn Summens sideswiped him with the golf cart, and he landed hard. As she pulled the cart into a tight U-turn, she saw the old professor laboriously reaching the bottom step as two dead figures lumbered toward him from either side.

"Hurry, Minister!" he wheezed.

"Sorry, Professor. This thing can't carry us both."

"Minister, please!"

It was true. The little cart barely reached ten miles per hour when she floored it. Just think how slow she'd go with that flabby old man weighing it down. She swerved around a blank-faced woman with bloodsmeared hands and pulled onto the street. The last she saw of Professor Builder he was in the grips of his two attackers, one on each arm and pulling in opposite directions. They were going to yank him apart.

She wondered how long that would take.

42

Jimmy and Ellen Sandiro had planned their vacation to paradise for eighteen months. They wanted it to be perfect. And everything had been perfect for the first few days. Sunshine, relaxing on the beach, delicious gourmet buffets and endless rum punch at the poolside.

Now this. The one night they decided to go out on the town, they got mugged, right in front of the piano bar.

"Jimmy!" Ellen shrieked and tackled the man who was holding Jimmy's ankle while four or five crazy people yanked on his skull. The man with the ankle refused to drop. Ellen refused give up. She locked her arms around the attacker's neck and heaved, trying to muscle him away from her husband.

The attacker staggered and dropped the ankle, then sort of shrugged Ellen right off him. She collapsed hard on the sidewalk and found herself staring at a face. A face on a head. A head on the sidewalk.

Jimmy.

Her scream was cut short as she was lifted by her

ponytail and she felt the horrific stretching of her vertebrae. Christ almighty, she didn't want to be a head on a
sidewalk!

Her ponytail was released and she cracked her head on
the sidewalk, mercifully blotting out her consciousness.

REMO'S STIFFENED FINGERS shot into the man's throat
with enough force to crush it. The man wordlessly released the woman's hair and staggered away, grabbing
at his throat in an attempt to take a deep breath again.
He was doomed to failure.

Remo grabbed a pair of attackers by the shoulders
and mashed them together. The next one got backed into
the wall—backed in hard.

Chiun had taken care of the others. He was standing
calmly with a pile of bodies on one side, a pile of the
freshly harvested arms and legs on the other.

"Giving them a taste of their own medicine?"
Remo asked.

"Yes, but I fear they did not appreciate the poetry of
my justice."

ANOTHER KNOT of mute, plodding figures had gathered
around a palm tree just off the main street. Two vaca-
tioning couples had somehow managed to shimmy up the
arched tree trunk and crowd together on top. Remo and
Chiun arrived just in time to see one of the men slip
halfway off the trunk. From there it was an easy job for
his attackers to grab him by the ankles and haul him down.

"I'll take that," Remo said, whisking the man bod-
ily out of the clutching, stained fingers of the attackers,

who turned on Remo with bloodshot, yellowing eyes and ghastly faces devoid of expression.

Remo put the surprised man on his feet and penetrated the knot of attackers in a blur of stiff fingers and kicking feet. He crushed a quartet of skulls in under four seconds.

Ignoring their dead companions, two more of them plodded toward Chiun, who stood waiting impassively until they were on top of him. Then he penetrated both foreheads with a finger, moving so fast the victims in the tree and the man on the sidewalk couldn't follow the movement. Their attackers had gone from dangerous to dead so quickly they were having trouble coming to terms with it.

Remo and Chiun left them still trying to figure it out and went on with their janitorial duties. The last of the mess that needed cleaning up was conveniently gathered all in one place.

There was a splash of blood and a torso on the steps on the side of the Union Island Museum of Natural History. The head and limbs that had once been attached to it were inside, dropped carelessly on the floor. The lights were on, and a silent crowd was inside admiring one of the exhibits.

"Real movie zombies never go to museums," Remo noted. "Of course, real movie zombies also eat people."

"Do not give them any ideas," Chiun cautioned.

Some of the figures gathered at the exhibit lolled their heads and rolled their eyes at Remo and Chiun, but turned back to the case.

"What's so damn interesting?" Remo asked. He stepped up onto the greeter's desk and got a glimpse of the legend on the case.

"Union Island Blue Ring Octopus. All right, now I'm totally confused."

"It is the source of the poison," Chiun said. "Not the laboratory fakery that we smelled on the tour bus, but the original, natural poison. These victims of the poison must sense its vapors."

"Yeah. Can't stop eating Union Island octopuses. The sign says it is now extinct. This was supposed to be the last known specimen," Remo related. "But the weird thing is the case is empty."

As that moment the crowd snapped the case off its base and threw it to the floor with a thud. The crowd began sniffing the display and the inside of the glass.

"Will you please finish this," Chiun directed.

"Yes, yes, yes." Remo lashed into them. It passed through his mind that these people didn't ask for this to happen to them. But he also knew they were irreparably damaged. Their humanity was erased. Their metabolism was crashing. They were mindless, dangerous hulks, and the poison was killing them fast. It was a mercy to end it now. Remo did so, quickly, then stood in the silence as the last body collapsed.

He bent and peered into the display case, giving a shallow sniff. He nudged a corpse and uncovered gray powder on the floor.

"Somebody took the octopus recently. Like today."

"Do not touch it," Chiun warned.

"Don't plan to," Remo said. "Whoever took it, I hope they were wearing rubber gloves."

43

Dawn Summens felt strange. Her cheeks and mouth were getting numb. She kept rubbing her face to stimulate circulation. Her lips were dried out and felt cracked, and she wetted them again and again.

Something on her face. Gritty.

Even at just ten miles per hour, she was having difficulty controling the golf cart. She drove out of town, swerving through bands of fleeing tourists. Everybody was headed for the docks where the cruise ships landed their tour groups. Grom would be there, and she had plans for Grom. Reassuringly she nudged the purse with her arm again, just to make sure it was still there.

A curve in the road became a major problem when she found her hands weren't responding to her brain's instructions. She gripped the steering wheel, but it refused to budge until she leaned her entire body. The cart swerved through the curve, but now the road curved back the other way. Dawn fought to steer through it. Her hands wouldn't work. She tried to lift her foot from the accelerator pedal but found it stuck there.

The golf cart puttered off the road and into a clump of weeds, where a thicket nudged it to a stop. Dawn fell on her side across the front seats. She tried to sit up, but her body wouldn't listen to her.

"Hello? I need help." She wanted to shout, but it came out a thin croak. "Hello?"

She could still move her hands a little and she extended her arm with great effort, only to find that the horn on the steering wheel was beyond her reach. Minutes later she could no longer move a muscle, and her mouth would no longer vocalize. She stared at the dashboard and the weeds above her and tried to think. She was lucid, but she was paralyzed. What was wrong?

Of course. The Union Island Blue. She had touched it. That was a big no-no. She had licked crumbs off her lips. And her body was still burdened with her earlier dose of GUTX synthesis. The charcoal would have passed through her system, and the counteractives she injected wore off hours ago.

A guaneurotetrodotoxin overdose meant a descent into living death, in which she would see, hear and feel even while her body ceased functioning. Finally the lungs would go slack. Unconsciousness would come as her brain starved for oxygen, and finally it would shut down.

Unable to thrash or scream or fight, she could do nothing except lie there and wait for it to happen. Her only consolation was that death should come quickly.

But it didn't.

44

Chief Spence jogged to the president, his clothes flapping in the wash of the helicopter rotor blades. "It's over!"

"What's over?" Greg Grom shouted above the roar as the big transport chopper settled on the helipad.

"The crisis! My men are combing the town. The mob has been wiped out."

"Wiped out? Who wiped them out?"

"I guess it was the citizens," Chief Spence said vaguely. He avoided telling the president the truth about the dead-eyed man who had run alongside his squad car and matched the description of one of the two said to have wiped out the mob.

"I'm going anyway," Grom declared.

"Don't you think you should stick around?" the chief asked. "The news will be all over this place in an hour."

"I don't care," Grom said nervously. "I have to go!"

Chief Spence picked up a megaphone and began

telling the tourists to turn around and go back to their hotels. The danger was past. Evacuation was unnecessary. The vacationers were complaining but relieved.

Greg Grom didn't feel relief. Not yet.

Finally the emergency transport chopper swayed and lifted off of the helipad. The lights of the cruise ship dock fell away and the blackness of the nighttime Caribbean Sea cushioned them. They'd be in St. Thomas in no time.

Somebody knocked.

"Hello? Can I come in?"

It was him. The one with the dead eyes was standing on the landing skid with his face pressed against the glass.

"Fine. I'll let myself in."

The rush of air filled the cabin and the dead-eyed man didn't close the door behind him.

"Who are you?" Greg Grom demanded.

"Remo...somebody. I forget exactly. Why do you care?"

"Are you going to assassinate me?"

"Oh, for sure. But first—" Remo grabbed the small carryon that was Grom's only luggage "—is this all of it? The poison?"

"Yes. Take it. It's all yours. It'll make you rich and powerful!"

"Like you?" Remo asked with a chuckle. "No, thanks." He hoisted the bag out the open door, and it tumbled three thousand feet into the sea.

"No!"

"Don't fret about it, Prez. You're going with it."

Remo grabbed Grom by the back of the neck and walked him to the open door.

"No!" Grom shouted again. This time it was a long, long "no" that ended with a splash.

The copilot burst into the passenger compartment. "What the hell is going on?"

"My friend," Remo said, "I'm just figuring it all out myself."

With a little persuasion, the pilot and copilot agreed to turn the helicopter around.

REMO FOUND the suite empty when he awoke in the morning. He lifted Chiun's trunks and wandered downstairs, past the all-you-can-eat breakfast where the sleep-deprived vacationers were having it out with the staff.

A woman in a floral swimsuit under a souvenir T-shirt was leading the resistance movement. "What do you mean no hash browns! How can you not have hash browns?"

The staff was confused about this, too, and tried to explain what they thought had happened.

"Stolen?" the woman cried. "Your hash browns were stolen? Nobody steals hash browns."

"Well, those were awfully good hash browns," an elderly woman in the crowd spoke up, and she was met with fervent agreement from the others.

"Was it you who stole them?" the outspoken lady demanded of the old woman.

"No. I was just saying they were worth stealing."

"It *was* you!"

The outspoken lady had to be restrained.

Remo found Chiun in the lobby, talking to the big blue parrot.

"It was Master Lu who actually decided to try to eat parrots. Lu made several bad decisions. For some reason he thought the parrot flesh might be suitable fare, comparable to duck."

The macaw shifted uneasily on its branch.

"Of course," Chiun continued, "those were ugly little gray parrots. The Romans imported them from Africa. You look like a much meatier specimen."

The macaw gave a small squawk and hopped several branches away.

"Finally found somebody you can win an argument with?" Remo asked.

"I wondered if you would be sleeping until noon. May we leave now?"

"The sooner the better. Say goodbye to your buddy."

"Perhaps I should bring it along."

"I am *not* going to eat parrot," Remo insisted.

"I did not intend to share it with you," Chiun replied. "But I think not. Farewell, ugly bird."

The macaw hopped forward again and cocked its great head with its big yellow eye patches. Chiun stopped. Remo watched the two of them regarding each other.

"Hello?" Remo asked.

Chiun held up a hand for silence, which lasted a full minute. Remo stood there impatiently with the trunks balanced on his shoulders.

"Ah, well, goodbye," Chiun said finally.

The parrot squawked. "Bye-bye! See you soon!"

They strolled out of the open air lobby, and Remo began loading the trunks into the first taxi in the lineup. All the while he heard the raucous voice of the bird drifting out. "Bye-bye! See you soon! Bye-bye! See you soon!"

"Hey, you weren't thinking of bringing it home as a pet were you?" Remo demanded.

"Of course not," Chiun said from inside the cab.

"Bye-bye! See you soon! Bye-bye! See you, Chiun! Bye-bye! See you soon!"

Remo got in. "Well, you sure seem friendly with the thing. It even knows your name."

"I did not tell it my name."

"It just said goodbye to you personally."

Chiun looked straight ahead. "I do not believe so."

The cab pulled onto the road and began driving in the direction of the Union Island International Airport. A few miles later Remo poked his head out the window and looked up.

With its great wings spread wide against the crystal morning sky, the blue macaw was an elegant creature. It greeted Remo with a squawk.

"No pet parrot!" Remo insisted, pulling his head in again.

"Of course not," Chiun answered stoically.

Remo saw the bird one more time, riding the updrafts a half mile from the airport. "See you, Chiun! See you soon!"

"Hear that?" Remo demanded as he hoisted the trunks from the cab.

Chiun went through the airport doors, ignoring him completely.

45

The white sheet they draped over Dawn Summens was translucent. She saw it all as it happened.

They put her on a stretcher and placed her in an ambulance. The drive into town was surreal. She could hear the engine sound and the whine of the tires on the pavement. The dappled sunlight of daybreak made the inside of the ambulance look almost cheery. The paramedics were discussing her and she heard every word.

"She sure was a hottie," one of them said. "It's too damn bad."

"Yeah. What a bod. What an ass."

"And not a bad rack."

"I always wanted to see them puppies."

"What's stopping you?"

They parked and wheeled out the gurney. Wheeled her up a ramp. It was the front entrance to the museum of natural history. The great hall had become a temporary morgue. Bodies were lined up, sheeted and tagged, in neat rows. They laid her at a place of honor, in the front row, and because her head was locked in a slight turn to the right she could see, through her thin sheet, that a cadaver was laid out next to her. The sheet was oddly distended, as if the remains underneath were somehow malformed.

"Well?" said one of the paramedics.

"Nobody else here," the other one whispered. "Now's our chance."

Dawn Summens should have been repulsed, but instead she was relieved when the paramedics pulled off her sheet. Now was her chance. She fought with all her will to move. A twitch. A blink. Anything to show them she was still alive.

"Aw, her eyes are open!" one of the paramedics complained.

"I told you. I couldn't close them," the other one said.

She saw them clearly. Could she move her eyeballs?

"Cover her face at least."

"All right."

The sheet was draped across her face while the paramedics took a quick gander under her shirt.

"Mighty fine."

"She sure was a hottie."

There! Her finger! She had moved her finger! Hadn't she?

The sheet was draped over her entire body again and the paramedics left. Dawn Summens heard only silence.

Through the veil of her cover she saw the sheet next to her move. From beneath it emerged a hideous black burned thing. Amelia Powlik grinned, which cracked more of the crust that had once been her face. She reached over and gently lifted the sheet from Dawn Summens's face.

"Hello, hello," Amelia sang quietly. "I know you're in there."

Paralyzed, unblinking, Dawn wanted to retch against the stench of scorched flesh and hair.

"Shouldn't have done that to me, Minister Summens," Amelia said. "Now I feel disinclined to be nice to you."

The sheet dropped back over her face, and Amelia Powlik recovered herself.

Dawn's mind whirled. An hour passed, and the sheet next to hers didn't move again, and her confusion turned to doubt. Had she imagined it? Had Amelia really moved? Was it even Amelia under there?

The door opened and the police chief, Spence, came in carrying Dawn's handbag. He had a couple of his officers with him.

"There she is," one of them said, pointing right at her.

"What were you thinking?" Spence asked her, then he went to the display case. He dragged on rubber gloves, then gingerly extracted the crumbling, battered Union Island Blue Ring Octopus out of her purse. He put it back on the rubber stand, where it belonged.

"It's all beat up," one of the officers said sadly.

"Help me put the case back on," Spence said.

The three men muscled the heavy case up and over the display stand, then latched it down. All the while Dawn Summens was shouting at them, thrashing her limbs, blinking her eyes. But it was all in her head.

As the cops headed for the door they heard a moan. The three of them rocketed straight into the air.

"Holy shit!"

"Look!"

Chief Spence spoke sharply. "Get the doctor over here! Tell him we have a live one! Oh Christ, look who it is!"

The doctor arrived in minutes. The paramedics followed him in.

"Water. Drink of water."

"Doc, can I give her some damn water?" Spence asked. "She's been asking and asking."

"Yes, just a little." The doctor began working over her while Chief Spence dribbled water on her blackened lips. Soon they had Amelia Powlik stabilized and on the gurney. Dawn's efforts grew weaker, but she kept willing herself to make a sound. Take me, too! Take me, too!

They never heard a thing, and all of them left to accompany Amelia Powlik to the hospital.

Dawn Summens was alone again, with all those dead people and one dead, dried-up octopus. The Union Island Blue Ring stared at her through the glass with its shriveled black eye. The great hall was utterly silent.

James Axler
Outlanders®

MAD GOD'S WRATH

The survivors of the oldest moon colony have been revived from cryostasis and brought to Cerberus Redoubt, leaving behind an enemy in deep, frozen sleep. But betrayal and treachery bring the rebel stronghold under seige by the resurrected demon king of a lost world. With a prize hostage in tow to lure Kane and his fellow warriors, he retreats to the uncharted planet of mystery and impossibility for a final act of madness.

Available February 2004 at your favorite retail outlet.

Or order your copy now by sending your name, address, zip or postal code, along with a check or money order (please do not send cash) for $6.50 for each book ordered ($7.99 in Canada), plus 75¢ postage and handling ($1.00 in Canada), payable to Gold Eagle Books, to:

In the U.S.	In Canada
Gold Eagle Books	Gold Eagle Books
3010 Walden Avenue	P.O. Box 636
P.O. Box 9077	Fort Erie, Ontario
Buffalo, NY 14269-9077	L2A 5X3

Please specify book title with your order.
Canadian residents add applicable federal and provincial taxes.

GOLD
EAGLE®

GOUT28

TAKE 'EM FREE
2 action-packed novels plus a mystery bonus
NO RISK
NO OBLIGATION TO BUY

Stony Man is deployed against an armed
invasion on American soil...

DAY OF DECISION

A Typhoon class nuclear sub has been commandeered by
terrorist dissidents. Halfway across the globe, members of
the same group have hijacked an airliner and rerouted it to
Somalia. Now the plane is heading toward its U.S. target—
with a nuclear payload. While Stony Man's elite cyber team
works feverishly to understand a blueprint for horror, Able
Team and Phoenix Force strike out from Afghanistan to
Siberia, tracking the nightmare to its source.

STONY MAN®

*Available in
February 2004
at your favorite
retail outlet.*

THE
DESTROYER

POLITICAL PRESSURE

The juggernaut that is the Morals and Ethics Behavior Establishment—MAEBE—is on a roll. Will its ultra-secret enforcement arm, the White Hand, kill enough scumbags to make their guy the uber-boy of the Presidential race? MAEBE! Will Orville Flicker succeed in his murderous, manipulative campaign to win the Oval Office? MAEBE! Can Remo and Chiun stop the bad guys from getting whacked—at least until CURE officially pays them to do it? MAEBE!

Available April 2004 at your favorite retail outlet.